MISTLETOE MISCHIEF

Marian had made the mistake of soundly trouncing the high-and-mighty Lord Gilbert Ingraham at a game of chess. Now he was claiming his revenge—under the mistletoe.

Marian opened her mouth to object and he kissed her. He stepped back a moment, put his hands on her neck, and kissed her again. The only way to steady herself was to put her arms around Ingraham, Marian discovered. And his back felt so good that she had to run her hands up and down it once, and then again.

Marian was beginning to sense that she was far less in control of the game of love than that of chess, especially since she was clearly up against a master. But if it were far more dangerous, it was also ever so much more delightful . . .

CARLA KELLY lives in Springfield Missouri. She is a public relations writer for a local hospital.

Marian's Christmas Wish

Carla Kelly

A SIGNET BOOK

NEW AMERICAN LIBRARY

A DIVISION OF PENGUIN BOOKS USA INC.

Copyright © 1989 by Carla Kelly

 SIGNET TRADEMARK REG. U.S. PAT. OFF. AND FOREIGN COUNTRIES
REGISTERED TRADEMARK—MARCIA REGISTRADA
HECHO EN DRESDEN. TN. U.S.A.

SIGNET, SIGNET CLASSIC, MENTOR, ONYX, PLUME, MERIDIAN
and NAL BOOKS are published by New American Library, a division of
Penguin Books USA Inc., 1633 Broadway, New York, New York 10019

First Printing, December, 1989

1 2 3 4 5 6 7 8 9

PRINTED IN THE UNITED STATES OF AMERICA

To my husband

Of all the agonies of life, that which is most poignant and harrowing—that which for the time annihilates reason and leaves our whole organization one lacerated, mangled heart—is the conviction that we have been deceived where we placed all the trust of love.

William Henry Bulwer,
British diplomat

Prologue

"Ariadne, you don't really think that Mama—our mama—has written to Percy, do you?"

Marian Wynswich looked to her elder sister for an answer, but Ariadne only frowned and twitched her shawl up higher around her shoulders. Marian rummaged through the wooden crate on the floor and pulled out another red streamer, one of many jerked off the walls and stuffed into the box after Papa had drunk too deep of Squire Edgerton's eggnog and took a fence too high coming home last Christmas Eve.

She shook off the streamer and handed the end of it to her sister, who pulled it from the box. "Oh, Ariadne, it is too bad," she exclaimed. "Everything is limp and wrinkled. Who would have thought that one year could do so much damage? It is too bad," she repeated, and then added in a softer voice, "And I do think Mama has written to Percy. I truly think she has begged him to come home from the treaty talks and bring a suitor with him for you."

Ariadne sighed. "At least he is coming home, my dear. I never thought he would receive permission, considering . . ."

". . . how very junior he is," Marian finished. "But Ariadne, *who* would want to hang around Ghent at Christmastime except the Americans, and heaven knows *they* can't be home in a week! And didn't Percy tell us last time he was home that just the poor folk who must make the fair copies, and the poor folk who must sign them have to see it through to the bitter end?" She tugged

9

another bow from the box. "How comforting that Percy is in the middle." She leaned forward and spoke almost in a whisper. "And I am sure he is bringing home a suitor."

"Marian! You can't be sure of that, you know you can't," Ariadne burst out, even as she lowered her voice and looked about to make sure that no one had overheard her unladylike exhibition. "Did Mama ask for your help in composing such a letter? You know what a dreadful speller she is and how her thoughts sometimes twist themselves in such an amazing way."

Marian leapt to her feet and stretched the streamer out across the floor. "No, she has said nothing to me. And she did not come to you, did she, for help to copy it out and make her blots and squiggles all right and tight?"

Ariadne shook her head, and her glowing chestnut ringlets danced about her ears. "Then what makes you think she has written to our brother about . . . you know . . ."

Marian sighed and stared out the window, where the rain thrummed down. "She has taken to giving us those arch little looks of hers. You know, the ones she employs when she is onto something and we are not." She pulled the streamer toward her again, gathering it into a tidy ball, her hands moving rapidly as her agitation increased. "Oh, depend upon it, Ariadne, she means for you to be married—or engaged, surely—before this Christmas season ends. And I say it is too bad!"

A long silence passed between the sisters. Marian returned her attention to the satin streamer, which she bound with a bit of twine and put aside. She peeked a look at Ariadne, beautiful Ariadne, who sat with her head bowed and turned a little to one side, her dark eyelashes brushing her pale cheek, her lips curved downward. The Wynswich women had abandoned their deepest mourning for pale gray now, and Ariadne looked like a dove, a dove that drooped and languished on Mama's favorite fainting couch.

Marian came to Ariadne, sitting beside her and wrapping her arms about her older sister in an oddly protective gesture. "Can you not see, Ari, dear? You must get Sam Beddoe to come up to scratch. Perhaps if Percy understood the way things are . . ." She sighed in turn and released her grip.

"But S—the reverend is so poor, my dear," Ariadne began.

"The worst part is that he is shy and has a hen's heart when it comes to the thought of facing our 'fearsome' brother," Marian interrupted, and then giggled. "Percy would stare his eyeballs out if he knew how terrified Sam is."

"I still contend Sam would be braver if he had more than a competence to live upon," said Ariadne.

Their argument always took them to this point, but no further. "Oh, let us face it, Ariadne. How on earth can Percy dredge up someone rich enough—no matter how Mama schemes—to put a little heart into this estate? And into us," she added under her breath.

There was no answer from the fainting couch. Without a word, both sisters returned to the Christmas box. To the side, in its own pasteboard container, was a thinner box. The Wynswich sisters looked at each other.

"Oh, I cannot," said Ariadne. "You open it."

Marian took a deep breath and pulled the twine that bound the box. She laid it flat on the floor and lifted out the wreath, hoping that Ariadne would not notice how her hands trembled. She felt her breath come in little gasps as she smoothed out the red bow and touched the circled branches, cunningly fashioned of silken leaves and copper wires. It was the wreath her father, Bertram Wynswich, had brought home from London and presented to his daughters with such a flourish. They had put it up the afternoon he rode over to Squire Edgerton's, and he never lived to see it on the door.

"Better late than never," she said, "especially since we must practice economy. I shall ask Billings to hang it at once. Don't be a goose, Ariadne. You know Papa would call you missish if you cried."

Wreath in hand, she marched into the front hall, grateful that no one was there to see her own tears glistening on eyelashes equally as long as Ariadne's. She dabbed at her eyes with the corner of her apron and set the wreath on the hall table, reviewing in her mind the black wreath of last Christmas and the black bunting decorating the doors and outer windows She clasped her hands tight in front of her and saw again the rain-soaked streamers that ran dark tears until the whole house seemed to mourn a death in that season of birth.

"And all for you, Papa," she whispered. "How could you do this to us?"

She glanced about her, hopeful that no one listened. There was only Ariadne in the drawing room, still draped gracefully on the fainting couch, indulging in the bliss of sobs and sniffles. Marian watched her, and a smile of wonderment came to her face. How do you do that, Ariadne dear? she thought. How is it that you can cry and still your face is beautiful?

With no rancor, but rather a grudging admiration, she reflected again how unfair life was. How was it that she, Marian Wynswich of Covenden Hall, could sob and rant and look like a thresher suffering from hay fever, while Ariadne only appeared delicate and mysterious?

She had accused Ariadne of practicing such art in front of the mirror, and while Ariadne had looked at her in surprise, she had not denied the accusation. In silence, Marian watched her sister on the couch and thought that it was high time she learned such an art. For one of us must nab a Croesus of a husband, she thought, and Ariadne, you would prefer the vicar.

Oh, the devil take matrimony, she thought crossly, and then repented immediately, at least in Ariadne's case. There was no one finer than Sam Beddoe, even if church mice did have more inheritance than he.

But somewhere we have to find a rich man, she thought, someone to take away that sting of Papa's years and years of borrowing to support his horses and his races, his bets and his opera dancers. Someone who knows something about the mysteries of 'Change, and who won't squander the tatters of the family fortune on treasure-hunting in the Azores, or nonexistent gold mines in Bolivia. Someone to keep Mama from writing desperate, tear-stained letters to dear Percy, who likely had troubles enough of his own, especially with Napoleon twiddling his thumbs on Elba and the rest of the world gone slightly cock-eyed.

She hesitated. Perhaps her mother had not written to Percy in Ghent at the treaty talks, after all. Perhaps if they lived tighter and held household better, it could wait just this little while. Surely things would look better in the spring.

Marian brightened and entered the room again. January was an excellent month in which to put away childish things and begin her own practice in front of the mirror. She would not squander her Christmas thinking of suitors, or family debts, or twice-turned gowns. Such cold-eyed reflections would be the business of January.

Marian Wynswich meant to enjoy this Christmas.

1

Marian's enjoyment lingered no longer than the first hour after luncheon. Lady Wynswich had already taken herself off for her afternoon nap, which caused Marian no dissatisfaction—in fact, quite the opposite. Her mother had been impossible during their meal in the breakfast parlor, eyeing both of her daughters with that superior air that spoke of hidden knowledge.

"My dear girls," she said, "Percy will be here by nightfall, depend upon it. I have told Billings to instruct the maid to air out his room *and* the best guest room." She had paused and looked around, her eyes bright with something very like mischief. "Ariadne, wouldn't you like to know what Percy has planned for you?"

"No, Mama, I would not," replied Ariadne. "Whatever it is can keep."

If she was disappointed at this lack of interest, Lady Wynswich did not show it. With a laugh that she quickly stifled with one hand, and with an airy wave of the other hand, she floated from the breakfast room and hummed her way up the stairs.

Marian cast a speaking glance at her sister. "I told you, Ariadne."

"So you did. I must talk to Sam, and soon!"

As she spoke, Billings entered the room and proved to the Wynswich daughters that Christmas was, indeed, a season of miracles. "Miss Wynswich," he said, speaking to Ariadne, "the vicar waits in the parlor."

"Touché," exclaimed Marian, and turned back to the remainder of her cold sandwich. "Go tell Sam to 'screw his courage to the sticky point,' as our brother used to say, and get on with his courtship."

"How odd that you should mention Master Wynswich," said the butler. "He awaits with the Reverend Beddoe."

The sisters looked at each other with dismay, and Marian returned the sandwich to plate, uneaten. "Good God, whatever has he done now," she said. "Ariadne, does not the term at Eton end one week from tomorrow?"

Ariadne nodded. A frown began to crease its way between her eyes. Automatically she rubbed at it. "What do you suppose that dreadful brother of ours has done now?" The light that had come into her face at Billings' mention of the vicar dimmed as her eyes narrowed. "Oh, if he is in the basket again, I shall go distracted."

"Yes," agreed Marian, "and Mama will suffer one of her celebrated palpitations, and cry and groan, and then take him to her bosom. 'How like Papa you are,' she will cry until we are all tired of it. Ariadne, I want to box his ears."

Ariadne rose. "Let us forge ahead, Mare. And do brush those crumbs off your lap. I wonder that you will ever be a proper lady."

Marian made a face at Ariadne's back and followed her into the parlor. When they were scarcely over the threshold, the vicar leapt to his feet. Marian watched in amusement at the blush that began probably somewhere deep in his chest and zoomed up beyond his hairline and onto the top of his head.

I wonder if he will do that when they have been married for years and years and their grandchildren are grouped around them, Marian thought. As he hurried forward to shake hands with Ariadne, Marian concluded that he would. And he will probably cast those cow eyes on her, even when they are in their dotage. I don't think I shall ever fall in love.

"The Misses Wynswich," he exclaimed, and then turned his attention to Ariadne. "There is no accounting for fate. I was coming here in the gig to discuss the hanging of the greens in the church next week, and whom should I encounter on the road but Alistair?"

And there you should have left him, thought Marian, even as she smiled and hurried to her brother, who sat rather far removed from the tableau, by the doorway.

Anyone even remotely acquainted with the Wynswiches would have entertained no doubts over Alistair's parentage. He was quick on his feet and slim as his sisters, and possessed his mother's lively brown eyes and his papa's curly chestnut hair.

Marian looked closer. What had the dratted boy done to his hair? "Alistair, turn around," she commanded.

Her younger brother did as he was bid. "This was not the greeting I expected from you, of all people, Mare," he said.

"Good God, Alistair," Marian exclaimed, "how could you?" She looked at her sister for support, but Ariadne and Sam Beddoe were involved in each other's eyes, so there was no artillery from that quarter.

Alistair shrugged himself out of his greatcoat and touched the back of his hair, which had been cropped until not a single wavy lock remained. "The Byron look was last season, Mare," he said. "This is a Brutus. At least, as close as Etheridge could come, working by a candle's glow after lights-out."

Marian sighed and held out her arms. "Alistair, you are a sore trial. Come give me a hug."

Alistair grinned. He grabbed his sister up in a bear's embrace and towed her around the room before setting her down. "Mare, you are getting shorter. Or did I grow?"

"You grew, Alistair," she replied, out of breath.

She glanced at Ariadne. Her sister and the vicar had found the sofa and were sitting there, staring at each other. No I shall never fall in love, thought Marian again. It is entirely too tedious.

She disengaged herself from Alistair and turned to her sister. "Ariadne, dear, I believe the vicar has come to talk about the hanging of the greens in the chapel?"

The vicar gave a start and blushed again. He seemed bereft of speech, so Marian continued, "Remember, sir, the fourth Sunday in Advent? Greens? Church?" She smiled at him wickedly. "Devon?"

The blush deepened. "Ah, yes, Marian. Ah, yes."

Ariadne gazed at him as though he had declared a deep

profundity worthy of encapsulation in Sunday's sermon. Marian sighed again, and took Alistair by the arm. "Come on, dear brother, let us go to the bookroom. Perhaps eventually they will remember what year it is."

She hurried down the hall, pulling Alistair after her, glancing up at the stairs to make sure that her mother had not come down yet. They would be safe in the bookroom. Lady Wynswich never came near it.

Marian sat her brother down and pulled up a chair next to him. "Alistair, what mischief are you in now? I know the term at Eton does not end until one week from tomorrow."

His calm self-assurance, an additional legacy from his father, deserted him for the first time. Alistair ran his finger around the inside of his grimy collar.

"Gracious, Alistair, don't you ever wash at school?" asked Marian. "Your collar is a disgrace."

He patted it and straightened his neckcloth, which was no cleaner. "Of course we wash! But you see, Mare, it was a wager. You know, who could go the longest without being called down. I won."

"I am relieved. Now what are you doing here?"

Alistair was silent a moment, as if considering all avenues of the strategy he had developed in the long walk from Picton to Covenden Hall. Looking into Marian's clear eyes and watching how her lips tightened together in such a thin line, he discarded them all.

"You see, my dear, it was another wager." He looked around him. "Etheridge wagered that I could not compose a set of bawdy lines to 'God Rest Ye Merry Gentlemen.' " He couldn't bear the look in Marian's eyes and transferred his gaze to the map of Europe on the wall beyond her shoulder. "And how was I to know that the Archbishop of Canterbury would be visiting his grandsons—and regular little mewling things they are, too—in the next set of rooms? He took exception to my composition. And really, Mare, I was't singing loud."

Marian opened and closed her mouth several times in perfect imitation of a mackerel.

"In fact . . . Oh, Mare, he cut up stiff about it. The dean

told me to take myself off." He slumped in the chair. "A letter is to follow."

"Oh, Alistair! I . . ."

"Do words fail you, sister?" he asked hopefully when she continued to stare at him, her eyes wide.

"Indeed they do not," she snapped. She jumped up and began to pace back and forth about the room.

Alistair watched her come and go. "I was hoping they would, actually, Mare. It is the season to be jolly."

She picked up a paperweight on the desk and would have thrown it at him, except that she feared the racket would have brought the entire household into the room. She slammed it down on the desk, marched in front of him, and slapped him on both shoulders. He reeled back in his chair and nearly spilled himself out.

"Alistair, you are a ninny! Percy is due here any minute from Belgium . . ."

It was Alistair's turn to imitate the mackerel. "Good God. I had no idea. Then he . . ."

". . . will read the letter. Oh, Alistair, he is bringing company, too, important company. And Mama will have hysterics."

They were both silent, Alistair waiting out the storm that he knew from long experience would end soon, and Marian unable to think of anything to say. She felt her Christmas plans coming down about her ears. First Percy and the would-be suitor, and now Alistair bumbling about. All it needed was . . .

Someone knocked at the door. Grateful for the diversion, Alistair opened it so fast that the boy outside gasped. He recovered quickly and came into the room.

It was the stableboy and he carried a cat in his arms, a particularly ugly cat, soaking wet, and obviously soon to be a mother. The creature was plastered with mud. Whether its coat was brown or gray, Marian could not be sure.

The boy looked from the sister to the brother. His face brightened. "Alistair! I mean, well, hello!" He looked back to the sister again. "Begging your pardon, Miss Wynswich, but I found this cat out by the main road. The dogs were teasing it. I thought you might . . . well, you know."

"Yes, I know. Hand it here, and thank you."

The boy relinquished his burden, grinned at Alistair, and executed a quick march from the bookroom before Marian could change her mind.

Marian sat down next to Alistair again and wrapped her apron around the cat. The babies in its belly squirmed and tumbled into each other as she rubbed the cat dry. The animal began to purr, and the sound was a balm to her jangled nerves. She smiled and scratched the cat under the chin.

"And I suppose you have a sad story to tell, too, if only you could talk," she said, addressing the animal. "Something about a misspent kittenhood and the perfidy of toms." Marian looked at her brother. "Since everything and everyone conspires against me this Christmas, we shall simply have to make the best of it." Her tone became decisive. "Alistair, you will take yourself off to the guest room. No, the second-best one. I'll contrive to bring you up some dinner later. It would be better, I think, if Mama did not know you were about yet, and your own room is too close to hers. She would hear you. If you will lie low, I may have the chance to talk to Percy before he finds out . . . or receives that letter."

"I think the archbishop is sending one, too," said Alistair.

Marian winced. "I wonder, brother, does the Church of England excommunicate entire families?"

"Surely not minors, Mare," said Alistair. "We are safe!"

"No, we are not, you great big looby! Oh, take the cot in the dressing closet. Who knows, but Mama may stick her head in the room. At least then she will not see you. And take this cat and clean it up. I will send up some food for it, too."

Alistair felt himself on more sure ground. "Mare, are you never going to outgrow your *tendre* for strays and waifs?"

She fixed him with a glare that made perspiration break out on his upper lip. "Alistair! Don't try me! Now take yourself up the back stairs, and for the Lord's sake, don't show yourself. Billings will fetch your valise."

Marian took off her apron, wrapped the cat in it, and handed the bundle to her brother, who kissed her on the cheek and darted out of the room. In a moment she heard him on the backstairs, whistling to himself. She groaned and rolled her eyes. "We got past the worst interview, didn't we, Alistair?" she said out loud. "Mama you can wrap around your little finger, and you will depend upon me to carry you through an interview with Percy."

She went to the window and pressed her nose against the glass. The action teased a smile to her lips. When she was a little girl and did that, Papa would rush outside and press his face against the glass and kiss her through the pane.

"Dear, foolish Papa," she said softly, her lips still against the glass. "Why did you leave me the burden of this whole family?"

Percy had no idea of the state of affairs at Covenden Hall. As much as she now dreaded his arrival, and what it might mean to Ariadne and Alistair, she longed for it. She yearned to cut away some of the weight she bore and pitch it onto his shoulders for a change. The treaty talks could go hang, for all she cared. "It is high time those Americans quit brangling and wrangling and you came home, Percy," she told the window.

She rested her cheek against the glass and closed her eyes. "Oh, Papa, I am weary of being the only sensible person in this entire household. It's not fair."

The bookroom was cold, and the chill finally penetrated through her dress. She went into the hall, standing still as Billings passed her carrying Alistair's valise.

"The second-best guest room, ma'am?" he asked.

She nodded and wondered only a second how it was that the servants knew entirely what was going on. "And not a word to Lady Wynswich, mind."

"Oh, no, miss," he replied. "Cook has already started on Alistair's favorite dinner. I'll see that he gets it."

She waved him on, marveling how the world loved rascals so, while the virtuous were only put upon. I shall ask the vicar to compose a sermon on the topic, she thought as she approached the parlor. That is, if his wits have returned in any quantity at all. Ariadne simply must bring him up to scratch so we can have good sermons again, sermons where he doesn't stammer and blush, track back upon himself, and stare continually at Ariadne.

The object of her thoughts stood at the parlor door, bidding farewell to Ariadne. He had possessed himself of his greatcoat and hat again, but he had not yet freed himself from Ariadne's handclasp. Marian watched them a moment and resolved anew never to fall in love. I have not the temperament for it, she decided as Sam finally let go and turned like a blind man toward the front door. Marian hurried to open it for him so he did not tumble into the frame.

After seeing her love safely out the door, Ariadne began a meditative progress toward her room.

Marian took her by the hand. "My dear, did you suggest to Sam that he approach Percy, and soon?"

Marian's words had the effect of cold water flung without warning. Ariadne's chin came up. "Marian, it is almost Christmas, and that subject will be a sore one to Percy. Why must you be so practical-minded?"

"Because someone must, Ariadne dear," Marian began, and then stopped. The one who needed stiffening was the vicar. Likely this would fall her task, too. She sighed and hugged her older sister. "It's just that there must be some strategy, my dear. Christmas may come and go, and you might find yourself pitch-forked into an engagement entirely of Mama's—or Percy's choosing." The stricken look in Ariadne's eyes almost quelled her own spirits, but she plunged on. "I shall talk to Sam myself, dear. Goodness knows someone must . . ."

Dinner was an unrelieved tedium and two hours late in the bargain, as Lady Wynswich fretted and stewed and held the cook at bay, waiting for Percy to arrive. "Depend upon it, he has forgotten us," she declared finally in despairing tones as she tore herself away from the window and cascaded gracefully onto her fainting couch. "Ariadne, my smelling salts!" She wept into her handkerchief. "I do not know what will become of us if Percy does not do as he ought."

Marian brought her the salts, uncapped them, and waved them expertly under her nose. "Mama, you know that is not the case. Likely he was held up and will arrive later. If you succumb to vapors, you know how that makes your eyes redden and your nose run."

Lady Wynswich recovered sufficiently to glare at her younger child. "You are an unfeeling girl," she stated, and motioned to Ariadne, who sat down on the sofa and began to chafe her mother's wrists. "Ariadne knows how to conduct herself. Marian, make yourself useful and watch at the window."

No one arrived. When Billings appeared in the doorway for the tenth or eleventh time, Lady Wynswich raised herself from her couch and directed her daughters to help her to her feet. "For we must keep up our strength. dear girls. Let us dine."

Dine they did, on food that had waited too long belowstairs. Lady Wynswich dabbed at her eyes and pushed away her half-eaten food. "Marian, how are we to manage with such a cook? Whatever will Percy's guest think? This venison is the ruination of every hope of our family."

"Mama, it is no such thing," Marian said. "It would have been excellent two hours ago." The stubborn glint returned to Mama's eyes, so Marian trod carefully. "I recommend, dear, that Ariadne make you a tisane and you go to bed. Now, do not protest! It is unlikely in the extreme that Percy will arrive any later. He was merely delayed and will be here in the morning."

The overdone venison had stripped Lady Wynswich of all fight. She nodded, fought back tears, and let herself be led away by her older daughter, uttering, "Unworthiest of sons" and "Unfeeling daughter" as she made her invalid's progress up the stairs.

Marian could only sigh with relief and wish herself elsewhere. She thought of Alistair in the second guest room, and resolved to pay him a clandestine visit, but her heart was not in it. He will rave on about Eton and the tricks he has pulled, and how he has outrun his quarterly allowance, and I shall grow quite distracted. Better to find a book and carry it upstairs.

How lonely the library was, how cold. Marian went straight to the Roman philosophers. Something bracing and practical would suit her frame of mind; this was not a time for Greeks. She ran her finger across several titles and changed her mind. This was not even a time for books, she decided as she touched the back of Papa's wing chair, drawn up before the dark hearth, and quietly left the room.

Billings sat in the hallway, his chin nodding over his chest. ''I will wait up awhile, miss,'' he said, ''in case Percy should come.''

She smiled at him and went to her room; she sat cross-legged on the bed in her flannel nightgown and wrapped her long black hair in rags on the hope that there would be a tiny suggestion of curls in the morning. The fact that she had not inherited the famous Wynswich hair was only another jostle of cruel fate, a circumstance that she seldom troubled herself about, but that seemed on this night only one more indication of disaster to come. There was no tidings of great joy in her heart when she finally closed her eyes.

It was well after midnight when she sat up in bed, wondering for only a second what had awakened her, and then realizing that Percy was home. She got out of bed and padded to the door. She opened it a crack and listened in appreciation to Mama's tears and admonitions, her exclamations of delight. ''Dear lady, you are in your element now,'' she said. Marian tiptoed into the hall, knelt on the landing, and peered through the railing.

Percy stood almost directly below her. Tears started in her eyes, but she brushed them away. He had taken off his hat, and the famous Wynswich chestnut hair gleamed in the little light. Lady Wynswich was clasped tight in his arms. ''How long you have been, my son,'' she murmured over and over as she held him close.

''Not so long this time, Mama. Only a year. And Mama, we have company.''

Two other gentlemen stood in the shadows of the front hall. Marian pulled her nightgown down over her bare feet. Two gentlemen? How dreadful. She had been right all along. Percy had produced not one, but two worthy suitors for Ariadne. One was quite tall, so tall that his high-crowned beaver hat brushed the greenery draped in the hall. The other man was much shorter and quite round. Marian fancied she heard his stays creak as he leaned forward to shake her mother's hand. She giggled and then put her hand over her mouth.

No one appeared to hear her except the tall man. He looked in her general direction and then tipped his hat to her and smiled. Or she thought he smiled. With the smallest wave of her hand, she got quietly to her feet and ran back to her room.

She closed the door on an agonizing thought that made her suck in her breath. Two gentlemen. One of them would surely be assigned to the second-best guest room.

Marian stood rooted to the spot and briefly considered the idea of confessing everything to her mother and revealing Alistair's whereabouts. Her courage deserted her. She stayed where she was, and prayed that whoever got the room would be too tired to do anything but go to bed, and leave the unpacking and any probable trips to the dressing room for the morrow.

She considered prayer for a moment and then discarded the idea. Not many Sundays past, the vicar had expounded on the folly of calling upon the Lord for help when one had not prayed for a long while. I will not be a hypocrite, she told herself as she climbed back in bed and waited for the ax to fall.

It did not. In a quake, she heard the gentlemen moving down the hall and into the guest rooms. Her mother and Percy stood outside the door talking quietly for a few more minutes, and then the doors to their rooms closed, too. All was silent. Marian relaxed gradually, sinking deeper and deeper into her feather-bed. Perhaps Alistair had gone down the hall to his own room, after all.

Her wish was not to be realized. A scream echoed and then reechoed from the second-best guest room. The door opened with a bang that rattled the window in her room. Marian leapt from her bed and flung back her door in time to see Alistair running down the hall, a sheet clutched around his middle.

Clad in his nightgown, the little round man stood in the middle of the hall. As she watched, horrified, he sat down and fell back in a faint. Marian darted into her room and snatched up the smelling salts that her mother insisted they all carry. She waved the bottle under the man's nose, even as Percy burst out of his room and Lady Wynswich came shrieking down the hall, shouting, "Murder! Murder!" in a voice not the least infirm.

The door to the best guest room opened and the tall man stood

there in the shadows. Marian only glanced at him and turned
her attention to the little man on the floor. Percy was at her
side now, his arm under the man's head. "Sir William? Sir
William? I say, are you all right?"

"He faints at card tricks, balloon ascensions, and military
reviews, my dear Percy," said the voice from the other doorway. "Or so my acquaintance through the years testifies. Give
him a moment. He will be fine." He stifled what sounded
remarkably like a laugh, and asked, "I want to know who it
was running down the hall. He is remarkably fleet."

Marian could not look at Percy. "That was Alistair."

"Alistair!" Percy dropped the little man back on the carpet.
"Alistair! Marian, he is not supposed to be here. Oh, what have
you been up to?"

By now, Lady Wynswich's cries had awakened Ariadne, who
came into the hall, saw the scene of carnage spread before her,
and burst into noisy tears of her own.

Alistair had collected himself and watched from the safety
of the landing. Draping his sheet around him in a more states-
manlike fashion, he came padding toward the group gathered
about the man on the floor.

"I was as surprised as he was, Mare," he said, and continued
his stately progress down the hall.

Percy could only stare in wonder at the devastation about him.
The silence grew until it almost hummed, and then it was
supplanted by another sound, the squeaks and mewings of tiny
kittens. With another muffled laugh, the shadowy man went next
door.

Marian put her hand to her mouth. "Good God! My kittens!"
She ran into the second-best guest room on the heels of the other
gentleman. He stopped and she bumped into him in the dark.

"Oh, I am so sorry," she gasped. "It's the cat. I forgot. Oh,
and kittens, too. Dear me, whatever must you be thinking? Percy
will murder me. He will ship me to Australia."

She stepped away from the tall man, grateful that it was dark
and no one could see her hair in its disgraceful rags, and her
flannel nightgown. She listened for the mewings and got down
on her hands and knees, feeling under the bed.

The tall man joined her. "Here they are," he said. "I can reach them if I stretch out. Hold out your hands, my dear, here they come."

She sat on the floor as he deposited two slimy kittens into her lap, followed by a cat, who was grunting softly. He sat down next to her on the floor. "I fear she is not quite through yet." He ran his hands over the cat's abdomen. "Perhaps you had better take her into another room. Sir William is decidedly fussy about his bedmates."

The thought launched him into silent laughter. He leaned against the bed and stretched his bare legs out in front of him. "Mercy," he whispered to her at last, "I don't know when I've been so entertained at three in the morning."

After another shake of his shoulders, he got to his feet and held out a hand for Marian. She gathered the kittens and cat into her nightgown and took her burden into the hall, the tall man's hand on her back to guide her in the dark. She looked behind her once. "Thank you for not cutting up stiff, sir," she whispered.

"To show you what a good fellow I am, I will put in a nice word to your brother, my dear. I do not think he will ship you to Australia. Are you Marian?"

"Yes."

"I thought so."

She stopped in surprise. "What do you mean?"

He laughed out loud. "Percy has already warned me."

Sir William was sitting up now. Lady Wynswich was reduced to hiccups, while Ariadne still sobbed. Alistair stood in his doorway, shaking his head over the follies of his elders

Percy turned to Marian, his eyes wide. He slowly shook his head.

"Welcome home, Percy," Marian said.

2

Mama Cat delivered herself of two more kittens on Marian's bed, grunting and grunting and then purring as she licked the new arrivals with her rough tongue. Marian rubbed the little ones dry with the hem of her nightgown, all the time rehearsing in her mind what she would say to Percy and Mama in the morning.

Before Percy had turned his attentions back to the little fat man wheezing on the carpet he had said to her, "Marian, the gold saloon, nine tomorrow morning." Mama had seconded his command, adding, "And not one second later," before returning to her own tearful apology to Sir William.

As she sat cross-legged on her bed and watched the kittens, Marian could have told Percy there was no need to hold star-chamber proceedings in the gold saloon. The thought of her mother out of bed and dressed at the unheard-of hour of nine A.M. had already put her into such a quake that she knew she would be far advanced in age—probably twenty at least—before the memory of it would dim.

Last night, as she had struggled in the dark hallway with the newborn kittens, Alistair had attempted to come to her aid. As he hurried toward her, he tripped over his sheet and sprawled on his stomach next to Sir William, affording the astounded company an excellent view of his bare parts. Philanthropy suddenly stripped from his mind, Alistair elected discretion over valor and beat a hasty retreat to his own room.

There had been only one advocate in the hallway. As she gathered her dignity and her kittens and skirted past the little man on the carpet, the tall rescuer of the kittens touched her on the shoulder. It was more than a touch; it was a reassuring squeeze.

Or so she had imagined. Marian resisted the urge then and there to cry "Sanctuary!" and hurl herself into the tall man's arms. It was curious indeed, but as she prepared to face the dragons in the gold saloon, she felt his protection around her still.

The feeling vanished the moment she raised her hand to knock on the door, forbiddingly shut. Instead of knocking, she put her ear to the door. All was silence within. There was not even the comfort of idle chatter from inside. Marian took a deep breath, knocked, and entered the room.

Lady Wynswich lay on the sofa, her vinaigrette clutched tight in her hand. The disagreeable odor of burned feathers filled the room like fog over Picton. Percy stood at the window watching his sister, his lips still set in the grim lines of last night. Marian looked at him and her heart failed her.

It wasn't the look of irritation that overset her. She had seen that look the time she took his best neckcloths to line a basket for a family of orphaned rabbits, or the day she ran away and had to be retrieved from a posting house ten miles distant. What caused her heart to flutter and then drift down toward her slippers was the look in his eyes.

Even at her father's funeral, when Percy Wynswich stood at the head of the casket and pitched in the first handful of dirt, she had not seen that look. Shock and sorrow, yes, but not flatout despair. It was not in his nature.

Despair stared back at her now. Her legs failed her. She groped for the chair nearest the door and sank into it. No one said anything. No one moved. Marian's eyes filled with tears.

Her own expression of anguish struck some chord in Percy. He came toward her, lifted her by the elbows from the chair, and took her in his arms. "Mare, don't ever look at me like that," he said as she sobbed on his chest.

Her mother had not envisioned such easy capitulation. She

cleared her throat several times until her children looked around at her.

Percy tucked Marian close to his side and began in gentler tones. "Marian, I have already spoken to Alistair, and he—"

"Oh, Percy," she burst out, "he has been sent down! I was so worried it would overset Mama. That was why I hid him. And as for the cat . . ." She stopped.

The despair had returned to her brother's eyes. He took her by the hand and led her to a chair closer to Mama. His hands were icy cold. He gestured toward the table.

She saw the letter. Her heart gave a last, weak plop and settled around her ankles.

"It is more than rustication, Marian. The letter is from the headmaster. Eton will not entertain Alistair Wynswich for one more term. Marian, he is out." He took her by the hand again. "And I do not know what to do."

"Come, come, son," Lady Wynswich said as she rallied and sat up on the sofa. "What is that to anything, really? Papa used to brag on the schools he went through. There are other schools. Probably better ones."

"And they are an expense, Mama," Percy said, his voice controlled. "And this estate . . ." He could scarcely continue, no matter how calm his voice. "This estate is so heavily encumbered with Papa's debts that we might all be permanently rusticated by the end of next quarter."

His words seemed to hover about the room for an age and then land on Marian's shoulders. Where she had longed for Percy to return from his diplomatic chores and lift some of the worry from her, he had only increased it.

She found her voice after a moment. "Oh, Percy, surely not! Surely a little more economizing, a little—"

"No, Mare. We're in the basket, under the hatches, knocked up." He waved aside Mama's indignation at his language. "Papa danced, and now we must pay the piper."

Lady Wynswich reached for her handkerchief. "Odious, odious boy," she said. "How can you speak so of dear Papa? Are you so dead to feeling?"

Marian's eyes flew to Percy as he shuddered under the force

of his mother's recrimination. She tried to take his hand, but he would not have it. He returned to the window again, and there he remained until he achieved some command over himself.

Lady Wynswich saw none of this. She sobbed into her handkerchief. "Marian, my smelling salts. Oh, where is Ariadne? Ariadne is such a comfort!"

Words were a waste. Marian pointed to the vinaigrette already clasped tight in her hand. Her mother glared at her. "Even Alistair would be a relief," she said in a whisper loud enough for Percy to hear. "He would not pinch at me and threaten doom. Alistair is always so agreeable." She stared at her elder son's back. "Not like some I could name."

"Mama, please," said Marian. "Don't . . . Oh, not now!"

Percy sighed and came back to stand by his mother. "My dear, finances are never pleasant for the Wynswiches, but they must be faced. The bailiff and I and Papa's solicitors have kept up such a correspondence this fall. They assure me that I can staunch the hemorrhage with a little money." He bowed. "Excuse my language, Mama, but that is the cold fact. We need some cash." He sighed again. "And that is why I agreed with you in your last letter. That is why Sir William Clinghorn is here."

Lady Wynswich looked at Marian in triumph. "You are not the only clever one in the family, my dear girl."

Marian raised her eyes to stare at her brother, and he could not meet her glance. He attempted a light tone. " 'Extraordinary times call for extraordinary measures,' says our prime minister." The tack failed and he abandoned it. "Sir William is looking for a wife, someone who will pour tea at receptions, take no untoward interest in affairs foreign and domestic, someone to do him credit at court functions and cause him no embarrassment. He doesn't have the inclination for an extended courtship. I suggested Ariadne and he is here."

There was something of defiance in his voice.

Marian raised her chin. "And if I were older, you would ransom me, too?"

"I probably would, Marian. We are that desperate."

She could not look at him. Hardly realizing what she did, she scooted her chair away from her brother. She regretted the gesture the moment she did it, but she could not take it back any more than Percy could take back the look on his face.

"Which brings us to this morning's interview, Marian."

His voice was formal, distant. Percy Wynswich might as well have been discussing some term of the Treaty of Ghent. He ameliorated his tone by standing behind her chair and placing his hands on her shoulders, but his fingers were so cold.

"I spent the better part of last night convincing Sir William to stay. He will be here in a matter of minutes. You are to apologize to him."

If he had expected a fight from her, she disappointed him. Marian nodded and then shifted her shoulders slightly. Percy dropped his hands and stepped back.

"And you are to do nothing else to throw this household on its side," he continued. "I am well aware of the influence you exert over your older sister. I would wish that Ariadne were not so biddable at times, but it will probably serve us well enough now if Sir William's wooing is to go forth—without any exertion," he concluded dryly.

Marian stood up slowly, as if unsure of her balance. "And it doesn't matter to you that she is agonizingly in love with our vicar?"

He regarded her. "And does our vicar have a fortune to waste on Covenden Hall?"

She returned him stare for stare. "You know he does not. Percy, how can you be so heartless?"

If she had suddenly ripped open his shirt and clawed out his heart, she could not have increased the pain in his eyes. He grasped her by the shoulders and shook her, even as his eyes filled. "I have been over and over the estate books until I am dizzy with it, Mare," he exclaimed, and then dropped his voice to a whisper. "And there is no other solution. After a while, given time, Ariadne will comform herself to the notion. You know she will."

"And we can have beeswax candles again," Lady Wynswich added her mite.

Marian sucked in her breath and stared at them both, her mother triumphant, even as she dabbed at her eyes, Percy dashing his hand across his own, his face a study in shame. She could only turn away and hug herself with her arms. Her fingers had grown as cold as Percy's and her head was beginning to ache.

The knock at the door roused her. Without another look back at her brother, she opened it.

Sir William Clinghorn stood in front of her. Marian looked him over and decided that moonlight became him more than the glare of morning, even a shadowy Devon morning with its misty rain. He was shorter and fatter and reeked of eau de cologne. And this toad is Ariadne's future, she thought even as she smiled at him, curtsied, and held out her hand.

He gave it a perfunctory shake and stepped into the room. The stays of his corset protested as he bowed to Lady Wynswich and Percy, folded his arms, and looked at Marian again, waiting.

She cleared her throat. "Forgive me, Sir William, for the hubble-bubble last night."

It wasn't enough. Still he glared at her. He was so fat that he had to clutch at the sleeves of his coat to keep his arms folded across his paunch. The eau de cologne was overpowering.

"I . . . I forget myself occasionally. I don't mean to, truly I don't."

"The folly of youth," tossed in Lady Wynswich, sitting up straighter on the sofa.

"Then I can take it that distempered freaks are not a condition of this household?"

"Only mine," she said earnestly, and then blushed as Sir William started to laugh.

It was more than a laugh. It was a donkey's bray, a hee-haw accompanied by the crack and sputter of his corset. "Oh, my, this is a ripe one, Percy," he managed at last. He pinched Marian's cheek until she squirmed. "You'll never find a husband for this one outside of a lunatic asylum."

Percy managed a tiny smile. "Come, come, Sir William, let us be charitable."

Sir William released Marian. " 'Tis the season, eh?" he

brayed in her face. He clapped his hands together. "Very well, my dear Percy." He winked at Lady Wynswich. "And now, if you'll call Ariadne, we'll make our acquaintance. Ariadne," he rolled the name around on his tongue like a bad taste. "What a name, Lady W.! Whatever were you thinking of?"

Marian felt Percy stiffen even as he took her firmly by the elbow. "Very well, Sir William, I shall go find her. Come, Marian."

She opened her mouth to protest, but Percy's grip tightened. Sir William was warming to his subject. "Has she a middle name, Lady Wynswich?"

"Elaine," Lady Wynswich said, and reached for her handkerchief again.

"I shall call her Elaine. Ariadne, indeed!"

Before Marian could say anything, Percy pulled her out the door and closed it behind him. He did not relinquish his hold on her until they were down the hall. He pulled her into the bookroom.

"Percy, he is odious! And . . . and . . . he has bad breath."

Percy released her. "And twenty thousand pounds a year, dear one. Mare, as long as he has breath—"

"But he's going to change her name! Percy, you can't do this."

"Don't rip up at me, Marian."

They glared at each other. "Oh, Mare," said Percy at last as he held out his arms again. "Give me a hug. We'll see what we can do."

She rested her head against his chest as he put his arms around her and talked into her hair. "I don't know what to do. I wish I'd never listened to Mama's letter. But here we are, and we'll just have to see what happens. I'll go find Ariadne."

He released her. "But don't you go causing another distempered freak, Marian. You're not too old to spank."

She took his words in better grace than she felt. "Very well, Percy. Do you think should I apologize to the other gentleman, the tall one?"

The first smile of the day crossed her brother's face. "I think not." He touched her under the chin. "And in the middle of that Cheltenham scene last night, didn't I hear him laughing? And upon my word, Marian, I have never heard him laugh. Not that treaty-making is jolly business. Lord Ingraham just doesn't laugh. No, I don't think he'll demand an apology . . . or pinch your cheek, either.''

''He had better not,'' she exclaimed, her hand going to her cheek. ''But why is he here?''

Percy shrugged. ''He was going to London and I just asked him on a whim. He chose not to go home this season.''

Marian opened her eyes wide. ''But why ever not?''

''Oh, I do not know. It may have something to do with . . . Well, Marian, I own I was surprised he accepted. But maybe he feels uncomfortable . . . Well, relatives can be a chore at times like this.''

His words mystified her. ''And do we become a chore?''

He looked at her and spoke with no hesitation. ''You cannot imagine how pleased I am to see you all again, even if we are all as eccentric as we can stare. Other families are so . . . so boring.''

Marian took Percy's arm and drew him down to her so she could kiss his cheek. ''Percy, I promise to stay in here until I am in a better frame of mind.''

He enveloped her in a hug that threatened her breath. ''Just stand by me, Marian, and promise me that you will remember that our guests are dignified and deserving of your deference. Sir William is a distinguished servant of our poor king, and Lord Ingraham, my God, Marian, he is renowned in international circles. Remember yourself.''

She remained where she was until she heard Percy's footsteps disappear down the hall. She went to the window and wrote, ''I will not be so impulsive,'' on the steamy glass. As she stood there, she sniffed the odor drifting up from belowstairs. Cook was making the Christmas pudding.

I shall go belowstairs, she thought, and stir in my Christmas wish. I shall wish that the Reverend Beddoe will suddenly inherit a fortune. And that Alistair will reform and lead a blameless life. And Percy will . . .

The smile left her face. Marian Wynswich, grow up, she

scolded herself. You would do better to wish that you could learn to stay out of scrapes.

No sudden flash of illumination brightened the bookroom. She sighed and picked up the feather duster. There was only one thing to do, and she would do it.

It had long been a source of family humor that whenever Marian Wynswich was agitated, she took herself to the library to dust books. Even her father knew to duck out of harm's way when Marian came down the hall, wielding the feather duster like Marshal Ney's baton. "God help us," he would say, "Little Blue Eyes is loose on an unsuspecting world."

And so I am, dear Papa, she thought as she entered the library, closing the door carefully behind her. The instinct was to slam it, but her mother was right: now that she was almost seventeen, it was time to put away some childish things. She allowed herself a sharp click of the lock to telegraph her displeasure to anyone lurking in the hall, but thought better of it and unlocked the door. No one in the Wynswich family read except her and Percy, and he was busy sealing Ariadne's doom with that silly little man.

"Percy, you are in my black books," Marian said out loud as she attacked the first book that came to hand, shook it, dusted it, and returned it to the shelf. She dispatched an entire row of books and then sat down in Papa's wing chair by the fireplace. She drew her legs up and sat cross-legged, daring her mother to come in and scold her.

But Lady Wynswich never came near the library. Marian leaned back in the chair and closed her eyes, wishing that Sir William would discover another attraction far removed from Devon and leave the Wynswiches to a merry Christmas.

"My peace is quite cut up," she said. "Papa, why did you have to die and leave us so poor?"

He could not answer, of course, no more than anyone could who drank overmuch eggnog, stuffed his horse at a fence, and landed on his neck with a crack. Last year, with its black gowns and improving thoughts, had been ten years long. She had planned so carefully for this to be the best Christmas ever, and here it was, turning to sawdust before her eyes.

"Drat!"

She got up and searched along the row of books until she found *The Odyssey*. At such an impasse, only Homer would do. She would lose herself in the wanderings of Odysseus, wishing herself anywhere but Devon.

A year had passed since she had opened the book. Marian rested the book against her cheek and willed away an enormous tide of sadness. When she was much younger, Papa had set a row of her favorite books along the lowest shelf, never mind that it threw the volumes out of order.

"She wants to read," her father had told the librarian—back when they could afford a librarian. "She should be able to reach her books without a ladder, or a rope swung from the ceiling."

The text was in Greek, of course. For all his rackety ways, her father had recognized a fine mind and taught her Greek. It was her pleasure and joy. Marian turned the pages, fanning them toward her. Poor, wandering Odysseus would be her solace when everyone else nattered about trying to snabble a husband for Ariadne. She retreated again to the chair, drawing herself into a little ball. She would begin with the tale of the Sirens.

The door opened. Marian started and then relaxed. It could not possibly be Lady Wynswich. She was probably even now raising herself from her couch of suffering to extol Ariadne's—Elaine's—virtues to Sir William. And she will titter and prattle until it is too much, thought Marian as she drew herself into a tighter ball and peered out from the wing chair.

It was the tall gentleman of last night. Lord Ingraham, Percy had called him. He was casually dressed in the garb of a country gentleman, but possessed of an air that spoke of more exotic places than Picton, or even Lyme Regis. She was struck by the excellence of his posture. His back was straight, and in consequence, he seemed almost to reach the ceiling.

Marian sighed, thinking of the hours and hours spent with a book on her head to achieve the same effect. No one would ever dare put a book on this elegant man's head.

He was broad in all those places that a man should have some width, and narrow where it served him best. This was not a

man who would require any subterfuge from his tailor to cut
a figure that would make heads turn.

I should not stare, she thought. It is vulgar of me.

His hair was black in places, as dark as her own, but peppered
liberally with gray. His nose was straight, even a little sharpish,
his lips set in a firm line. Ariadne would have sighed and called
his bearing noble; Marian thought him old.

And yet he did not have the walk of one well on in years.
His walk, while firm, had a spring to it. Marian concluded that
he must be younger than he looked, and turned back to Odysseus
roped to his mast.

Her disinterest lasted only a moment. This was not a man
to be ignored, even for Odysseus. She watched Lord Ingraham
out of the corner of her eye as he crossed the room to the window
and stood, rocking back and forth on his heels, looking out at
the bleakness of the landscape.

" 'Ah, lovely Devon, where it rains eight days out of seven.' "

Marian covered her mouth so he would not hear her laugh.
She had not thought her rescuer of last night would resort to
nursery rhymes. After another moment spent in contemplation
of England's dreariest scenery, he turned the other way toward
the books. Marian's hand tightened over her mouth.

Her eyes widened but she made no sound as she made herself
smaller in the chair. His cheek was scarred with the imprint
of a crisscross. She looked closer. It appeared almost ike a
tattoo, except that it was red and raw-looking, a burn such as
she could never have imagined. Her stomach did a flip even
as her heart went out to him.

Still he did not see her. His eyes were on the books. He ran
his finger across the gold binding of Lord Wynswich's
Shakespeare and then traveled farther to the poetry of Ben
Jonson, the essays of Donne, the plays of Marlowe.

She watched as he squatted down, his back still rod-straight,
to look at the lower shelves, her shelves. He pulled out her well-
worn copy of Blake, rose to his feet, and cleared his throat.

"Do you recommend the Blake, my dear, or does it depend
on the weather?"

Marian squeaked in surprise. He turned to look at her. Slowly she sat up and put her legs on the floor, smoothing her dress down and wishing last night's rag curls had done their duty.

"Sir, if we depended on the weather in Devon, we would never have the heart to even open a book. I recommend the Blake."

He nodded. "The Blake it will be, my dear. Don't let me disturb you." He made no move to come closer, but selected a chair across the room, carefully turning it so the scarred side of his face was away from her view when he sat down. He crossed his legs and opened the book.

Marian put down *The Odyssey* and rose to her feet. The gentleman did also. "Oh, no, don't bother," she protested. "I was . . . I was supposed to be dusting. Please don't bother."

He nodded and sat down again, but he did not open the book.

Marian picked up her book and gave it a fierce dusting. "Sir, how did you know I was here? I was ever so quiet."

"You were. Do you know that when you stand at the window, your glance takes in the mirror over the fireplace? There you sat, all gathered together, watching me. I thought at first that you were a maid, but as a rule . . . ." He craned his head slightly to look at the book in her arms. "As a rule, maids don't trouble themselves with Greek. I think you must be the altogether singular Marian Wynswich. I believe we have already met."

Marian came closer and he motioned to the chair opposite his own. She sat in it without a word, too shy to speak, feeling anything but singular. Drat Percy again.

"Is it that you are not allowed to talk to strangers?" he asked at last.

She found her tongue. "Oh, no, no. I just . . . Percy tells me I am not to rattle on and cut up everyone's peace. Oh, truly I did not mean to cause Sir William distress!" She put her hand to her mouth. "And now I am rattling on. I had better leave, sir."

"Oh, don't." He leaned forward and held out his hand to her. "Let me introduce myself. I am Ingraham. Gilbert Ingraham."

She took his hand. His clasp was firm and warm. She shook his hand and, before a thought of discretion crossed her mind,

reached out and touched his cheek, resting her fingers for the
tiniest moment on the burn that desecrated his face.

If he was surprised, he did not show it. He did not move as
she traced her finger over the scar, her eyes filled with concern.
He scarcely breathed. His eyes were on her face as she gently
pressed his cheek and made him turn it toward her.

"Does it hurt?" she asked. "What do you do for it?"

"It always hurts. The surgeons tell me I can do nothing for
it." He made no move to pull back from her fingers.

She inched her chair closer, her eyes intent on the burn. "Do
you know," she began slowly, "I have concocted a salve that
I use on animals. It is remarkably efficacious and . . ." She
stopped and took her hand away from his face as though it
burned still. "Whatever must you think?" she said, and then
was silent, wishing herself anywhere but in that quiet library
where the tall man regarded her with a look remarkably like
amusement.

Marian closed her eyes. If Mama learns of this, she will
plunge the entire household into spasms, Percy will shoot me,
and Ariadne will swoon. She opened her eyes, and the man
continued to regard her. He leaned back and crossed his legs
again. The slight smile on his face put a little heart back into
her and she took a deep breath.

"Forgive me. I cannot imagine why I did that."

"Perhaps you were concerned?" he asked. "And Percy did
tell me you were singular, Miss Wynswich. Please don't leave.
I wish you would tell me more about your salve for animals."

Marian gripped her hands together in her lap. The room felt
warm and close, as if too many logs burned in the fireplace.
She glanced at the hearth. There were no logs at all. "It is
merely something I put together," she said. "It works
wondrously well on cuts and scrapes."

"And do your patients tell you so?" he quizzed. "If they
do, then you are probably even more singular than Percy
imagined."

She relaxed. "You are bamming me, sir," she protested.
"But I deserve it. Mama and Percy tell me that I am entirely
too impulsive." She sat up straighter. "And, yes, I know it

works well. My animals are able to sleep and eat again." She
laughed. "Some of them even follow me about, which is a sore
trial at times."

He joined in her laughter. "Which brings us, I suppose, to
your kittens. Did they survive their precipitous eviction?" He
leaned toward her in a conspiratorial fashion and she was
irresistibly drawn to do the same. "Sir William is a bit of a
dog in the manger. He won't even share a coach willingly, which
made our journey from Ghent rather a trial. How could we
expect him to suffer the confinement of a cat?"

Marian blushed. This was hardly a topic to discuss with a
gentleman. Even loyal Ariadne would throw up her hands in
surrender and march from the room, denying all kinship. Marian
struggled on.

"Imagine, my lord, two more kittens were born on my bed.
When the rain stops, I will remove them all to the stables. And
now, sir, I really must leave you." She rose, feeling absurdly
small next to Gilbert Ingraham. She admired the buttons on his
waistcoat and then stepped back quickly. She was standing much
too close.

He bowed to her. "Miss Wynswich. I am pleased to have
made your acquaintance in daylight hours. If you have some
of that salve, I think I would like to try it. That is, if your dogs
and cats won't cut up stiff at my intrusion." He bowed again.
"And I promise not to trail after you."

She giggled. "If you promise, I will give you some. You must
apply it to your face at night, and it will loosen some of the
tension of the scar." She raised her hands again to his face and
then put them behind her back. "As a rule, however, burns
do not heal well. It is a sad fact, but true." Marian was backing
toward the door as she spoke. "And, sir, forgive me for being
so forward. I seem to be making a habit of apology this morning.
In your case, I do mean it."

He followed her to the door, moving slowly, as if afraid she
would bolt. "There is nothing to forgive, Miss Wynswich. Do
you know, most women look away like your mother, or speak
of something else, anything else. You are the first who has cared
enough to offer help."

He would have said more, but the door banged open and Alistair hurtled into the room. "Marian, Cook has summoned us below. You know what that means."

He vanished as quickly as he had come, and Lord Ingraham blinked in surprise. "Does he do nothing but run about?"

It was on the tip of her tongue to apologize for Alistair and his rackety air, to beg forgiveness because the library was cold and the furnishings shabby, to beg Lord Ingraham's tolerance of their eccentricities.

She did not. "Lord Ingraham, let me put it to you this way: we are intent upon keeping Christmas this year and the pudding awaits."

A smile played about his lips, and the wonder increased in his eyes but he said nothing.

"We are all of us singular, my lord."

The light in his eyes encouraged her. She took a deep breath and stood as tall as she could. "Percy announces that we are poorer than church mice. This could be our last Christmas together in this house. I plan to enjoy it. You may enjoy it, too, and you had better like wishing on Christmas pudding and caroling and dragging in the Yule log, and even getting a little bosky on eggnog."

His smile grew wider. "Pray go on, Miss Wynswich. I am all ears."

"Not discernibly," she replied.

Alistair darted down the hall again, tugging Ariadne after him. "Oh, hurry it, Mare. You know Cook won't wait."

Sir William puffed and chugged after Ariadne, but the effort was too extreme. He abandoned the chase, shrugged to Gilbert Ingraham in the library door, and let himself back into the gold saloon.

Marian waited until the saloon door shut. "If you wish to stand on ceremony, Lord Ingraham, this is not the house to do it in. I am going to make a wish on our Christmas pudding."

She turned to go, but Gilbert Ingraham stopped her, tucking her arm in his. "I haven't done this in more years than I care to claim. Lead on, Miss Wynswich."

The kitchen smelled of citron and orange peel, mingled with

sultanas both golden and brown. Alistair loomed over the pot, stirring the brown mass, his eyes closed, his lips moving. "Done," he declared, and handed the wooden paddle to Ariadne. Her face was serious, her eyes troubled, as she stirred the pudding around and around.

Percy followed them down the stairs. He saw Lord Ingraham waiting his turn by the hearth. "Marian, you promised me," he said in an undervoice to his little sister.

Ingraham bowed and released his hold on Marian. "And she promised me a pudding wish, Percy. I suggest you go next, as I have to consider the matter further."

Marian held her breath and watched as a whole series of objections paraded across Percy's face. "Very well," he said at last, and took the spoon from Ariadne. He stirred it, his eyes on his little sister. She could not read his expression, but her heart lightened as she watched him.

He made his wish, released the spoon, and it stood upright in the pudding pot. The Wynswiches all said, "Ah!" at the sight of the pudding well done. With an elaborate bow, Percy turned to his guest. "Lord Ingraham, it is your turn. Marian will be last because she is still quite out of my good graces." He pulled out his pocket watch. "For at least another fifteen minutes."

Marian grabbed his arm, pulled him toward her, and kissed his cheek. He winked at her, and her heart grew lighter still.

Lord Ingraham observed the proceedings, a thoughtful expression on his face. He took the spoon, bent over the pot, and sniffed deep of the pudding. "My God, this is magnificent," he murmured. "I close my eyes?"

"Only if you want your wish to come true." Ariadne's voice was so wistful that Marian's heart drooped a bit.

"Oh, I do want it to come true," Lord Ingraham said. "I do, above all things."

"And you mustn't tell, at least, until it has come true. Nobody tells," explained Alistair. "At least, unless you tickle my sisters to death and make them confess!"

"Alistair, really," said Ariadne, coloring up prettily and looking away.

"Very well, then." Lord Ingraham closed his eyes and stirred the pot. The smile on his face grew. As Marian watched him, she found herself smiling along with him and then laughing out loud when he opened his eyes, declared, "Done," and took her hand and placed it over the spoon. "Make it a good one," he said.

She began to stir. She had planned all along to wish for Ariadne and Sam, and Alistair. Even during the summer, when it was warm and she was tired of black gowns, she had thought of the Christmas pudding and planned a special wish for Percy.

Marian did none of these things. She closed her eyes and stirred the spoon 'round and 'round with each word that came into her mind: I wish Gilbert Ingraham will have the best Christmas.

3

Nuncheon with Sir William was an unrelieved tedium, so breathtaking in scope that Marian resolved to give up food for Advent.

She had meant only to duck into the breakfast room, where the Wynswiches took most of their meals, scavenge the sideboard for bread and cold meat, and then prepare her kittens for a wet trip to the stables. She knew Cook was still busy belowstairs readying the Christmas pudding for steaming; the nooning could only be haphazard.

She erred. Cook had been at work early to devise a more elegant repast. Lady Wynswich presided at the table, with Sir William at her left and Lord Ingraham on her right.

"Come, come, daughter," said her mother as Marian stuck her head in the room. "Find yourself something and join us."

Lady Wynswich's tone commanded obedience. Marian hurried to the sideboard, filled her plate, and moved to her usual place, which would have put her next to Sir William.

Her mother took instant exception to this. "Marian, Marian, how forgetful you are," she exclaimed. "Over here by Lord Ingraham, please! Ariadne—Elaine—will be along momentarily." This last comment was addressed to Sir William.

He paid little heed to his hostess: his eye was on Marian's plate, with its two slices of Cook's thick bread, the mound of meat, pink and steaming, the jellies, the creams. He looked at Lady Wynswich with that tight little smile Marian was already beginning to dislike.

"Lady Wynswich, it is no wonder that your family is hanging out over the chasm. When one's daughters eat so much . . . I mean, what does it admit to economy?"

Marian blinked and looked at her plate. It was no more than she usually ate, and even then, she knew she would be in the kitchen before dinner, pleading more meat and bread to hold her over until the advanced hour of six o'clock.

When Sir William continued to stare at her plate as though it were alive and writhing about, Lady Wynswich spoke.

"Marian, my dear, perhaps you should return some of that to the sideboard. Doesn't our vicar Mr. Beddoe speak to us from the pulpit about starving children in London?"

She stood her ground. "Mama, there is a starving child here at Covenden Hall."

Lord Ingraham made an odd noise deep in his throat and brought his napkin hurriedly to his lips. "Sorry. I have a touch of dyspepsia once in a while. Goodness, where are my manners?"

Marian looked at him. His eyes twinkled at her over the napkin, and she knew it would not be safe to look again. Without a word, she took her maligned plate to Lord Ingraham's side and sat.

Sir William would not abandon his train of thought. He shook his head at her and cast his whole attention upon his hostess. "Only assure me, Lady Wynswich, that Elaine consumes more ladylike proportions?"

"Indeed she does," replied Lady Wynswich. "She'll give you no cause to blush, Sir William."

Satisfied, he returned to his soup.

Marian created a sandwich and cut it in half. "But do you know, Sir William," she said as she spread a dab of jelly on it. "I heard Ariadne belch once. But it was only once, and she apologized so prettily afterward. I do believe, sir, that there were tears in her eyes."

Sir William choked over his soup and Lord Ingraham retreated to the safety of his napkin again.

Her mother sat in stupefied silence as Marian daintily cut her sandwich into tiny bites and ate them delicately off her fork. Sir William continued to cough and sputter as Marian put down her knife and fork and wiped her fingers neatly.

"Sir William, if you will raise both arms over your head and breathe deeply, you will feel quite the thing again," she advised serenely.

"Marian," said Lady Wynswich, her tone glacial. "That is quite enough."

"And so I was telling Sir William," Marian continued.

Recovering sufficiently to draw a breath, Sir William stared at Marian, who gave him her sunniest smile and took knife and fork to the other half of her sandwich. He opened his mouth to speak, when Lord Ingraham intervened.

"Lady Wynswich, these are charming watercolors on your walls. How well they suit," he said.

"Do they not?" agreed Lady Wynswich, eager to put Marian's food behind her. She would not look at Lord Ingraham, but cast her eyes instead upon the paintings. "Ariadne painted those only this summer. She is highly accomplished. Do you not agree, Sir William?"

Sir William gave the paintings only the briefest scrutiny. "I, madam, am partial to oils," he said, and then tittered. "Of course, one becomes used to such delights in the great galleries of Europe, which, I am sad to say, have been so long closed to our fair isle by the machinations of that evil beast Napoleon. Thank God he now resides on Elba."

Marian stared at him in admiration. She opened her mouth to compliment him on the grandeur of that sentence, when Lord Ingraham trod upon her foot. The napkin came to his lips again. "Hush, brat," he ordered behind it.

"You should see Ariadne's oils," Lady Wynswich prevaricated, and had the grace not to look in Marian's direction, even though her next comment was directed to her younger daughter. "Whatever is keeping our dear . . . Elaine?"

"Ariadne has the headache and will not be down," said Marian calmly as she extracted her foot from under Lord Ingraham's and crossed her ankles.

Her mother paused with her fork in midair, smiled, but did not look in Marian's direction. "Then why did you not tell me, dear? I would have seen to her at once."

Marian chewed and swallowed. "Mama, it was never my

wish to interrupt your conversation. And I know you would not wish me to call attention to myself.''

Lady Wynswich was left with nothing to say.

Lord Ingraham filled in the gap with all the skill of the treaty table in Ghent. ''Lady Wynswich, such excellent soup! I do not know when I have had better.''

''It is but a simple fish soup, Lord Ingraham,'' she said, her eyes looking everywhere but at the diplomat.

Marian watched her mother, a frown on her face, and then glanced at Gilbert Ingraham. She could see only his profile because she sat on his right side. Her mother had the full effect of his scar, and she would not look. Marian thought of Lord Ingraham's words in the library, and she burned with shame for her mother.

Lady Wynswich's attention was drawn then to a commonplace from Sir William.

Without thinking, Marian touched Lord Ingraham's sleeve and leaned toward him. ''Thank you for your valiant rally,'' she whispered, and then lowered her eyes. ''And please, please forgive my mother.''

''Forgiven already,'' he whispered back. ''One does become inured, or so I am discovering.''

''Discovering what?'' asked Lady Wynswich, her attention drawn across the table again, even though she gave Lord Ingraham only the briefest glance. ''Marian,'' she chided, ''you know what Papa used to say: 'Out loud, or not at all.' ''

''That is my doing,'' apologized Lord Ingraham. ''I merely commented I am discovering what a thoroughly charming family you have. I am also congratulating myself on the wisdom of accepting your son's Christmas invitation.''

''Have you not a wife and children of your own?'' Marian asked.

''Oh, no,'' he replied, and then chuckled. ''I seem to have kept myself too busy in foreign places for such a complication. I have a mother in Bath and two sisters near to her. We are Wiltshire folks, actually, for there my estate is located.''

''Oh, but this is not so far, Lord Ingraham,'' Lady Wynswich said to the distant wall. ''I wonder that you would choose us over a holiday with your loved ones.''

"It is my choice this year," he replied. "For all that Percy and Sir William and I know we could be summoned to Belgium in a moment's notice, although I suspect we were withdrawn for . . . other purposes. Vienna, perhaps. It is better if we stay together this holiday"

Lady Wynswich returned some vague answer and still would not look at Lord Ingraham.

Marian felt the blood rush to her face. She yanked her napkin off her lap and slapped it on the table, rising to her feet even as Lord Ingraham stood up and took hold of her so she could not brush past him.

"Lady Wynswich," he said as he tightened his grip on Marian's wrist, "Marian reminds me. She has promised to let me help her take the kittens"—he bowed to Sir William—"your kittens, Sir William, to the stables. You'll excuse us both, I trust. I am confident that Sir William will keep you tolerable good company. Come, Marian, you promised."

Before Lady Wynswich could return either a protest or an acquiescence, Marian found herself in the hall. Lord Ingraham did not release his grip until they were on the stairs, and then he rested his hand on the small of her back to continue her forward movement.

"Are the kittens still in your room?" he asked finally at the top of the stairs. "Marian, have a little patience with people!"

"But she was so inexcusably rude," she said, horrified at the tears that sprang into her eyes. "She avoids looking at you as if you were . . . were leprous. Oh, it mortifies me!"

He took her hand again, brought it to his lips, and kissed it. "My dear lady, are you always so quick to spring to the defense? Do you not think I am old enough to defend myself?"

"Yes! I mean, no . . . Oh, I do not know what I mean," she said, and dabbed at her eyes. "I own I was not altogether kind to Sir William, either. Oh, I cannot imagine what you must think of us."

He only smiled and bowed. "My dear Marian . . . Do you mind if I call you Marian? Miss Wynswich seems too formal, and after all, that is still your sister's title. Marian, I am going to my room to put on my boots. Assemble your kittens and let us be off."

She stood where she was. "Do you know, Lord Ingraham, no one has ever kissed my hand before. Except Alistair, and he only does it to make me angry."

His hand on the doorknob, Lord Ingraham looked back at her. "Then I declare the local swains utterly devoid of feeling, sense, and duty. Now, hurry up, Marian, and don't stand there with your mouth open. You'll catch flies."

But she still stood there, shaking her head.

"Now, what?" Lord Ingraham asked, the amusement almost palpable in his voice.

"Percy admonished me only this morning to remember how well-bred you are, how exalted . . ." She stopped. "Oh, why the devil do I not mind my tongue!"

He laughed. "Never tell me that Percy said I was 'exalted?' "

"Oh, no, no. That was my word. And he is wrong, or you have changed remarkably in a short space." It was her turn to laugh. "But Papa used to say that the Wynswiches have that effect on some."

The kittens, all tumbled together, were sleeping off a mighty feeding in the basket by her bed. Marian pulled on her oldest riding boots and cloak and picked up the basket. Whatever is the matter with me? she asked herself as she put the basket down for a peek in the mirror. Her cheeks were bright. "Drat!" she said, picked up the mother cat, and added her to the basket.

Ingraham waited for her in the hall. He took the basket from her and pulled her hood up over her hair. "Lead on," he said.

The rain was letting up, but the stableyard was a quagmire. "Does it truly do nothing but rain in Devon?" Lord Ingraham asked as he carefully picked his way through the mud.

"The summers are quite pleasant, my lord," she said, and resolved herself to remember herself. The resolution lasted only a moment. She stopped suddenly in the middle of a puddle, her hands on her hips. "But, my lord, I like it here in Devon, and you would, too, when the mist clears and the tree frogs sing after a spring rain."

He laughed, and she blushed and then hurried ahead of him into the stables so he would not notice. She waved to the stableboy and led Lord Ingraham to her workroom, pausing for just a moment to breathe deep of the horse smell, and remind herself all over again to set a good example and not give Percy pause to scold.

"There, over there." She gestured, and Lord Ingraham set the basket down where the straw was spread around. "Papa let me have this room for my patients."

Mama Cat took momentary exception to the barn owl that watched her, unblinking, from a perch nearby. She arched her back at him, but the owl regarded her only a moment more and then elaborately turned his back.

"I found him two years ago with a broken wing," Marian explained as she removed her cloak and shook off the rain. "He can fly, but he does so rather reluctantly. And he keeps the mice down. I have named him Solomon, of course."

"Of course." Lord Ingraham removed his coat. "And who is this frippery fellow?" he asked, squatting down to pat a black puppy, who licked his hand and then rolled over on his back in blatant invitation. Lord Ingraham scratched where he was bid, and the puppy groaned with pleasure.

Marian knelt down beside him. "You would not have recognized him six weeks ago, my lord." She gently pulled at the puppy's ears. "He was a bag of bones, you see. I found him in a box beside the road. The rest of the litter was dead. It is shameful the way some people use animals, my lord."

"And will you find a home for him?"

She nodded and gave the puppy's ears a final tug. "He is to be the vicar's Christmas present."

"Lucky man," declared Lord Ingraham. "And does the vicar know?"

She twinkled her eyes at him. "He will on Christmas, my lord."

Lord Ingraham stood and pulled up Marian. "You are an abominable child. Now, where is this famous salve that you have promised?"

"It is here," she said, and went to the shelf. "I have made it out of goose grease and other more felicitous ingredients." She sniffed it. "I added a bit of lavender water, or else you would smell rather like a nesting box, my lord. Sit down, and I will apply it."

He sat on a stool and she draped a towel around his shoulders, anchoring it with a pin. "Just in case," she explained, "although I trust you will sit still and not dart about as most of my patients do, my lord."

"Not even if you should step on my foot. And do, please, stop calling me 'my lord.' My name is Gilbert. Or you may call me Lowell, or Mason, which my friends do. After two daughters and many years, Papa had quite given up on a son, and he lost his head at my birth. I have any number of names. You need only choose."

She rested her hand on his shoulder. "Oh, dear, my papa had no more imagination than Marian Wynswich, my lord."

"It is enough. In fact, now that I know you, it is quite enough. I am serious, Marian. 'My lord' sounds much too old, and I'll have you know I'm not a day above twenty-eight." He met her look of frank surprise. "It is entirely the doing of this salt-and-pepper hair of mine, Madam Skeptic, which you can blame entirely on the life I have lately led."

Marian unstoppered the jar. "Sit still." She touched his scar. "I will call you Gil, my lord." She dipped her finger in the salve and spread it slowly over the burn. "Now, if you will wait a moment, it will soak in . . . Gil."

"Very good. No one calls me Gil, so it is entirely your name."

She outlined the scar, scrutinizing it. "How odd, my lord—I mean, Gil. Such a strange pattern. I do not understand. And look there on your temple—is that a fainter scar? I could not see it for your hair. Whatever were you doing, sir? Percy would dub me vastly impertinent, but I suppose I cannot help that."

He smiled at her and gestured to the stool nearby. "Sit down, Marian. I had the misfortune to be aboard HMS *Defiant* when we were attacked in midocean by a French fleet, returning from Haiti, I believe."

Marian's eyes widened. "My word, sir, whatever were you doing there?"

"Attempting a return from a peace mission to Washington. Such a wretched swamp for such a beautiful city! Too bad we burned it. At any rate, we were returning from Washington and were set upon and burned to the waterline. I had the misfortune to trip and slip myself on a grate so hot it was practically glowing. Hence the pattern.''

Marian's eyes filled with tears.

''Here, here, my dear,'' Lord Ingraham said, and touched her cheek. ''The ship heaved only a second later, and I found myself pitched into the ocean.'' He dipped his finger in the salve and touched it to the burn. ''The oddest thing happened. About the last thing I remember as the water closed over me was my face hissing. And the smell, of course.'' He shuddered. ''That is something one doesn't forget.''

''When did all this happen?''

He thought back. ''It was July, about six weeks before we burned Washington. I remember particularly because the French ship took us aboard and I woke up a few days later to a celebration of Bastille Day. I drank more rum than I should have, of course, but you know the French.''

''However did you escape?'' she asked, her eyes still wide.

''There was no trick to it. The captain could see no use for a slightly singed diplomat. I was set ashore in the Azores. It was easy enough to hail a passing ship bound for Plymouth.'' He looked at her for the first time since he began his recital. ''I don't look in too many mirrors anymore, but then, that never was my style to begin with.''

Marian sat in silence, her lips pursed.

''You appear ready to make a pronouncement,'' Lord Ingraham said. ''Our acquaintance is brief, but that much I know about you already.''

''I was merely going to observe . . . I think I know why you have chosen to avoid Bath this Christmas season. Do they not know at home?''

It was Lord Ingraham's turn for silence. To Marian's eye, he appeared less sure of himself, and for a moment he did seem young to her. Impulsively, she took his hand and held it tight.

''It will fade, you know,'' she said when she trusted her voice. ''But, sir, it is Christmas, and you should be home. You know you should.''

He freed his hand and stood up. ''No, Marian, not this year. Maybe next year. Such things are difficult.''

He sat down again and without a word she applied more salve to the burn. He reached up and stopped her hand.

"But it will not fade overnight, Marian."

"No."

She wiped her fingers on the towel and put the stopper back in the bottle. "But only think how dreadfully you will be missed, Gil."

"Next year."

The stable door opened. The door to the workroom was partly ajar, so Marian tiptoed to it. "Oh, it is Percy. He will come to take you away and show you around the estate."

"Oh, but I will not go," said Lord Ingraham as he dabbed at the corner of his chin, where the salve dripped. "Besides that, he has Sir William, I'm bound, and surely Sir William is company enough." He winked. "If we are silent, my dear, he will never know we are here."

They both stood by the door, listening as Percy showed Papa's horses to his guest, explaining in his careful way their excellent bloodlines, their prime points.

"But, my dear Percy," they heard Sir William say, "whatever can your mother be thinking of to keep these prime goers here all year, unridden and eating their heads off? Is it not a peculiar extravagance? I do not wonder that your estate is all to pieces."

Marian set her lips tight together. "And next he will prose on about my eating habits. He thinks to tell us how to manage," she told Lord Ingraham. "He is right, of course, and that is the sorrow of it." She sighed. "Mama refuses to sell them. She cries and sighs and takes to her couch when the solicitor comes, or when the bailiff and I attempt to get her to listen to reason."

"And this falls to your task?" he asked, his voice low.

"Oh, yes! And I am a thankless child." She stifled a laugh. "I thought I would lose all countenance when Mama pointed at me after one of those quelling interviews and declared, 'How sharper than a serpent's child is a thankless tooth!' Ariadne and I were in whoops about it for days. Poor Shakespeare suffers at Mama's hands." She looked at him.

"Speak, by all means, Marian."

"*King Lear* is scarcely my favorite, I must admit. Really, Gil, why doesn't that wretched Cordelia just say what she thinks?"

It was Lord Ingraham's turn to smother a laugh. "Why, indeed, Marian? Cordelia's a regular spineless wonder. Why did I never see that before I met you?"

"But setting Shakespeare aside—which Mama has always done—we are in the basket and Ariadne will be sacrificed on the altar of duty."

"And another thing," Sir William was saying, "do you not think Ariadne is a trifle short?"

Marian looked at Lord Ingraham in amazement.

"I do not know that there is anything we can do to correct this oversight," said Percy from the other room, his voice a study in seriousness.

"Perhaps the rack?" Lord Ingraham whispered to Marian, and then clapped his hand over her mouth when she started to laugh. He held it there, even as his own shoulders shook.

Sir William made his ponderous progress down the row of loose boxes, commenting on this horse and that horse, animadverting on the spendthrift ways of some, and raising questions about the wisdom of a connection with the Wynswiches. Soon their footsteps receded into the distance, and the stable doors were slid in place again.

Marian was long through laughing when Lord Ingraham removed his hand. She sat on the floor, her knees drawn up, her chin resting on them, as Mama Cat coiled around her and rubbed against her legs. "I had such high hopes for Ariadne, and now Percy thinks to marry her to that silly fat man." She shook her head. "Percy tells me I must not speak so. And so I should not." She wagged her finger in his face. "But, sir, I will never marry. From all that I can see, it is an uncomfortable business. Now sit down again, and hold still."

Lord Ingraham obeyed and she smoothed the salve in another layer over his cheek again. "Marian," he asked suddenly, "how old are you?"

"I am almost seventeen," she replied, and started when he

winced. "Am I hurting you? I would not for the world."

"No, no. Your fingers are wondrously careful." He swiveled his head slightly to regard her. "How soon are you seventeen?"

She shrugged. "In March, but it hardly signifies. We cannot afford a London Season for Ariadne or for me, and besides, I did not inherit the Wynswich looks. But I did have such plans for Ariadne and the vicar."

The cat jumped into Lord Ingraham's lap, turned around several times, and settled herself. He fingered her fur thoughtfully. "Surely there is someone in this wide world who prefers black hair to chestnut, and blue eyes to Wynswich brown," he said. "But I see a mulish look in those blue eyes, and I am reminded that marriage is an uncomfortable business, as you put it."

"It must be," she pointed out. "Only look how long you have avoided the altar of duty."

"Yes, I have, haven't I?" he agreed. "Perhaps I have not sufficiently applied myself."

"I know it is different with men," Marian said generously. "Mama used to say that when Papa received love notes from his opera dancers."

Lord Ingraham let out a shout of laughter. "Marian, what will you say next?"

She stuck out her tongue at him and returned to her contemplation. The rain was beginning again, the soothing sound of it making her eyes droop. It reminded her how tired she was, how little sleep she had snatched the night before. She hardly noticed when Lord Ingraham put his hand on her shoulder. She leaned against his hand for the briefest moment before he took it away.

"Does nothing ever go the way we plan?" she asked. "I did so want to have a wonderful Christmas."

"So you shall, Marian," he said.

She thought he was going to say something else, but the door slammed open. The cat hissed and leapt off his lap and into the basket of kittens. The owl ruffled his feathers.

"Mare! There you are!"

Alistair let out a crack of laughter. "Lord Ingraham! Did you

let Marian quack you?'' He pulled off his coat and shook it over
Marian, who made a grab for him. He danced nimbly out of
reach. "Mare, did I see Percy and that funny little man ride
off in the gig? D'ye think Percy will show him all around? Lord,
I feel sorry for Ariadne.''

He went over to the shelf and picked up another bottle,
opening it and holding it under his nostrils. "Marian, a dose
of this and Sir W. would cock his toes up stiff.''

"Alistair," she exclaimed, and took the bottle from him. "It
would likely only give him a headache to remember. But do
not wave it about. Alistair, you are a dreadful nuisance.''

She appealed to Lord Ingraham. "Sir you must forgive us
both our rudeness.''

Alistair snorted, and she whirled about. "For that's what it
is, Alistair!''

Gilbert merely smiled and watched them both. Marian stared
down Alistair, and he laughed and put up both hands to ward
off his sister.

"Alistair," she declared, "I am so much better when you
are not about! Even Mama remarks upon it.''

"She will now blame me for her manners, my lord," Alistair
explained. He frowned and was silent a moment. "Better we
should blame our own dear Bertram Wynswich, eh?'' he said
quietly.

His serious tone stabbed at Marian's heart, but she nodded.
"Mama had the raising of Percy and Ariadne," she explained,
too shy to meet Lord Ingraham's glance, which had not wavered
from her face. "That was before . . . before she took to her
bed so often. Oh, there were such times we had . . .'' Marian
began wistfully, and then stopped as she recalled herself to the
moment. "But truly, Percy and Ariadne are everything that is
proper.''

"And dull occasionally," added Alistair.

"Alistair, please!'' Marian flared. "Well, I own at
times . . .'' She smiled to herself, a quick grin chasing across
her face and gone in no time. "So Mama turned me and Alistair
over to Papa, and he always encouraged us to speak our minds.''
She looked down at her hands. "Plain speaking is a hard habit

to break, my lord. There's something so . . . so *free* about it. Ah, well.'' She finally raised her eyes to Gilbert Ingraham's. "And things do strike me funny. Well, I am determined to do better in the New Year. It is time I grew up.''

Lord Ingraham touched her cheek. ''But not too fast, please? I confess to being bored around diplomats who never, ever, say what is on their minds.'' He bowed. ''It is a pleasure to meet a female with both hair and wit.''

Alistair laughed as Marian blushed. ''Oh, Mare, aren't you the silly one! And you had better get used to having me around, especially if I cannot convince Percy to let me ship off to sea as some man o' war's 'Young Gentleman.' '' He appealed to Lord Ingraham. ''My lord, I know I am old enough to go to sea, but Percy will have none of it.''

''Perhaps if you went to school and did well, he might reconsider,'' Lord Ingraham suggested.

''You don't know Percy,'' Alistair said morosely, and sat beside his sister.

''And there are other schools beside Eton,'' continued Lord Ingraham.

Marian watched him. Again he appeared on the verge of saying something more, but he did not. How good he is at that, she thought. I would blurt out whatever came into my head, and then regret it. I must ask him how he keeps his own counsel so well.

She knew she would not. She also knew that Percy would rake her over the hearth for dragging the elegant Lord Ingraham into the stable for a dose of her dog-and-cat salve. He would look at her in that patient way of his, and the despair in his eyes would make her squirm again.

She handed the bottle of salve to Lord Ingraham and stood up, brushing the bits of straw from her skirt and mumbling her apologies for taking up his time. ''For I do forget myself,'' she concluded, ameliorating the effect by adding, ''when I remember.''

Lord Ingraham looked from the sister to the brother and back again. ''You two are surely the most abominable children I ever met. You must be a sore trial to Percy and your mama.''

"Oh, we are," agreed Alistair, not in the least put out, "although Marian is forever telling me to behave as I ought, and Ariadne . . ." He turned to Marian. "That was what I came here for. Do you know that the vicar is in the house seeking an audience with Ariadne?" His face fell. "But I do believe he got Mama instead."

"Oh, Alistair, no," exclaimed Marian. "Could you not rescue him? Only think what Mama is telling him about Sir William!"

Her brother grabbed his coat and fled the workroom. Marian threw on her cloak and followed after him, Lord Ingraham right behind.

4

The vicar's gig waited in the front drive. As Marian and Lord Ingraham came around the corner of the building, Alistair was already up the front steps in time to hold the door open for the vicar. Other than a slight lift of the eyebrows, Mr. Sam Beddoe barely acknowledged Alistair's presence. He dragged down the front steps, his head drooping down into the top of his overcoat, like a turtle retreating into its shell. He did not see them; even if he had, Marian thought, he would not have known them.

Sam stood there a moment beside the gig, as if wondering what it was doing there. Eventually he recognized the horse as his own and climbed in. He sat there in the rain another long moment before he spoke to the horse and started down the lane.

Alistair looked back at Marian and Lord Ingraham, shrugged, and went indoors.

"Mama has told Sam about Sir William, depend upon it," Marian said, and then to her own amazement, she burst into noisy tears.

She could not have explained why, but she was not at all surprised when Lord Ingraham took her into his arms right there in the drive and held her tight, his hand on her hair, her face pressed against his chest. She was not even surprised at herself when she put her arms around his waist and sobbed heartily into his already wet coat.

"Poor, poor Marian," he said softly, "we are ruining your Christmas, are we not? What can I do to make it better?"

His voice was amazingly soothing. If the rain had not commenced to drum down, Marian would have been content to remain where she was. "I wish Sir William would go away," she sobbed. "And I wish, oh, I wish the vicar would inherit a fortune." She stepped out of Lord Ingraham's generous embrace. "But now I am being foolish beyond belief, Lord Ingraham."

"Gil," he reminded her.

"No. Lord Ingraham," she repeated. "I am too forward by half. I cannot fathom what you must think of me, sir." She wiped her face. "But it would be wonderful beyond anything if my wishes came true."

"Done," Lord Ingraham said in a low voice.

She started toward the front steps and then stopped. "Beg pardon?" she asked.

"Oh, nothing, Marian," he said. "Hurry inside before you catch a cold."

Percy waited for her in the front hall, his lips tight together again, no humor in his eyes. Marian stopped where she was, just inside the door, her hands clasped together in front of her. Gilbert stood next to her; unconsciously she moved closer to him.

Percy stared at her. Marian gazed back timidly. "Percy, you are back so soon."

"It was too wet for Sir William," he replied in crisp tones. "Devon weather displeases him." Percy folded his arms across his chest. "Marian, the bookroom."

"Oh, but, Percy," she began, "you must understand about lunch—"

"The bookroom," he repeated.

She opened her mouth to protest, but Lord Ingraham put his hand on her shoulder and she closed it.

"Percy," he began, "before you take her off, let me tell you how much I am enjoying my visit with you and your family. Such warmth, such friendliness! I own I do not know when I have laughed as much."

Percy could only gape at him in surprise. "My family?" he repeated.

"Oh, yes, and especially Marian and Alistair. How you must enjoy the pleasure of their company. I truly envy you."

Marian marveled at the diplomat's art. Under the protection of Lord Ingraham, she looked at her brother, who was looking back at her with an expression less perilous than the one that greeted her.

"I do enjoy their company, despite their hey-go-mad ways," Percy said, relaxing, and for a moment Marian saw the brother she remembered, the one less burdened with care. She almost said something, but reconsidered. This could be one of those times to remain silent and let another take the lead.

Lord Ingraham did not fail her. "And if you would, if you had the time before dinner, could I make a request?"

"Certainly, sir. Only ask."

"That chestnut in your stable. The one with a blaze? Could you show him to me? I want a good horse, and I like the looks of that one, provided, of course, Lady Wynswich will consent to part with him."

Percy's interview with Marian was forgotten. "Only let me put on my riding boots, and we'll try out that horse. I think a ride about the place would be welcome, that is, if you don't mind the rain."

"Not at all. People tell me that Devon is lovely, even when it's wet."

Percy looked at his sister, coaxed a smile out of her, and started for the stairs. "You, sir, have been listening too long to Marian. I'll be right back."

Lord Ingraham seemed to remember himself and removed his hand from Marian's shoulder. "There, brat, I saved your bacon. Promise me you will exercise a little discretion this evening at table."

"I will never say a word, sir," she replied, and felt suddenly shy. "You were magnificent, my lord. But do you really want to buy a horse? You needn't go that far."

"I am looking for a prime goer. If I am posted to the United States, as I hope I am, I want to bring along my own mount. And frankly, my dear, your papa's stables were famous."

"Yes, they were," she agreed, pleased that for the first time, the thought gave her no sadness. She tugged at his sleeve. "And do you know, once the Prince Regent himself came here to look over Papa's stable?" She glanced about her for Percy, and lowered her voice. "But he was too much of a nip-farthing to buy one." She considered the subject. "And I do not think we had a horse big enough to hold him up, now that I consider it."

"Marian, do you always say what comes to mind?" asked Lord Ingraham.

"Why, no, sir. Only just a moment ago when Percy was acting the perfect dragon, I refrained. I thought you might rescue me."

Gilbert threw back his head and laughed. "You are utterly incorrigible. I wonder that anyone tolerates you."

Marian released her grip on his sleeve, opened her mouth, and then closed it again. Lord Ingraham gave her an inquiring look, but she shook her head. "I shall be circumspect, sir. Good day to you."

He took her arm. "Not so fast, my dear. Will you come riding, too?"

She made a face. "I am such an indifferent horsewoman. It was one of Papa's crosses, I assure you, but horses are so big! I think any horse I rode would feel my fear and bite me out of spite. Thank you, no, sir."

"I wish I could teach you to ride, Marian."

Marian darted away from him. "Unless that is your Christmas wish, sir, it will not come true. And now, farewell. I have other things to attend to." She started up the stairs, go halfway up, and leaned over the railing. "But thank you, Gil, for . . . for everything." She laughed. "Only think what your friends would say if you were caught tutoring a schoolroom chit in riding! You know they would laugh."

"I'm already thinking about my friends," he replied mildly, and kissed his hand to her. "Hurry, brat, before your brother comes back and changes his mind and hauls you off to the horrors of the bookroom."

Marian changed quickly into dry clothes and wrapped a towel about her hair. Mama was asleep in her room. Marian heard Percy and Lord Ingraham in the front hall again, and then the door closed. Sir William was nowhere in sight.

"Ariadne? Ariadne?" she asked softly as she knocked on her sister's door.

"Go away."

Marian entered her sister's room. It was no more than she expected. Ariadne sat drooping in the window seat. Marian watched her for a moment—so still, so delicate—and felt a tug of irritation. Dear, dearest Ariadne, she thought, sometimes you do so remind me of Mama. This is a time for action, not vapors.

She almost spoke her thoughts out loud, but reconsidered. I should be silent. That is what Gil would be.

Quietly she entered the room and sat down in the window seat across from her sister. She wrapped her arms around her knees and just sat there.

Ariadne's eyes were red. She held a handkerchief to her nose and blew it every now and then, little dainty sniffles.

"Oh, for the Lord's sake, Ariadne, give it a good blow," Marian said finally, casting aside her brief hold on diplomacy.

With a look half-mutinous, half-pitiful, Ariadne blew her nose until her curls shook.

"That's better," Marian said. "Now, what are we to do?"

"I do not know what we can do," exclaimed Ariadne in tragic accents. "Mama has told the vicar that I am to entertain an offer from Sir William. I am sure Sir William lurks below; I dare not leave my room."

"Oh, stuff," Marian said prosaically. "Sir William is far too fat to lurk."

"It was merely a figure of speech," Ariadne said. "Marian, Sam will never offer for me now. You know he is too timid."

"Then we must stiffen his spine . . . some way or other."

Both sisters fell silent. Marian unwrapped her hair and began to comb her fingers through it.

Ariadne got up and came back to the window seat with a brush. "You will snarl your hair something wretched, Mare," she said, and started to brush it. She applied herself diligently to the task, humming as she brushed, and soon Marian's hair fell, straight and gleaming, to her waist. Ariadne kissed the top of her sister's head and sat down.

Marian fingered the ends of her hair, coaxing a curl where

there was none. "Ariadne, tell me truthfully, in words with bark: am I even a little pretty?"

The question surprised them both. Ariadne looked at her in amazement.

"I mean, I know I do not have the Wynswich looks," Marian stumbled on as she felt her face grow red, "but do you think I am attractive?"

For a moment the light came back into Ariadne's eyes. She leaned against the dormer wall and regarded her sister for several long moments. "I have always thought you were pretty, Mare. True, your hair is black, but what is that to anything? It is so long and thick. And do you not admire blue eyes? They are so much more interesting than brown. And you have such a lively way about you." Ariadne tilted her head to continue her perusal. "In truth, you look a great deal like Mama, back before she took to her bed every time the wind blew or anyone made demands. I would say you are pretty." She kissed Marian again. "Goose, what is it? Are you going to catch a husband so I do not have to? Is that it? Too bad there is no one here for both of us!"

Marian drew up her dignity. "You know I have no wish ever to marry, and besides, my dear, you already have someone who loves you amazingly. The matter simply must be brought to a head. I believe I will think on it."

Ariadne smiled for the first time as she pulled Marian to her feet. "Then go along with you and think! You were always better at that than anyone in this disordered household, excepting Percy, of course."

"Of course," agreed Marian, "although I cannot imagine what maggot was in his head to bring us Sir William Clinghorn on a platter."

The mention of Sir William brought the frown back to Ariadne's face. "Oh, Marian, do apply yourself."

She applied herself all afternoon in her room, adding a little more wood to the fire than she usually permitted herself, resting her stockinged feet on the grate, and pulling her skirts up to her knees to catch the little drafts of heat that billowed up.

Think as she would, the matter of giving unsought advice to

the parish vicar was a tangle she could not resolve. For most of the afternoon, she found herself thinking instead of Gilbert Ingraham.

Such a life he had led. I have been no farther than Lyme Regis on occasion, and once to London, she thought. And he has been to the United States of America on a special mission, in a desperate sea battle, shipwrecked and cast ashore on foreign soil. How blue his eyes are. And Percy says he is an earl, and Mama says he is exalted, but he is ever so much fun, and not at all stuffy. And he is tall and calm and rational and orderly and entirely what I would imagine a diplomat to be.

When the wood was ashes, she did not add another log. Marian wrapped herself in her favorite blanket and lay down. I shall think better this way, she thought as her eyes closed.

The room was in shadow when she woke, but it was not the shadow of night. She folded her arms across her stomach and listened. The rain had stopped and there was the softest sound of snow falling. She threw back the blanket and ran to the window.

Snow cast its gray and white shadows all over Covenden Hall. It fell straight and heavy, and covered the mud of the front drive, turning the soggy ground into something magical. Marian closed her eyes and listened. I can truly truly hear snow fall. I wonder if Ariadne knows that you can hear snow? As she pulled on her shoes and tried to smooth the wrinkles from her dress, she decided that it would not be a matter of interest to Ariadne.

Marian's stomach rumbled; she wondered what kind of mood Cook was in. She tiptoed down the backstairs to the kitchen and looked about her in satisfaction. The Christmas pudding, wrapped and rewrapped in cheesecloth, steamed in its pudding pot. A tray of ginger cookies tempted Marian. She took one and bit into it, uttering a little cry of delight.

Cook shook a wooden spoon at her as she ate another and then another.

"Cook," she asked, her mouth full, "will you make toffee and marchpane?"

"You know that I will," assured Cook, and then glanced

about her. "Only do not tell Sir William Clinghorn. He would call it a fearful extravagance."

Marian swallowed. "Whatever do you mean? Why should it matter to him?"

It was all the avenue Cook needed. "Such nerve I never hope to see," she exclaimed. "Who should walk up and down in here this afternoon, like the devil in Job, peeking in pots and pans, looking in the pantry, and all the time cluck-clucking about waste and what he calls 'Wynswich management?' "

Marian put back a ginger biscuit, her appetite gone. "Oh, Cook, it is not true!"

Cook glared back. "Only ask Billings, if you doubt me! He will tell you a tale of Sir William snooping about in the wine cellar even. He thought to remove a Richelieu '73, but you know how Billings gets when there is iron in his gizzard."

"Oh, dear," Marian said. Visions of Billings defending his wine cellar waved in front of her eyes.

"And the parlormaid tells me that man has already sifted through the linen closets. And all this while Lord Wynswich was out riding with the tall man."

The other servants had been listening. They gathered about the long table, nodding and adding their mites to the conversation. Marian heard them all, nodding and cluck-clucking herself in all the appropriate pauses, but her thoughts were elsewhere.

How dare that wart act as though he already owned Covenden Hall? It would be a long dinner and a much longer evening. She wished herself in the wine cellar next to the Richelieu.

Sir William had done his work well. A subdued group of Wynswiches gathered in comparative order for dinner and were only five minutes late, Alistair breathing heavy and bringing up the rear as he straightened his neckcloth.

Sir William snapped open his watch when Billings, his face wooden, announced dinner. He waggled his finger at Lady Wynswich. "Punctuality, my dear lady, is a gift from heaven. You fail your children when you do not enforce it."

Lady Wynswich could only stare. Alistair began to cough. He ran to the window and flung up the sash, breathing deeply as the snow settled into the room. When he turned around again, all eyes were upon him. Alistair closed the window and looked at them. "It was merely a touch of . . . of . . ."

"Insanity?" Marian filled in helpfully.

Sir William stared back, goggle-eyed. "There is nothing, nothing, I say, that would compel me to sever my ties here faster than the thought of nurturing the hobgoblin of insanity in my bosom."

Lady Wynswich uttered an inarticulate moan. Percy raised his eyebrows and began advancing on his sister.

She was saved by Lord Ingraham, who came bursting into the room, pulling on his coat. He stopped immediately, gave his coat another twitch, and became a diplomat again "Do excuse my tardiness, Lady Wynswich," he began. "I lay down on that marvelous feather bed and quite forgot about the time. And then I lay there, just listening to the snow. Sir William, do not you find Covenden Hall refreshing?"

Sir William was left with no recourse but to bow, creak, and smile. He pocketed his watch and held out his arm to Lady Wynswich. Percy followed with Ariadne, as Lord Ingraham appropriated Marian.

"My dear Miss Wynswich," he said as he tucked Marian's arm in his, "you will forgive my gaff?"

She hung back from the dinner procession and stood on tiptoe to whisper, "You did that on purpose! I would wager that you are never late to anything. And didn't I hear someone just waiting on the stairs?"

He bowed. "Sir William is a terror for punctuality. When I saw Alistair running for the dining room like he was rounding a wicket, I knew that he—and you—would require assistance"

He chuckled, and looked about him to make sure no one else was listening. "The impulsive shade of Bertram Wynswich must be watching me, too! That's the first time I ever took off my coat once I was out of my room and on my way to dinner, but it seemed like the only way to help Alistair."

He bowed. "Consider it a gesture in the spirit of Christmas, when charity should be extended, even to little brothers."

Marian patted his sleeve and smoothed out a wrinkle. "Are you *never* at a loss?"

He gazed down at her and there was a peculiar look in his eyes. She thought perhaps his cravat was too tight. "I am at a loss now, my dear, and have been for some twenty-four hours. Now, close your mouth, for I will say no more on that subject. And I advise you to only open your mouth for the food."

Dinner was a near-run thing. Marian did as she was bid, maintaining a discreet silence. Even when Sir William began to eye her plate as she put away dish after dish, she said nothing. Sir William was left to murmur, "Prodigious," under his breath, before turning his whole attention to Ariadne, who answered him prettily enough but kept her eyes on the plate before her, and pushed around her food.

Tiring of that finally, Sir William directed his conversation to his host. He moved himself back from the table and rested his hands on his paunch. "Percy, I spent an afternoon in your library."

Percy smiled. "It was Papa's pride, Sir William. There is none like it in Devon, I am sure."

"Yes, I found something quite out of the ordinary there, myself," agreed Lord Ingraham. "Only this morning."

"Did you, my lord?" Sir William purred and then pounced. "Well, Percy, do you know what I discovered in your library?"

He paused for effect and looked at them each in turn, his stare landing last on Lady Wynswich.

"I found Rabelais," he concluded, his voice full of accusation.

Lady Wynswich stared back, her mouth a perfect O. "I am sure I do not know how it got there, Sir William," she declared when she could command her voice. "But you know that in the country, little woodling creatures do sometimes invade even the best of homes in the winter. I shall speak to the parlormaid in the morning."

The silence was stunning. Marian gripped the seat of her chair, knowing that if she looked at Lord Ingraham or made even the slightest sound, she would lose all countenance and disgrace herself for all time. She knew that Lord Ingraham was struggling, for she heard an inarticulate sound deep in his throat.

"Mama, it is a French author," Percy said, with only the slightest quaver.

The magic word had been spoken, the word that unleashed Sir William Clinghorn. "Ah, madam, and such a book he wrote! I wonder that you would pollute the library with it. Ladies have been known to read it and faint."

"But I did not faint," Marian said into the large silence that followed his pronouncement. "I thought it quite humorous."

All color drained from Sir William's ample cheeks. "Good God, Lady Wynswich, what is this?"

Marian raised her chin and looked him right in the eye. "It was almost as entertaining as Boccaccio's *Decameron*, but not half as fun as Chaucer and that wonderful housewife of Bath." She turned to Lord Ingraham. "Did you not say you were from Bath, Lord Ingraham? I daresay it has changed since Chaucer's time."

He did not fail her. "Indeed, Miss Wynswich, and it is lovely this time of year. You would particularly enjoy the carolers." He directed his attention to his hostess. "Lady Wynswich, is there the possibility of shopping hereabouts? I need to purchase some Christmas items, myself, now that Marian reminds me."

The conversation creaked into gear again and lurched on for the remainder of that course, Lord Ingraham regaling those assembled with the events of his last Christmas, spent in St. Petersburg.

Marian opened her mouth once to enter the fray again, but a discreet elbow from Lord Ingraham reduced her to silence. She glanced at him. She wouldn't have thought such a big, comfortable-looking man to have such sharp elbows.

Marian remained in silence, not even eating, thinking about other dinners, dinners where Ariadne and Mama would discuss some nuance of fashion or county gossip, and she and Papa would wrangle with each other over something one or the other had read. Percy would join in, when he was home, and they would sit at the dining-room table long after Ariadne and Mama had left to other pursuits. Papa would push back the plates, and the candle would gutter low while Marian opened books on the table and argued.

She glanced at Percy, who also sat quietly, twirling his glass by the stem, watching her. Percy, she thought as she smiled at him, I wish you could remember this side of Papa as well as I do. Papa was improvident and shocking in many ways, I suppose, but he loved us, and, oh, I am starved for his conversation.

Nothing about Percy's demeanor indicated that he shared a single reminiscence. He continued gazing at her thoughtfully. As if wondering how to dispose of me, she reasoned to herself. And who can blame him? Why am I such a bagpipe? So contentious? She sank lower in her chair and resolved to quit the family circle when the meal was complete.

Soon the conversation was spinning off on its own, and Lord Ingraham took himself out of the lists. He finished his dinner as Sir William prosed on about economy as the backbone of English society.

"I didn't mean to quell you entirely," he whispered to Marian finally when she remained sunk in silence.

"It is nothing. I was merely thinking . . . about Papa." She raised her eyes to his. "When Papa was at table, there were so many things to talk about."

"Great ideas?" Lord Ingraham asked gently. "Not whether Lady X dampens her petticoat, or why Lady Z's latest baby resembles the Regent?"

She nodded, but said nothing more. When Lady Wynswich finally signaled to her and Ariadne that it was time to leave the table to the gentlemen, she rose with gratitude.

Lord Ingraham rose, too, as the ladies made ready to withdraw. "Marian," he said, "don't disappear before we're through in here."

"I am sure Percy would prefer it."

"Don't," he repeated, "just don't."

While the men lingered at the table over their brandy, Marian bore in silence her mother's scold in the parlor. "Marian, I do not understand what maggot riddles your brain at times. If we can fix matters with Sir William, and Ariadne does as she ought, we can all be comfortable again."

"Except for Ariadne," was Marian's only reply.

Ariadne said nothing, only retreated to a corner of the room.

And why do you not leap into the struggle, my dear sister? Marian asked herself as she listened to her mother out of one ear. Are you so passive that you will allow yourself to be pulled into this distasteful marriage? Is Covenden Hall that important?

The thought was disquieting in the extreme. With a sigh of her own, Marian found her workbasket where she had tossed it the night before, and hitched herself close to a branch of candles, wondering how it was possible for threads to tangle so amazingly all by themselves. It would be an evening's serious application to straighten them all out.

The gentlemen joined them a half-hour later, Sir William much rosier from an application of Papa's smuggled brandy. Even Percy was smiling. Out of the corner of her eye, Marian noticed Lord Ingraham look her way. There was no chair near hers, and he did not seek to join her company, particularly after Alistair flung himself down on the floor beside her and pulled out a handful of snarled yarns.

"Mare," he announced to the room, "how d'ye muddle these things so completely?"

On another evening, she would have made a grab at his hair and pelted the skeins at him, one at a time. She sat and watched her brother. "I suppose I must apply myself, Alistair."

Percy started and looked toward her.

From his place seated beside his host, Lord Ingraham remarked, "Alistair, to some it is given to do other things. Perhaps this is your sister's case?"

"Exactly so, Lord Ingraham," said Lady Wynswich, relieving Marian of any reply. "And so I tell Marian," she enlarged, speaking to him but avoiding even a glance in his direction. "She could learn to knot a fringe, or paint a watercolor like Ariadne, or even practice on the pianoforte. She has a beautiful voice."

"Lady Wynswich, there are even accomplishments beyond those," he replied.

"Not for a lady," Lady Wynswich announced, and her tone invited no disagreement.

There was a general pause while everyone waited for someone else to begin a conversation.

Sir William looked about him. "I say, does anyone in this household play chess?"

He asked the question with the air of one already doomed to disappointment, as if chess were as far removed from the better homes of Devon as Ultima Thule from the Antipodes.

Marian put down her yarns and sat up straighter. "I play, Sir William."

Sir William only smiled at her indulgently. "I had a real game in mind, Miss Wynswich, although I am sure you play prettily."

"Prettily," Alistair said in a low voice. "You'll be bloodied, drawn, and quartered."

"Hush, Alistair," Marian said. "I play a real game, sir. Only let me get the pieces and show you." She put down her work-basket and moved to the cupboard where the pieces were kept.

Lady Wynswich cleared her throat. "My dear Sir William, Marian is a most indifferent player. Aren't you, my dear?"

Marian's fingers froze on the chessboard. She turned around. Ariadne watched her, a guarded expression in her eyes. She does not want a scene, thought Marian. She never wants a scene. She glanced at Alistair. He wants me to challenge this detestable man. She looked at Percy. And my brother wishes me to Jericho. Her gaze shifted to Lord Ingraham. And what is in your eyes? I wish I knew.

"Yes, Mama," she replied in a low voice, "I am much too indifferent."

Sir William was willing to forgive. "Some morning, my dear, when I have nothing else to do, I shall endeavor to instruct you. It will be well worth your time, if you are interested in chess."

"Marian would love that, Sir William. It would be such a treat for you, wouldn't it, daughter?" said Lady Wynswich. "But now, I am sure Percy would be delighted to challenge you, Sir William. Perhaps, Marian, you would see to the tea tray? I cannot imagine what is keeping the parlormaid."

Other than the fact that we let her go six months ago, thought Marian, I cannot imagine either. "Yes, Mama, I will see to the tea," she said, and beat a hasty retreat into the hall.

She leaned against the wall, fists clenched, waiting for her anger to recede. I cannot go back in there again, she told herself, I simply cannot. And I cannot endure one more minute of this horrid Christmas.

The door opened and Lord Ingraham came into the hall. He nodded to her. "I seem to recall that tea trays are notoriously heavy. But what's this? Marian, my goodness."

She rubbed at the tears that spilled down her cheeks. "It is nothing, my lord. I am being what Mama calls 'fractious and distempered.' "

Before she could move away, he took a handkerchief, wiped her eyes, and then put it over her nose. "Blow, brat. Much better." He leaned one hand on the wall so she could not bolt. "I have a suspicion. Tell me if it is true."

She nodded, but raised her eyes no further than the watch fob on his waistcoat.

"I want to know . . . Marian Wynswich, look at me." He put his finger under her chin and forced her to look him n the face. "Are you not permitted to win?"

She shook her head. "Mama reminded me only yesterday that I must not even beat Alistair anymore, now that he is growing up." She grabbed the handkerchief and blew her nose fiercely. "And I could beat Sir William to flinders! I know I could!" Marian sobbed out loud.

Lord Ingraham took her by the hand and pulled her farther from the parlor door. He sat her down on the staircase and said not a word as she cried, blew her nose, and pocketed his handkerchief.

"I'll return it tomorrow," she said. "Forgive me, Lord Ingraham."

"The last time I checked, my name was still Gilbert," he said mildly. "Gil to you, as I recall."

Marian managed a watery smile in his direction. "Very well, then, Gil. I do not know what has gotten into me this day." The stairs were cold; she inched closer to him. "And this is not at all the Christmas I imagined."

"Nor I," he replied, and moved to put his arm around her.

Before he could quite accomplish it, Marian leaned forward, her head turned to one side, listening intently.

"Marian, I—"

"Hush, Gil," she ordered. "Oh, do listen!"

The sound was a murmur at first, a murmur so low she

wondered if her ears were deceiving her. At first she could hear
only Lord Ingraham's quiet breathing close to her ear, and then
the indistinct hum turned into music. She rose and started toward
the door as the music turned into words.

"Our mighty Lord He looked on us and bade us awake and
pray."

She turned back to Lord Ingraham, who still sat on the stairs,
a bemused expression on his face. "Oh, can you not hear it?
'The life of man is but a span, and cut down in its flower,' "
she sang, even as her eyes misted over again and she ached for
Papa. " 'We're here today, tomorrow gone, the creatures of
an hour.' "

"Marian," he began again, and started toward her, his hands
held out.

Singing louder, she took his hand, even as the parlor door
opened and Alistair came into the hall, a smile on his face.
" 'My song is done, I must be gone, I stay no longer here.'
Oh, sing, Gil!"

She flung the door open wide and pulled Lord Ingraham after
her into the snowy evening. The parish choir stood there,
bundled to the eyebrows, candles brave in the breeze. The little
ones bobbed and curtsied and Marian clapped her hands.

" 'God bless you all, both great and small.' Sing, Marian,"
teased Lord Ingraham as he sang and took her hand again.

" 'And send you a glad New Year,' " she finished.

"Bravo, bravo," said Alistair from the hallway. "Mare,
move out of the way. You're blocking the view."

Marian motioned the choir into the hall and followed with
Lord Ingraham, who still held tight to her hand.

"Better?" he whispered in her ear.

Marian grabbed him and hugged him. He laughed in surprise
and then picked her up and planted a loud kiss on her forehead.
The younger carolers whooped, even as their elders shushed
them.

Marian laughed. "Put me down, sir," she commanded as
Percy and Mama came into the hall.

"Not until you kiss him, too, miss," said the boldest caroler.

Marian rested her hands on Lord Ingraham's shoulders and

spoke softly to him. "Oh, I could not. It is too forward, even
for Marian Wynswich." She took his face between her hands
and rubbed her cheek against his. He smelled faintly of brandy
and of nothing more than Gilbert Ingraham. She took a deep
breath. It was altogether pleasant. "And now you must put me
down, sir," she said into his ear.

"Very well," he agreed, his voice as soft as hers and a trifle
unsteady. "For now," he added.

He was obviously a bit mizzled with brandy. Marian couldn't
even be sure she had heard him, but she did not mind. It was
Christmas again, and nothing else mattered.

5

The choir members looked at one another, nodded, and began "God Rest Ye Merry Gentlemen," in at least three different keys, which blended miraculously into one by the end of the first verse.

Marian turned around and watched the snow coming in the front door, deckling her hair until it was peppered with white like Lord Ingraham's. Everywhere the world was white. She closed her eyes and savored the moment, grateful that this year the wreath on the door was green and red, instead of black.

She remembered Lord Ingraham, who stood so close to her. "Do you know, sir," she whispered, "you really should be home with your family."

"Not this year, Marian," was all he would say.

The choir sang another song and then the leader held out the subscription book to Percy.

"What custom is this?" whispered Lord Ingraham.

"Oh, do you not do this in Wiltshire? The choir goes about collecting. It is our tithe for listening to them all year." Marian leaned closer. "Even when they are not worth hearing. They come here first because Covenden Hall is the biggest house. Whatever Percy gives will set the challenge for the other householders."

"And they go on?"

"Yes, and sing and sing and end up at last at the vicarage, where they count the money."

"Marian, go get on your boots," Lord Ingraham said suddenly. "We're about to join the choir."

She looked up at him in delight. "I have always wanted to, and never was I permitted. Oh, do you think . . ."

"I can square it with Percy. We need a breath of air."

Marian excused herself and hurried up the stairs as the choir sang "Master in the House." She paused only long enough at the top of the stairs to see Lord Ingraham speak to Percy, and to see her brother nod. She danced into her room, tugged on her boots, found another wool dress to pull over the one she wore, and grabbed up her cloak and a muffler.

She ran down the stairs as Lord Ingraham was ascending them.

"We'll catch up with the choir," he said.

She sat down on the steps to wait for him. Cook brought up ginger cakes and figs from the kitchen as the choir members talked among themselves and backed toward the door.

Marian's stomach rumbled loud and long. She stood up to make sure that Cook had a few cakes left on her tray.

"Was that you? Good God, Marian, Sir William is right about your 'prodigious' appetite." Lord Ingraham came down the stairs, pulling on his overcoat with its many capes.

She blushed. "It has been two hours since dinner. I am famished! And Cook knows those are my favorites."

He reached over the banister and plucked a handful of little cakes from the tray, which Cook held shoulder-high, and handed them to Marian, keeping one for himself. "We cannot have you fainting with hunger in the Devon countryside. Only think how that would reflect on the family."

She ate the cakes as he buttoned his coat.

Percy sauntered over. "Lord Ingraham, are you sure that you wish to take this distempered female off my hands for the space of an evening?"

"It is purely selfish, my friend," the diplomat replied. "I am restless and would like a walk. Marian will see that I return to the right hearth."

Percy nodded. "Make sure that she behaves, my lord."

Lord Ingraham began to wind his muffler about his throat. "You would ask a miracle?"

Marian laughed and took the muffler ends from him "You are both rudesbys! Bend down, Gil. You must wind this around your face, as high up as you can, to protect your cheek."

"Yes, your worship," Ingraham said. "Percy, is she always so demanding?"

"Always," he answered. Marian looked at her brother anxiously, but there was a light lurking in his eyes. "She orders us all about shamelessly."

"And you permit this?" Ingraham quizzed.

Percy bowed and then pulled the cloak's hood up around his sister's face. "Very often, my lord, she is absolutely right. Have fun, Mare."

The air was alive with swirling snowflakes that seemed to blow in all directions, as if the wind couldn't decide where to take them. Lord Ingraham offered his arm to Marian, who tucked herself close. "Mind that you do not take excessively large steps, for I could not keep up."

He slowed obligingly. "Do you know, my dear, I am so bored with sitting in stuffy parlors and whiling away the evenings. It smacks of Ghent and dull treaty talks, and being pleasant to all people, and saying the correct thing until I am ready to call them all out—lord, princes, ambassadors, and Americans."

"But you would never, never do that."

He shook his head. "No, although the Americans are a special trial—such fractious people, Marian. How could we ever have thought them English? I am learning to be silent, even when I do not wish to be. Especially when I do not wish to be."

They continued and Marian thought about what he had said. "That was for me, wasn't it?" she asked quietly as they approached the next great house.

He slowed his stride. "You will be breathless if I do not remember. Yes, I suppose it is for you. And it is for me."

Marian stood still. "Oh, but you never say the wrong thing, or do the wrong thing, or embarrass your relatives, or become a laughingstock to your friends." When he said nothing, she peered closer. "Do you?"

"I might have said no yesterday, but today I am not so sure. Maybe I am not so sure about . . . Well, never mind." He teetered on the edge of saying something more, but did not.

"Look now, the door is opening. Hurry up, brat."

He broke into a run, and Marian chased after him, grabbing at his coattails. She arrived, out of breath, in time to join in singing the last verse of "Good King Wenceslas," to the doctor, who was standing in the doorway while his wife buttoned his overcoat. The doctor looked at the tithe book that the caroler thrust at him, filled in an amount, dropped his coins in the box, and hurried down the steps, muttering something about babies not waiting.

He stopped long enough to point a finger at one of the tenors. "You, Jim Plant, d'ye promise before these witnesses to sing on key four Sundays out of five?"

The tenor nodded as the others laughed. The doctor took another coin from his pocket and flipped it at the man. "Then have a Merry Christmas!"

Marian clapped her hands. She stood in front of Lord Ingraham and straightened his muffler again. "Gil, would you not rather be home?"

He pulled the strings of her hood tighter about her face and smiled down at her. "No, for the hundredth time, you nosy baggage, I would rather be here."

She was not satisfied, but the choir was cutting across the doctor's lawn, heading toward the home of Colonel John Quatermain, Ret. She grabbed his hand and pulled him after her.

By the time the choir reached the environs of Picton, it was in better tune than on many a Sunday. The tithing box had a pleasant jingle to it as the carolers hurried along, already anticipating the remainder of the evening in front of their own hearths.

By now Marian had lost one of her mittens, and her bare hand was deep in one of Lord Ingraham's pockets. "For that is what happens when you insist upon wearing a cloak, Marian, and have no pockets of your own. I'll share." He insisted upon putting his arm about her so she would not pull her hand out, and as he was adding to her own warmth, she made no objection.

The snow had ended an hour before. They trailed along behind the other carolers and Marian stopped and looked up at the sky, where the stars had come out in a frosty twinkle. "Oh, Gil, how beautiful," she exclaimed.

"I agree," he said, but he was looking at her and not the stars.

She prodded him. "No, look up there! I know that is Orion, because Percy says he hunts only in a winter sky." She sighed and drew in closer to Lord Ingraham. "It is almost perfect."

"And what would make it perfect?" whispered her escort in her ear.

His breath tickled her ear and Marian felt a little ripple of pleasure down her back. It was accompanied by an odd feeling, one that she had never experienced before, one that warmed her toes. She would have to ask Ariadne about it. She withdrew her hand from Lord Ingraham's pocket.

"Sam Beddoe offering for Ariadne. Before it is too late."

Ingraham only smiled and nudged her into motion again. "Let us see what we shall see at the vicarage," was all he would say.

The vicarage was full of carolers when they arrived, out of breath from running the last block.

Sam welcomed them in. "Marian! How did you convince Percy—"

"It was Gil's doing," she said, pulling him forward. "Mr. Beddoe, this is Lord Gilbert Ingraham, Earl of . . . Dear me, I forgot."

"I sometimes wish I could, Marian. Earl of Collinwood, Mr. Beddoe. My seat is in Wiltshire, near Bath."

"Ah! Excellent country, my lord," replied the vicar "Or so I remember it."

"I, too, sir. I am seldom there, what with the world situation as sticky as it is. If Collinwood falls down about my ears someday, I can blame Bonaparte."

The vicar laughed politely, as he was expected to, and welcomed them into the parlor, where the choir sat about the hearth counting their money and downing Christmas brew.

Lord Ingraham intercepted a pint pot that one of the baritones passed to Marian. He took a sip and shook his head at Marian.

"Not for you, brat. Your brother would have my ears, hooves, and tail if I brought you back bosky to Covenden Hall. Sir," he inquired of the vicar, "have you something else for members of the infantry?"

Marian watched as Ingraham and the vicar moved toward the sideboard, and then stood their, heads together, over a glass of ratafia. The vicar nodded and motioned the earl to follow him down the hall.

"I like that," Marian said out loud. "There goes my refreshment." She went to the sideboard and retrieved another drink, wishing she could follow the gentlemen down the hall. They were already deeply engaged in conversation as they walked along, and she knew her presence was neither wanted nor required.

"I shall be discreet," she said into her glass, "as seldom I am."

She returned to the parlor as the choir members pocketed their bounty, wished each other Good Christmas, called their farewells down the hall to the vicar, and left for their own homes. Marian came closer to the fire and added enough wood to warm her feet through her boots. How still the parlor was. The clock ticked over the mantelpiece, managing somehow to sound self-conscious in the quiet room. Only five days to Christmas.

Marian listened for Lord Ingraham's footsteps, wondering why it was that she already knew what they sounded like. She sighed and wondered why he was so opposed to Christmas by his own fireside. For even if they do not know the extent of his injury, she reasoned, surely it does not matter. Already, in less time than a day, that scar was a matter she seldom considered, even when she looked at him.

The clock chimed eleven. The sofa invited her, so she curled up one end of it, carefully arranging her cloak over herself. She was asleep in moments.

"Marian, wake up, you goose."

She opened her eyes. Lord Ingraham was bending over the end of the couch, looking down at her. "Thank goodness," he said, his ready smile lurking. "I was about to resort to a mirror to ascertain if you still breathed."

She sat up. "Silly! I am merely a sound sleeper." She looked about her. The room was wreathed in shadows. The smell of the vicar's Christmas punch lingered in the room, mingling with the garland of greenery that warmed itself over the mantel. "How pleasant it smells here. Oh, Gil, isn't Christmas simply the best time?"

She thought he would return some casual answer, but he sat down on the sofa and regarded her with some seriousness. "It used to be the veriest pleasure. Papa would be home from one country or another . . . Oh, yes, we are a family of diplomats. Mama was very like you, decorating everything that stood still and overseeing every detail. It was always so much more pleasant to be home than to be at school . . ." His voice trailed off. He looked down at his hands. "Perhaps I do not spend enough time at home."

Marian drew in a breath and opened her mouth to speak, but he beat her to it. "But not this year. Come, Marian. Your brother will have given us up for dead."

She did not argue. He draped her cloak about her, resting his hands for the smallest moment on her shoulders and then giving them a pat.

Sam showed them to the door. "Until tomorrow, then, my lord?"

Marian brightened. "Oh, Sam, you will visit us tomorrow? You will not let Sir William steal your march?"

The vicar put a finger to his lips. "Not a word, Marian. Especially not to Ariadne. When, sir?" he said to Lord Ingraham.

"Midafternoon. That should be ample time. Courage, Mr. Beddoe."

The vicar bowed and came up with a grin on his face. "The same to you, my lord."

They were out the door before the earl remembered. "I almost forgot," he said as he dug into his pocket and pulled up a handful of coins. "For the choir."

The vicar took the coins and looked long and hard at the amount of them. "My lord, they are not a very good choir."

Ingraham waved away his protestations. "Mr. Beddoe, merely remember that all things are possible on Christmas. Or so Marian would dictate."

And you could even be home for Christmas, my lord, Marian thought as he took her hand and hurried down the steps into Picton's main thoroughfare.

The village was deep in sleep. Many lights flickered in

the butcher shop as they walked by, crunching the snow underfoot.

The doctor turned the corner by the shop and pulled up his horse. "Care for a ride, my lord? Miss Marian?" he asked as he tipped his hat to Marian. "We can crowd together." The doctor nodded. "With your condescension, my lord."

Ingraham shook his head. "It's a lovely night, sir. Were you successful?"

The doctor nodded and spoke to Marian. "The butcher has a daughter at long last, my dear. Good Christmas to you both."

They walked into the quiet of the December night. Marian longed to ask her escort what had transpired in the vicar's study, but an unaccountable shyness settled over her and she did not. She hurried to keep up with Lord Ingraham, who seemed to be thinking of things other than his stride. The wind ruffled a skiff of snow in front of them and an owl hooted in the spinney nearby.

Ingraham stopped. "Oh, I do not mean to hurry so fast."

"Hold still a moment, then," Marian said, out of breath, "and I will wind your muffler tighter. You must not neglect that. And you must not forget to put on that salve before you retire for the night."

"Yes, your worship," he said, and bent down while she wound the scarf tighter. He looked right into her eyes. "Aren't you just desperate to know what is going on?"

She stared right back. "Of course I am! You know I am, and I think you are perfectly dreadful not to tell me."

"Well, I will not." He softened his words with a hand on her shoulder as he started her into motion again. "I will only be silent because it is wisest. But no matter what happens tomorrow, my dear Marian, do trust me."

She let herself be pushed along. Midnight in a snowy field was hardly the time for mutiny. "Very well." A dreadful thought occurred to her, and she stood stock-still, her eyes wide. "Gil, you do not think that Sir William took advantage of our absence to propose?"

"I think it highly likely. He never was one to waste much time."

Tears stung her eyes.

Without a word, he wiped her eyes with the corner of his muffler. "Now trust me, brat," he said softly. "The vicar and I had a good talk. I wished him godspeed in his wooing and he wished me the same."

Marian clapped her hands, instantly diverted. "Gilbert Ingraham! And are we to wish you happy, too? I do wonder that you can bear to spend Christmas in Covenden Hall." She put her hands on his chest and gave him a little push. "It is a wonder to me that you could bear to be away from your lady love. I do not understand men at all."

He started her moving again. "And what would you do in my case, Miss Wynswich-who-knows-everything?"

"I would fly to her side and not rest until the matter was settled to my complete satisfaction."

He chuckled and she blushed, grateful for the darkness.

"That is, if I were ever to fall in love and marry. And I have already told you, I plan to do neither."

"I seem to recall your mentioning that."

Covenden Hall was dark when they tramped up the front driveway. Marian opened the door a crack. There was a single candle burning on the hall table. She tiptoed in behind Ingraham. She closed the door quietly behind her.

"Where are you?" he whispered, and touched her arm.

He is so close I could just reach up and kiss him, Marian thought, and then wondered why she had such a silly thought.

He cleared his throat. "Marian, I . . . I want to . . ."

She never knew what he wanted to do. A hand snaked out of the darkness and grabbed her ankle. She shrieked and reached for Lord Ingraham, and heard a crack of laughter that made her lips come together in a firm line. She flailed out in the gloom of the hall, grabbed a handful of hair, and hung on. "Alistair! You wretch! Let go!"

She heard a smother of laughter, this one from Ingraham, who groped to a chair and sat down, holding his sides.

Alistair released his grip on her ankle and Marian sat down suddenly on the floor, which only increased the strangled sounds coming from the chair.

Alistair pried her fingers from his hair and got to his feet, leapnig nimbly out of reach. He touched a candle to the one on the hall table and held it over his sister. "I told Percy I would wait up for you," he explained, his tone virtuous, his eyes lively. He held out his hand. "Truce?" He pulled Marian to her feet.

"Alistair, you are worse than a Turk," hissed Marian. She turned on Lord Ingraham. "And you! How can you sit there laughing! Did you never have any pestilential brothers?"

"If it is any consolation, I am not laughing at you, but myself for thinking . . . What I was thinking? And no, I never had brothers, pestilential or otherwise, and I wish I had," he said, as unrepentant as Alistair.

Marian came closer to him. "You were about to say something when Alistair so rudely interrupted."

"It was nothing that won't keep a little while, Marian," he said, and then adroitly turned the subject. "And you, sir, tell us of this evening."

Alistair sat in the other chair. "That bag of wind—beg pardon, my lord, but you know he is!—that bag of wind proposed tonight. Oh, Mare, you should have been there. He got down on one knee and you could have heard his stays creak from here to Lyme Regis. He sounded like a frigate in a high wind."

After a moment of thoughtful silence, Lord Ingraham spoke. "And did you witness this?"

"Through the keyhole, my lord," responded Alistair. "I thought Mare would want the details."

Marian rubbed her arms and tugged her cloak tighter about her. "It is cold. And Ariadne?"

"She thanked him quite sweetly for the honor he did her, and said she would think about it."

Marian poked her brother. "Move over." She sat down on the chair with him. "And tomorrow Mama will preach and preach, and Ariadne will acquiesce. Depend upon it." She appealed to Ingraham. "What am I to do, sir? I believe this family will drive me distracted. I scheme and plot for everyone to be happy, and they just won't be!"

"Are you through?" said Ingraham finally.

"No! I am hungry, too," said Marian, with all the dignity

at her command. "Alistair, is there any beef left from dinner?
I am agonizingly hungry and it was all I could think about as
we walked home."

"And I thought you were attending to what I said.'

Marian smiled in the earl's direction. "I was, silly! But I am
hungry, too, and when things do not go well, I especially like
to eat."

"I shall have to remember that," Ingraham murmured.

Alistair pulled Marian to her feet. "Mare, I took the liberty
of making you a beef sandwich. It is in your room. For I know
her habits, my lord," he said to Gilbert.

Marian kissed her brother. "Alistair, you do redeem yourself.
Good night then, sirs! I shall eat and consider this wrinkle in
the morning."

"Good night, my dear," said the earl. "And now, Alistair,
I particularly wanted to talk to you this evening . . . this
morning. You have spared me the necessity of waking you."
Marian paused on the stairs. Ingraham waved her on. "Away,
you abominable child."

She sniffed and started up the stairs again.

The earl bounded up the stairs after her. "Just remember what
I said about trusting me, Marian. No matter what happens
tomorrow."

She stared at him, mystified. He stood two steps below her
and she could look him in the eyes. Again she felt that curious
tug at her heart. It was more than a twinge, but less than a flutter,
she thought. I shall have to figure out what is the matter with
me all of a sudden. I shall put my mind to it when Christmas
is past and Gil has left.

"Good night, Gil," she said as she reached out and touched
his cheek lightly.

Before she could take her hand away, he planted a kiss in
her palm. "Just remember, Marian."

I must be hungry, she thought as she floated up the stairs.
That's it, surely. I am merely hungry.

6

"Marian! Marian! Wake up, I say."

The deck of the burning frigate shivered as a new explosion shook it. Marian clung to the ratlines and the ship settled in the water. Gilbert was yelling at her to jump, prying her fingers from the ropes, but she could not throw herself into the water.

"Marian! Ariadne, how can she sleep like this, all wound up in her coverlets? Wake up, I say!"

Marian opened her eyes. Her mother was pummeling her and tugging at the sheet that she had twisted around herself. Marian sniffed. Wood smoke. The fireplace glowed cheerily. Lady Wynswich stood before her, dressed for travel, panting a little from the exertion of waking her.

"Merciful heaven, Mama," Marian exclaimed. "It is . . ." She craned her neck to look at the bedside clock. "Is it seven-thirty only? Mama? Are you well? This is two mornings in a row that you have left your bed before noon."

"Don't be pert with me, young lady," her mother snapped, obviously both wide awake and irritated into the bargain. She plumped herself down on the bed as Marian sat up and rubbed the sleep from her eyes. She looked beyond her mother to Ariadne, who stood at the door, pale but composed, and cloaked and bonneted. "I do not understand," Marian muttered, and tried to burrow back under her blanket. "Wherever you are going, I choose not to come."

Lady Wynswich slapped her smartly on the rump. "Pay

93

attention, girl! Percy received a note early this morning from our solicitor in Lyme Regis. Bonebrake requests his presence, mine, and Ariadne's in his office at eleven of the clock.''

"How very odd," Marian said. She reached for her robe. "Whatever could it be about?"

Her exertions accomplished, Lady Wynswich stood up. "How can we know? I am sure that he means to evict us, even before next quarter." Her eyes filled and her lips quivered. "Evict us, before Christmas? Heartless! Percy declares it is not so, but I put no faith in solicitors, Marian, none whatsoever! They are forever bearing bad news.''

"Mama," Ariadne began in a soft voice, "you know that is not so." She touched her mother on the shoulder and handed her the vinaigrette.

Lady Wynswich sniffed deep and coughed. "Percy says it is fortuitous, for now we can discuss arrangements for Ariadne." Her recovery complete, she glanced at Ariadne. "You will be such a lovely spring bride, my dear. It is something I have devoutly hoped for.''

"Yes, Mama," Ariadne replied automatically. There was no animation in her face, no glimmer in her eyes.

"And what am I to do, Mama?" asked Marian as she buttoned up her robe.

Lady Wynswich took Marian's hair and tugged it out from the collar of the robe. "I wish you would braid this mass at night! It tangles so wondrously." She shook the handful of dark hair. "You will never catch a husband like Ariadne if you let your hair go every which way.''

Marian tossed her head and made no attempt to find logic in her mother's speech. "Do you leave me in charge, then, Mama?" she asked, searching for the twisted thread of her mother's discourse.

Lady Wynswich shuddered. "I fear it must be so. Only behave yourself, miss! Lord Ingraham, for whatever odd reason, has taken a fancy to you, so I fear no trouble from that region. But if you are not completely courteous to Sir William, I'll— I'll think of something truly dreadful. Now get up and get to breakfast." She kissed the air over Marian's head and hurried to the door, shooing Ariadne before her. "And try not to eat everything except the cutlery."

The door closed and Marian sank back down again, animadverting to herself on her mother's injunctions as she fingered her hair. She bounced to her feet and stared long and deep into her mirror. In a moment, she was brushing her hair, wondering if perhaps her mother was right. For if I braid it tight every night, it will assume some sort of wave. I shall consider it, she thought as she swept it back from her face and secured it with a bit of twine.

Such activity called for a riband. She tiptoed into Ariadne's room, rummaged in her tidy vanity, and unearthed a red riband. She tied it handedly so it covered the twine, and surveyed the effect in Ariadne's mirror. I do wish my eyes were brown, she thought, but blue is not so bad. Thank goodness I never threw out spots, like the doctor's daughter.

Marian put on the green woolen dress she had been saving for Christmas Day, struggling with the buttons up the back, wishing for Ariadne's help. Another trip to her sister's room brought to light the lace collar Ariadne had knitted. She patted it down. "The perfect touch," she said out loud, and then giggled. "I could slay dragons in this dress."

Marian felt the soul of elegance as she descended the stairs, gathering the skirt up in back to keep it from dragging on the steps. She had begged and pleaded with her mother and the seamstress to make it just a little longer than her other dresses, ignoring Ariadne's "But, Mare, you have such neat ankles," and Lady Wynswich's "My dear, you are not seventeen yet."

She held her back straight and glided down the hall, feeling older, mysterious even, a Circe misplaced in George's England, a siren who could topple governments and change the course of history.

Sir William glared at her over the rim of his breakfast cup of tea as she swept into the breakfast parlor.

Alistair choked on his ham. "Mare, what a rig-out. If you've ever had a riband in your hair before, I disremember"

Lord Ingraham stood at the sideboard, contemplating the eggs and ham. He chose both and took the plate to his seat, and then held out Marian's chair for her. "A very lovely rig-out, I might add," he whispered in her ear as he quickly did up the one button she could not reach.

"Thank you," she whispered in turn. "You see, sir, my arms are not long enough."

He shrugged and seated himself beside her. "They reach to the end of your wrists, do they not?"

Marian winked at him. "You, sir, are a complete hand!"

The earl groaned and rolled his eyes.

Sir William glared at them both as he set his cup down heavily. "I do not approve of punning in females, Miss Wynswich, particularly over breakfast."

Marian bit back the reply that rose to her lips. I will be polite today, she told herself as she smiled sweetly. "It was raving distempered of me, Sir William. Do forgive my unruly tongue."

Sir William harrumphed and addressed his plate.

Marian got her own breakfast and sat down to eat it. There was scarcely enough on her plate to lay the dust of a long night's drought, but she resolved to visit the kitchen in midmorning to check on the Christmas pudding and whatever else Cook would allow.

Alistair finished first and pushed back his chair. "I am off to the stables, Lord Ingraham. Do you care to accompany me? I recall you mentioned something about a canter around the place, and the sun is shining."

"Very well, lad, I will join you. In a moment." He drained his teacup. "Sir William, what are your plans this day?"

Cook's muffins had settled Sir William into better tune. "I do believe I will search over the rest of this enchanting house. for I do admire old things, Miss Wynswich," he said to Marian. "Tell me. The part that you seem not to use—how old is it?"

"Papa said it dates to the reign of Henry the Eighth. You know, the one who was a husband so ill-suited to his wives."

Sir William sprayed muffin across the table.

Marian flicked her napkin about her dress, goaded on by her demon. "Of course, he was older than all except the first, and from what Papa told me, a little stout. Perhaps he suffered from ill humors."

"So it would seem, Marian," Lord Ingraham said, as he trod upon her toe. "Do excuse us, Sir William. Come, Marian." He took her by the elbow and lifted her out of her chair and into the hall before she had time to put down her fork.

He pinned her back to the wall. "Marian Wynswich, behave yourself," he admonished. "There's heavy business afoot today, and if you rock the boat, I will personally pull your fingernails out one by one."

She stared back. "Is this part of British diplomacy?"

The earl let go of her. "It should be in Devon, I am convinced. Mind your manners, brat." He flicked her cheek with a careless finger and opened the door to the breakfast parlor again.

She continued her breakfast in silence and took one last sip of her cold tea. "Sir William, will you require my escort this morning?"

"I think not, Miss Wynswich." He favored her with a smile, and little bits of egg dropped to the table. "And perhaps I should call you Marian?" He looked at her as coyly as a well-stuffed walrus could look. "For I do believe we soon will be related."

"What—whatever you desire," Marian said faintly, resisting the urge to run gagging from the room.

"All that I will require . . ."

Is a block and tackle to rise from that chair, thought Marian.

". . . is some paper and a pencil. In case there is anything worthy of note to inventory."

She looked at him sharply. And see what you can carry off as soon as you and Ariadne are wed, she thought.

He returned her look serenely, as if Covenden Hall were already his. "I have already told you how I love old houses, Marian. Indeed, I would never contemplate this marriage if I did not love old houses."

Well, I like that, she thought.

"I merely want to record such details as I can about wainscoting, mullioned windows, and the like."

Marian found the required pad and pencil in the top drawer of the sideboard and placed them before Sir William.

"Thank you, Marian. Should I require your assistance in my

perusal of this charming old manor, I will sing out.''

With a quick curtsy, Marian fled the breakfast parlor. Her first impulse was to take a spanking rapid walk through the shrubbery until her irritation exhausted itself, but the ground was still snow-covered and appeared highly unreliable. She went instead to the library, which was located in the newer wing of the house and considerably removed from the Henry the Eighth section.

The garland of holly she had been stringing two days before remained on the table, so she applied herself to the task, but not before noticing that someone had been sitting in her father's chair and had left her copy of Blake open on the seat. Marian felt her irritation slide away. How singularly sad that all house guests were not as amiable as Lord Gilbert Ingraham.

Marian applied herself diligently to the garland, determined to wrestle with a solution to Ariadne's dilemma. She wondered instead if Lord Ingraham had remembered to apply the salve to his cheek last night and in the morning.

The holly pricked her finger. I really must pay attention, or else I . . .

What she would do vanished from her mind. A scream of impressive dimensions split the quiet of Covenden Hall. It seemed to linger on the air longer than humanly possible and then resolve itself into a crescendo of barking laughter that caused Marian to drop the garland and cover her ears. The ghastly noise was followed by another scream, one that she remembered from her late-night difficulty with Mama Cat and Sir William.

"Good God, Sir William," she exclaimed, and ran into the hall.

The shrieks came again, louder even, as if doors had been opened. The screams sounded like those of the orangutan that she and Alistair had observed, openmouthed, at a fair in Lyme Regis when they were both much younger; it had given her nightmares for a week.

"Courage, Marian," she told herself as she darted back into the library and snatched up the fireplace poker. "You are in charge."

It was hardly a spine-stiffening consideration. She heard Sir William again, his voice high-pitched, and ran faster. She looked about for allies, but not a single servant was in sight. They are never about when you need them, she thought grimly.

The great room of the old wing was deserted. It had been tidied and dusted; the unlit Yule log already rested in the cavern of a fireplace, awaiting Christmas Eve. She took this in at a glance as she stopped, panting, at the foot of the staircase. One scream and then another, followed by the curious rattling of chains, greeted her. The sound was directly overhead.

Wave after wave of gooseflesh circulated around her back. She took a firmer grip on the poker and started up the stairs. "I'm coming, Sir William," she shouted, though her voice could not compete with the rattle of chains, as if someone dragged them about the floor. "Never fear, sir, never fear," she squeaked.

The stairs took a little time. For every one she ascended, she retreated two at the maniacal laughter and the pleadings of Sir William. By the time she reached the top, her heart was pounding so loud that she knew if she looked down, she would see it leaping about in her chest.

The sounds stopped and the door slammed open. Marian shrank back against the wall and raised the poker over her head.

Sir William leapt from the room as if shot from a cannon, fell to his knees, and crawled on all fours toward her. With a mighty swoosh of wings, an enormous bird flew out the door and circled about Sir William, who drew as much of himself into a ball as he could, and cowered there.

The bird—it seemed more apparition than fact—fluttered about and then glided smoothly down the stairwell. With another scream, Sir William scuttled behind her, jabbering something in an unknown tongue. He clutched her around the legs and she nearly fell down.

"Sir William, do unhand me," she said, and pried his fingers from her legs.

Alternating threats with appeasements, she freed herself. Against every instinct, she peered into the little room and was

rewarded with the merest glimpse of a shadowy figure that
lurched about, laughing.

The outside door below opened and Alistair and Lord
Ingraham took the stairs two at a time. Marian sank back in
relief. Sir William burst into tears, grabbed her about the
middle, and tried to bury his face in her lap.

"Sir William, this is highly improper," she hissed and tried
to pull him away. She looked at him. The seat of his pants had
split from his exertions. His wig was tumbled over one ear,
revealing a head as bald as an egg.

As Ingraham pulled Sir William away from her, Alistair took
the poker from Marian and knelt down to speak to the cowering
man, who could only sit and stare, his eyes bugging out and
his mouth opening and closing.

"Sir William, you were in rare danger. How were we to know
that you would come to this room? Oh, it is too terrible to
contemplate what would have happened if we had not stepped
in."

With an oath of his own, Alistair sprang to the doorway and
brandished the poker. "Never fear, Sir William," he declared
as he stepped inside the door and closed it behind him.

Marian gasped and clapped her hands over her ears, but she
could not drown out the clanking of the chains, and Alistair
crying, "Back! Back, you fiend," and flaying about him with
the poker. Before she realized it, she had retreated to the safety
of Lord Ingraham's open arms.

He seemed willing enough to enfold her in a tight embrace,
even as he talked in soothing tones to Sir William and convinced
the man he should get to his feet, in the event that immediate
flight was required.

The din from the room lessened, only to be followed by gusty
tears, and Alistair saying, "There, there now, Uncle, did the
fat old man give you a fright?"

Marian stiffened and looked up at Lord Ingraham, who still
clutched her to his chest. He looked down at her, gave her a
slow wink, and put his finger to his lips.

Suddenly it was all amazingly clear. After a rapid, sideways
look at Sir William, she burst into tears of her own and clung

tighter to Lord Ingraham. "Oh, my poor, poor uncle," she sobbed. "Oh, Sir William, whatever did you do to him? He is generally quite harmless. Oh, I cannot bear it." She sobbed louder and louder until her voice began to crack like that of the man behind the door.

Sir William stared at her.

Ingraham held her away from him and shook her until her hair came out of the riband. "Stop it, Marian," he ordered. "Remember yourself!"

His voice had a slight, all-too-familiar tremor, and she did not dare look at him. Instead, she collapsed in his arms and sobbed quietly, noting to herself that for a man somewhat stricken in years himself, Lord Ingraham had a wonderfully well-muscled chest.

Alistair came out of the room finally, closed the door firmly behind him, and turned the key in the lock. He leaned against the door panel and slid down to the floor until he slumped there. He buried his head in his hands for a brief moment, then drew himself together and took a deep breath.

"Sir William," he began, as if the words were torn from him, "I am horrified that you had to discover . . ." He looked at Marian, his eyes desperate. "Oh, Marian, how can we tell him? What will he think of us?"

Marian yanked Lord Ingraham's handkerchief from his breast pocket and buried her face in it. "Oh, Alistair, you must tell him, for I cannot."

Indeed I cannot, she thought.

Alistair got to his feet and stumbled toward Sir William, attempting to take hold of his hands. The man drew back in fright and Alistair turned his face away. "Sir, I fear you have discovered—oh horrors, how can I say it?—the Wynswich secret."

The silence was broken by the sound of stertorous breathing from behind the door and then little scratchings at random on it, some high, some low. Sir William shook like blancmange, and Marian would have owned up to another rank of shivers down her back if anyone had closely questioned her.

"Alistair," said a trembling thread of a voice, "I'll get you for this, just see if I don't, some night when you think all is safe. You, and that funny little fat man, too."

Sir William moaned out loud and scooted closer to Lord Ingraham. "Who-who-who-who," he stammered in remarkable imitation of an owl.

Alistair forced back a sob. "Sir, it is my uncle, Papa's dear brother. The estate would have been his, as eldest son, but he was found to be completely mad." He turned pleading eyes on Marian, her face still safely smothered in the handkerchief. "Oh, Marian, how dare we admit to this excellent gentleman, so soon to become part of our household, about the—I cannot bear it!—the tainted blood of the Wynswiches?"

Whatever color remained in the formerly sanguine Sir William drained away. He closed his mouth and set his wig on straight again. "Do you mean to tell me, young man, that there is a streak of madness in this family?"

"Oh, it is more than a streak, sir," offered Alistair. "It is more like a broad stripe." He forced a smile. "But, Sir William, I am happy to report that it skips a generation, and Ariadne is quite, quite normal."

Lord Ingraham shifted Marian to his other arm, but he did not release her. "Sir William, this is not an uncommon occurrence among older, titled families." He managed a little laugh. "Why, you will find queer stirrups among the best houses in England."

Sir William shuddered. "Then how grateful I am, my lod, that my title is a courtesy only and my relations are untainted by the fumes of madness."

"They are only tainted by illogical syntax," murmured Lord Ingraham into Marian's ear, for which she trod upon his toe.

Sir William was only just warming to his subject as his color and choler returned. "For all that we may smell a trifle of the shop, my lord, but there is not a looby among the whole crew."

"Then you are to be congratulated," Alistair said. "Ariadne will be privileged indeed to become a part of your untainted family."

Sir William yanked his wig down tighter about his ears. "My dear Alistair Wynswich, there will be no marriage."

Alistair staggered about on the landing and then dropped his head in his hands. "Oh, Marian," he sobbed, "speak to him. Reason with him."

Marian abandoned the safety of Lord Ingraham's arms and sidled toward Sir William, who backed up against the wall. "Sir," she began prettily, "only think how disappointed Ariadne will be." An odd little laugh rose in her throat. "And how sad you will make us." She laughed a little more, and her laughter was joined in precisely the same key by the creature behind the door. She threw herself to the floor in a flood of tears and mad laughter.

Sir William pointed a finger at her and edged down the stairs. "Legislation," he shrieked. "There ought to be legislation concerning women like that one, I tell you. And you say it skips a generation? Not in her case." He backed down the stairs. "If I had been misguided into an alliance with this demented family, hell's foundations would quiver."

Ingraham leaned over the railing to watch Sir William's descent. "Oh, perhaps not precisely quiver, my man. Shake a little perhaps, but quiver? Surely not."

"You can afford to be light and airy, my dear Lord Ingraham," said Sir William, drawing himself up, even as his ripped stays dropped his belly lower and lower. "You were not contemplating a union with these denatured Wynswiches."

"No, I was not, was I?" the earl said affably. "Sir, what will you do?"

"I will leave at once. Wild horses, et cetera et cetera." he declared. He jabbed the air with one hand and with the other grabbed for his pants, which were entirely split out the back. "How dreadful of Percy not to say something to me."

"Sir William, have some charity," Ingraham admonished in tones appropriate to a restless child. "Consider the embarrassment to Percy, and he a most excellent fellow! I am sure that the least said about this to him, the better. Indeed, haven't you been posted to Poland? I doubt your paths will cross with overmuch frequency, except at special court functions, when no one speaks the truth."

Sir William tugged at his pants. "Yes, thank goodness! I shall be polite to the poor fellow, cordial even. But never, never will I associate with this family again.''

Alistair burst into noisy tears of his own.

"Oh, cut line, you hellborn babe," snapped Sir William. "When you have collected yourself, direct your butler to inform the stables that I want your gig to take me to Picton. I shall wait there for the mail coach. I go to pack. Good day to you all.''

He turned and continued at a dignified pace down the stairs, his rump winking out of his ruined pants, his stays popping everywhere like ruptured barrel staves. The conspirators at the top of the stairs could only stare at him.

He slammed the door behind him, and except for the flutter of the owl downstairs, searching a way out, all was quiet.

Marian sat up, straightened her dress, and folded her hands in her lap. She looked at no one.

Alistair walked over to Lord Ingraham and shook his hand. "Sir, I can only ask: were you ever thrown out of boarding schools at an earlier age?''

Lord Ingraham coughed and had the grace to look away. "Oh, no. I was a well-mannered, highly regulated, extremely proper fellow until two days ago—God, is that *all*?—when I entered this house.'' He leaned over the banister again, as if searching out Sir William. "I can only speculate that something of what my colleague says about this family may be true. Are you *both* bewitching me? I don't pretend to understand any of this!'' He rested his forehead on the banister and began to laugh.

Marian shook her head, tugged at Alistair's trouser leg, and forced him to sit down beside her. "Who is in that room?'' she whispered.

Alistair jumped up. "I almost forgot!'' He unlocked the door and stuck his head in. "Daniel, you can come out now, to the thanks of an entire nation.''

"The stableboy! I should have known,'' muttered Marian. "Oh, Gil, do be quiet!''

Ingraham shook his head and tried to speak, failed, and sat down on the stairs. "Oh, Marian,'' he wheezed, "you were magnificent, a regular Sarah Siddons. That high-pitched laugh of yours, and the way you threw yourself at his feet!''

The stableboy came out of the room, rattling the chain draped about his waist. He grinned at Alistair. "I haven't had so much fun since the time you and Marian sent your cousins looking for King Arthur's treasure in the kitchen midden."

"That was a good stroke, wasn't it?" agreed Alistair modestly. "This was our crowning achievement, I vow, and it wasn't even our idea. We owe our complete success to Lord Ingraham."

The stableboy looked at the earl in admiration. "Coo, my lord, you should have been a Wynswich."

The earl finally regained a semblance of control over himself. "No, not that," he declared. "I haven't the stamina for it."

"Was that your note this morning to Percy?" Marian asked.

Ingraham nodded. "Wrote it with my left hand and made it properly lawyerish."

"And when he returns and wonders what is going on? What, then?" she accused.

"What's the trouble, Mare?" Alistair asked. "Are you jealous because you've finally met your match?" He cast another admiring look at Lord Ingraham. "No one likes to be shown up, sir," he explained generously. "She'll come about soon enough."

"Of that I have no doubt." He looked at his watch. "And soon your excellent vicar will be here to await Ariadne's return and ask Percy for permission to become leg-shackled."

"And that was your doing too, wasn't it?" asked Marian, in better charity with the Earl of Collinwood.

"I only had to remind him last night that if he wanted something, really wanted it, he would have to forge ahead." He sat on the railing. "Of course, this means you will likely lose Covenden Hall. I couldn't arrange a sudden legacy for the vicar, and truth to tell, I don't think he would have allowed it anyway."

Marian smiled. "He would not. I would rather lose Covenden Hall a hundred times over and see Ariadne happily married."

"But where will you go, dear lady?" he asked.

She shrugged and stood up, looking him straight in the eye. "I refuse to worry about that eventuality until after Christmas."

They remained in the old part of the house until they heard

the front door slam and saw Sir William ride past the window in the gig.

The stableboy gave a low whistle. "Gor, he still looks like a fire-breather." He poked Alistair. "But you should have seen him when he came in that room. I was curled up on the daybed, and he didn't even see me. He commences nosing about, and even fingering the curtains. And then I moans and groans, and he nearly did himself an injury."

Even Marian had to giggle.

Suddenly the earl put out his hand. "Listen! Is Sir William returning?"

All eyes turned to the windows downstairs. Instead of the gig, it was the family carriage, that shabby reminder of higher tides with the Wynswiches.

Alistair looked at Gilbert. "My lord, it would appear that they are back—rather sooner than we expected."

Ingraham nodded. "And I would wager, my young friend, that our spurned suitor may have exchanged a few words with his host on the road."

Alistair began to back carefully and slowly down the hall. "Come, come," admonished the earl lightly. "You were so brave with your mad uncle."

"Ah, my lord, but this will be my mad brother. Daniel, let us choose discretion a considerable distance beyond valor and test out the backstairs."

They were gone in a clatter and a clank of chains.

Marian retreated toward Lord Ingraham and reached for his hand, which he promptly provided. "Your hand is so warm," she exclaimed. "One would think you are used to dissembling on a daily basis, to be so calm."

"Perhaps I am more used to it than you think," he replied quixotically. "But come, come. Let us face the wrath. I will not desert you," he said, and added a rider, "particularly since you are less deserving of his wrath than usual, in this instance."

"Oh, I like that," she said, but did not let go of his hand as they went quietly down the stairs and back into the newer part of the house.

They arrived in the main hall at the same instant Percy, eyes blazing, face red, slapping his gloves from one hand to another, stomped in the front entrance. Marian stood rooted to the spot. All of the earl's urgings could not propel her forward.

"There you are, you wretched sister." Percy roared, his mother and sister right behind him. "Let me remind you that you are not too old to strop."

Marian, eyes wide, stood speechless. Then the library door opened and the Reverend Sam Beddoe stood before the assembly.

Marian sniffed. She knew that Lord Ingraham did not smell of Christmas wassail. She leaned closer to Sam. The fumes were rising from the vicar, who listed at an angle in the ibrary doorway, his hand tucked in his shirt front like Napoleon.

"Sir! You cannot speak that way of the sister of the woman I adore. After all, you blaggard, these are modern times. You touch one hair of Marian's or Ariadne's head, and I, sir, I personally will call you out."

Triumphant and pint-brave, the vicar took another look around at the openmouthed inmates of the hallway. He shook his fist at Percy Wynswich, an act that set him off-balance. He teetered for a moment on one leg, smiled a benevolent smile on these misguided members of his flock, and pitched faceforward onto the carpet.

No one moved. In another moment, the vicar belched and began to snore.

Ariadne shrieked and threw herself on the floor beside the vicar. Lady Wynswich swooned into her son's arms. Marian looked at Lord Ingraham, who bowed to her and held out his arm.

"My dear, let us retire to the library for a moment. I feel sadly inadequate to this occasion. Do close your mouth, Marian. You look like a grouper."

7

There was no question of a retreat to the library, no matter how welcome the idea. Ariadne sat on the floor, her arms clasped around the vicar. Her eyes entreated her sister. "Marian what can be the matter? Tell me he is not ill?"

"He is not ill," said Marian, on her knees beside the vicar, who continued to snore. "He is merely . . ." She leaned toward her sister and whispered in her ear.

"He would never," declared Ariadne, clasping her beloved parson to her bosom.

"I think that under the circumstances, he would," Lord Ingraham added. "My dear, consider the strain he has been under."

"Well, perhaps you are right," Ariadne said reluctantly. She sniffed the air. "And he does smell like Papa used to. "

"Sister," admonished Percy, who was rubbing his mother's wrists.

"Well, he does," she said with more spirit than Marian could remember hearing before.

Ariadne turned her attention to the earl, who knelt beside Marian. "My lord, what should we do?"

"Allow me to shoulder this man and take him down to the kitchen." Lord Ingraham leaned toward Marian. "Do you feel Cook can stand the excitement? The vicar will profit, I feel, from liberal infusions of black coffee, the blacker the better."

When no one disagreed, the earl picked up the vicar and balanced him over his shoulder like a meal bag.

Sam roused himself long enough to protest, then sighed and returned, upside down, to the generous embrace of Morpheus.

Percy was having better success with his mother. A pass of the vinaigrette under her nose brought her around in time to see Lord Ingraham start down the passageway with the parish good example dangling down his back. "How very odd," was all she said.

"Odd, indeed," echoed Percy, his voice more grim. He helped his mother to her feet. "I trust you have ample explanation, Marian. Sir William held us up at the Picton crossing to tell an incredible story of a mad uncle, and chains clanking, and something about the Wynswich secret. I never would have believed it, except that he came from Covenden Hall, and we left you in charge."

Percy was in no mood for disagreement, but the spark of injustice flared in Marian's bosom. "Percy, I am innocent," she declared in a loud, clear voice, her head high. A crack of laughter from Lord Ingraham as he descended the stairs dampened her protestation. "Well, I am, Lord Ingraham," she flared, and chased after him. "And you are perfectly beastly to tease me."

"Marian, remember yourself," Percy said in failing tones. "You are addressing the Earl of Collinwood."

"Earl, indeed!" Marian snorted as she followed Ingraham down to the kitchen, Ariadne close at her heels. "You're not to be trusted, Gil, even if you were a tinker."

"No more are you. What a pair we make. Come, Marian. Summon your persuasive resources and beg Cook for coffee."

In a few moments, all the Wynswiches sat at the kitchen table as Ingraham propped the vicar into a chair, took off his already drooping collar, straightened his blouse, and roused him sufficiently to down two cups of coffee.

Sam Beddoe shuddered and sat up. He put his hand to his head and patted it gingerly, carefully, as if it were two sizes too large. With considerable effort, he looked about him, taking in the Wynswiches, Lord Ingraham, and Cook, who watched him, all with varying degrees of interest on their faces.

His eyes looked upon Ariadne, and her quiet beauty seemed to fill him with the resolve that he needed even more than the coffee. He rose to his feet, wobbled there a moment, and then placed a hand on Ariadne's shoulder. He cleared his throat, and his eyes went momentarily blank.

Lord Ingraham cleared his throat, too, and recalled the vicar to his duty.

"Sir Percy, I wish your permission to offer for Ariadne."

Percy opened his mouth to speak, and the vicar waved him to silence.

"I'll have no disagreement, sir. Where, you ask, is my fortune?" He slapped his chest dramatically and nearly toppled. "Sir, it is in my heart. My love for your sister is worth more than rubies."

Percy tried again, and again the vicar, warming to his topic, dismissed him.

"What, you ask, is my future?" His hand went gingerly to his head again. "Sir, it is my brains. I mean to be Archbishop of Canterbury one day."

Marian sighed in perfect delight. Lord Ingraham rested his hand on her shoulder. She glanced at him in surprise, but the earl appeared to have his whole attention on the drama playing in front of his eyes. He ran his thumb softly against the junction of her jaw and the motion was soothing, soporific even, with just an edge of pleasure that she felt down to her toes. She inclined her head toward his hand, enjoying that same sensation she remembered from last night on the stairs, and hoping that he would not become suddenly aware of what he was doing and stop.

"But, Vicar, I—" Percy attempted, and got no farther.

"Nay, sir, say nothing. I may appear to have no prospects, but, sir, Ariadne will not starve."

"I should hope not," said Lady Wynswich. "Now, if you were required to feed Marian, this would be a different matter."

Marian felt rather than heard the earl's chuckle. "Shh," she said softly and reached up to touch his hand.

The silence around the table was broken at last by Percy. "My dear Reverend Beddoe, we had rather hoped for more than that.''

Sam's head went up. He struggled for a moment against the fumes of last night's wassail, and then the natural dignity that was his alone took over. "I know, my lord. I will open my home to Lady Wynswich and Marian, too. I wish that I had the means to keep Covenden Hall in the family, but I do not.'' He paused, less sure of himself, until Ariadne patted his arm. He looked down at her and his courage returned. "Sir, there will be no shortage of love for Ariadne. If this counts for anything, then there will be no wealthier family in all of Devon than that of the vicar and his wife and children.''

"Bravo," said Ingraham softly.

No one heard him except Marian. All eyes were on Percy. With a slight smile on his face, Percy motioned the vicar to sit down. "Vicar, may I speak now?''

Ssam nodded, his eyes stricken, his face reddening.

"On our way to Lyme Regis this morning, Ariadne assured me that she would marry no one but you. She became quite insistent.''

Marian gasped and reached for her sister. "Ariadne! You are a great gun, after all.''

Ariadne twinkled her eyes at her little sister. "Mare, you're not the only one in the family with a backbone.'' Her glance lingered next on the vicar. "Someone must keep this man sober for Sunday sermons and parish visits.''

It was as close to a joke as Ariadne had ever come before. She blushed and hid her face in the vicar's shoulder.

"I have something to say about this matter," Lady Wynswich said.

The room grew silent again. With a frown on his face, Percy took his mother's vinaigrette out of his pocket and placed it on the table. She snorted and pushed it away.

"No one has consulted me on this affair," she said, with a pointed look at Ariadne, "but I will tell you this." Everyone leaned forward, including Cook. "I do not think Sir William would have suited us precisely. And, after all, we could not depend on Napoleon making threatening noises on Elba and keeping our diplomats far from home, now, could we? At some future date, we might have been forced to deal with him here in Covenden Hall, and that would have been too, too bad."

After a moment of amazed silence, Percy burst into laughter. "Mama, Mama, you're—"

"A great gun, too?" she said. "Of course I am." She got to her feet, and the others rose, too. "Come, Ariadne. Only think of all the plans we have to make. There's nothing quite like a wedding to take one's mind off eviction."

Percy groaned. "Mama, you have such a way with words." He directed his attention to the vicar, whose eyelids were beginning to droop even as he struggled to stay awake. "Vicar, I believe that we have an empty guest room now. I recommend that you repair there for a nap."

"Allow me," said Lord Ingraham, offering his arm to the vicar. "I will see you safely there." He looked at Cook. "And if Cook will permit, I will mix you something that will help."

"Really?" asked the vicar.

"Immeasurably. Come, sir."

"Excellent," Percy said, rubbing his hands together. "And let us all convene in the old hall when it is dark. I think I want to light the Yule log early this year."

Marian clapped her hands. "Percy!"

He leaned across the table and kissed her on the forehead. "I am a great gun, too, sister. I believe we have something to celebrate, and it needn't wait for Christmas Eve." He waggled a finger at her. "But do locate Alistair for me. I am all eagerness to find out more about the Wynswich secret."

Ingraham bowed. "You can lay a considerable portion of the blame for that at my door, Percy."

Percy returned the bow. "I fear this disordered household has ruined you, my lord."

"I am certain of it, too. We will speak of this later. Percy. Marian. Your servant."

The others left the kitchen, but Marian remained, idly toying with the strengthening beef broth which Cook set before her. She sipped it thoughtfully, with less than her usual gusto, wondering about Ariadne. *Just when we think we know* somebody, they do something altogether surprising, she told herself. It must be that love has made Ariadne bold. There must be a lesson in this.

Marian considered for a moment the very real prospect of eviction, and then discarded it. The vicar said he would open his home to them. She looked about her in the low-ceilinged kitchen, close and cozy with the cooking smells of centuries. I shall miss Covenden Hall, she thought, but the fact gave her no start or pang. It would be enough that Ariadne would be happy.

She wandered out to the stables and looked in on Mama Cat and kittens. Alistair or the stableboy had restored Solomon to his perch in her workshop. He sat, eyes unblinking, uttering only an occasional who-who, as if in apology for his unseemly part in that morning's activities. His condescension complete, Solomon even permitted her to touch his feathers and feed him a mouse.

Marian strolled slowly through the stables, talking to her father's horses. Her mother would likely fetch a good price for them, if she could hold on until spring, when outdoor interests waxed again and sporting men took to the fields with their hounds. She sighed. Alistair would convince Percy to let him go to sea, and Percy would return soon to his diplomatic duties. Marian leaned on the loose box holding the gelding Lord Ingraham said he would purchase. And he will take you to America.

The thought filled her with a sudden rush of sadness. The empty feeling nearly took her breath away. Tears welled in her eyes and she blinked them back. What a goose I am, she thought. I don't even care for horses. What can be the matter? I should be so happy.

But she was not. She had rarely felt more miserable. I am not hungry, she thought as she closed the stable door behind her and picked her way across the slushy yard. It must be that I am tired.

Covenden Hall appeared deserted. She went quietly up the stairs, grateful that no one was about. She passed the second-best guest room and paused for a moment with her ear to the door. Sam Beddoe snored long and loud within.

The door opened suddenly and she nearly fell in. Lord Ingraham reached out to steady her. Marian looked beyond his hand on her arm to the vicar, sprawled out on the bed.

"Gil, do you think he stayed up all night after we left, drinking his Christmas punch?" she whispered.

"I think it very likely, Marian," he whispered back. "It must take a great deal of courage to propose."

"Surely it is not such a difficult thing. Surely you must have proposed to dozens of women."

He drew back in surprise. "Madam, I am not a Turk."

Marian smiled up at him. "But did you not say last night that the vicar wished you happy?"

"That does not mean I have put the matter to the test yet, madam," he protested. "After all, it is an event that a man wants to do correctly. Wait for the right moment."

Marian wished that he would not stand so close, and yet she felt that if he moved away, she would follow him. How contradictory.

"You will put the matter to the test soon?" she asked, and then looked down in confusion. "Of course, it is not my business. It's just that I, oh, I . . . " Her words seemed to be dragging her down into a regular Devon quagmire.

"Pray continue, Marian," he said.

"I shall not," she declared with some asperity, and then stepped away from him a little. "But I should, shouldn't I?"

"Undoubtedly."

"I mean, it is the height of rudeness to dangle one's thoughts for all to see and then not complete them."

"Most assuredly."

She looked him directly in the eyes. "It is just that I wish you well, my lord. That and no more. And I wish you would return to Bath," she finished, her words tumbling out of her. "Only think of those who love you, sir."

His glance did not waver. "That is precisely what I am doing, Marian. And I will not go to Bath this Christmas."

"You're dreadfully stubborn," she raged. "I am glad I do not have to face you across a treaty table."

"Yes, I suppose I am stubborn," he agreed. He took her face in his hands and kissed her on the forehead. "And you are an abominable, nosy brat.'' He released her as quickly as he had kissed her. "Run along, now. I have a matter to discuss with your brother, if he has quite recovered from the parson.''

She looked at him, her cheeks red but her eyes filled with interest.

"And I will not tell you what it is, save that it touches on your wretched brother Alistair. Go away, now.''

With a laugh and an airy wave of her hand, Marian danced down the hall to her room, pausing at the door and then looking back. He had not moved. He still regarded her with that curious smile.

"Until tonight, Marian?''

"Oh, yes. I wouldn't miss it.''

Dinner was a hasty affair, quickly gotten over. Percy, Lady Wynswich on his arm, led them into the old hall, which twinkled with lights from many branches of candles. "You see, my lord, this is the only fireplace big enough for the log,'' Percy explained to Ingraham, who trailed behind with Marian.

"We have such a fireplace at Collinwood,'' replied the earl. "And, no, I should not be there,'' he whispered to Marian, who had opened her mouth to speak. She closed it and glared at him until he laughed.

The butler had arranged Lord Wynswich's silver punch cups around the large silver bowl, and was wiping off the last of the Lafite 'Ol. "I was sure that the occasion called for Lafite, my lord,'' the butler explained to Percy, who nodded.

"But all the bottles, Billings?'' Percy asked him.

The butler shook his head. "I have held back a half-dozen, in the event that Miss Marian someday finds her way to the altar and you feel the necessity for another celebration.''

Percy released his mother and grabbed Marian around the waist. "Now, that would be cause for rejoicing, but where will we ever find a man to make such a sacrifice of his reason?''

Marian blushed. "Percy! For that rude crack you must allow me to light the Yule log.''

He removed one candle from the branch on the table. "I suppose I must, my dear. Here you are.''

"And does one make a wish on the log, too?" Lord Ingraham asked.

"No, silly," Marian replied. "That is only the Christmas pudding." She looked at Ariadne. "Did your wish come true today? You may tell us if it did, you know."

Ariadne cuddled in closer to the vicar and nodded. He kissed her and everyone applauded. Marian reached for Percy's hand. "Come, brother."

He took her hand, holding it tight as she knelt by the fireplace and touched the candle to the tinder surrounding the enormous log. The tinder crackled as the little flames jumped around the log and finally the log began to burn. Marian blew out the candle and looked at Percy.

He cleared his throat. "I wish Papa were here to say it."

"I know," she said, her voice tight and far away. She clung tighter to his hand. "But it is your turn, Percy."

Percy looked into the flames for a long minute.

Marian reached her hand up and placed it on his shoulder, holding him close to her, resting her head for a moment on his back. She held out her other hand. "Come, come, let us join hands."

The earl took her by the hand and held his out for Lady Wynswich, who struggled with tears. "Lady Wynswich, be so kind," he murmured.

"It is never the same," she said, her voice uncertain. She grasped his hand.

"No, it is not," he agreed. "But here we are."

They all joined hands in front of the fireplace, when the Yule log had caught in good earnest. The warmth was welcome, the smell of the wood the nearest thing to heaven.

Marian looked at Ariadne, and she nodded.

" 'May the fire of this log warm the cold,' " Percy began, his voice unsure. Then he looked at Marian. " 'And may the hungry be fed. May the weary find rest,' " he continued, his eyes on the earl. " 'And may all enjoy heaven's peace.' "

No one said anything. The Christmas spell and Lord Wynswich's spirit rested on them like a benediction for just a moment. Lady Wynswich sneezed. "If there is a worse drawing

fireplace in Devon, I declare I do not know of it,'' she exclaimed, and everyone laughed.

Percy signaled Billings to fill the cups from the punch bowl.
When everyone had a cup in hand, he held his high. ''I propose
to honor Sam Beddoe,'' he began, ''who has so courageously
decided to ally himself with the Wynswich family''—he looked
at Alistair—''and all its secrets. I'm convinced there is not a
braver man in this part of England. Hear, hear.''

A toast for Ariadne followed. Alistair sidled up to his sister.
''Percy could go on for hours like this. D'ye think the govern-
ment encourages diplomats to carry on like this?''

''I daresay,'' Marian said. ''Alistair, it is almost perfect.''

Alistair took another sip of his punch. ''Almost, Mare?
Almost?''

''Well, yes. I wish that Lord Ingraham could be convinced
to hurry off to Bath, where his relatives are.'' Marian held out
her cup for another dipper of punch. ''But he will have none
of it. And he as much as told me there is someone he is redding
up his nerve to propose to. Oh, I do not understand men.''

Alistair regarded her thoughtfully. ''I could put my mind to
this, Mare. Really concentrate on a solution.''

She shook her head. ''Even I must go down to defeat on
occasion. We were lucky to squeak through this morning's
bumble broth. Such good fortune seldom comes twice in the
same day.''

But what a pleasant thought, Marian considered as she sipped
her punch and watched Lord Ingraham. Her mother seemed to
have forgiven him his scar. She had pulled him a little to one
side and was carrying on at length. How patient he is, she
thought as she leaned against the fireplace and watched him.

How foolish she was to have thought him old. It was only
his salt-and-pepper hair that made him look old. There was
nothing ancient about the spring in his step, or the quick way
his eyes darted about a room, or the way his lips just naturally
curled into a smile. I wonder if he likes children.

The thought made her look down into her cup and swish it
around suspiciously. My thoughts are certainly traveling far
afield, she thought. It must be the punch. She set the cup down

hastily and moved toward the stairs, where she sat.

Marian rested her chin in her hands and watched them all: Ariadne and the vicar talking and laughing with the others, but never farther away from each other than a hand's touch; Alistair with his beautiful Wynswich hair, all cropped up the back; her mother and Percy close, disagreements forgotten, at least for the moment.

Lord Ingraham looked back at her.

She sat up as he came closer and joined her on the next step up. "My legs are too long for that bottom step," he said. "Some of us are less economical than others."

She only smiled and returned her chin to her hands.

"At a loss for words, Marian?" he asked finally, his voice low.

Marian shook her head. "I was merely thinking how much I love them all, for all their faults and silly notions . . . and for all of mine." She spoke seriously. "For I have many faults, my lord." She scooted up a step until she sat next to him. "But they love me anyway. I do not pretend to understand it."

"Love is a powerful emotion," her companion murmured.

She nodded and rose to her feet. She held out her hand to him. "Good night, sir. If I stay here much longer, I will indulge in a bout of tears, and everyone will be maudlin."

He made no attempt to dissuade her. "Good night, Marian," he said, and kissed her fingers.

She withdrew her hand reluctantly. "Don't . . . don't forget your salve."

It was an easy matter, once in her room, to shuck off her clothing and climb into bed. She knew she would sleep long and heartily. In the morning, Percy, her mother, Ariadne, and the vicar were to attempt Lyme Regis again, this time to permit their solicitor to draw up the marriage arrangements.

And then you will be happy, Ariadne, Marian thought as she brushed her hair until it crackled, and tied on her sleeping cap. But for tomorrow, I will have the house practically to myself. If Mama refuses to sleep until noon these days, I shall.

* * *

"Marian? I say, Mare, are you awake?"

Marian glanced and turned over in her bed, tucking her arms about her pillow, folding it in a tight embrace.

"Mare. Mare? We really have a matter to discuss—and quickly, too. Oh, do wake up."

Alistair. His words finally penetrated her brain and she opened her eyes.

Sunlight streamed in the window. Alistair must have pulled back the draperies. Marian yanked her pillow over her head. "Go away," she muttered. "Surely it can wait."

"Mare, listen to me. Mare, if you go back to sleep, I shall be forced to do something drastic. Oh, God, what am I saying? I already did that." He sat down on the bed, shaking her. "Mare. You'd better wake up."

"Go away."

He would not.

With one last sigh, Marian rolled over and looked up into her brother's face. She peered closer and rubbed her eyes. This was not the face of someone indulging in light fancy. As she stared at him long and hard, Alistair began to gnaw his lower lip.

She sat up. "What are you up to, Alistair?" She took off her sleeping cap and shook out her hair. "Alistair, answer me."

He got up from her bed. "Maybe you had better just come with me."

"Where?" she asked suspiciously.

"To Lord Ingraham's room."

She stared at him and drew the blankets around her. "Are you all about in your head, brother? What makes you think for one second that I would go in this state to Lord Ingraham's room?"

Alistair backed toward the door. "Do you recall what I said last night about really concentrating on the problem of getting Lord Ingraham home to Bath?"

She nodded, watching the expression in her brother's eyes as little prickles of warning began to gather together in her brain.

"Alistair, if you have done something to Lord Ingraham . . ." She held her breath.

He wouldn't look at her. "We can bounce him onto the next mail coach to Bath and he'll never know what hit him."

"Alistair . . ." she began, her voice low and threatening.

"I drugged him, Mare."

8

In one quick motion, Marian threw back the covers and leapt from her bed. She grabbed up the hem of her nightgown so she would not trip over it, and raced to Lord Ingraham's room, Alistair hot on her bare heels.

Lord Ingraham lay on his bed, his shoes off, his pants unbuttoned. His arms were flung wide across the bed, which looked unrumpled, as though he had not moved all night.

"What did you do?" Marian asked in a quiet voice. Alistair didn't answer, so she asked louder. "Alistair, you had better tell me right now."

He hung his head. "After you left, and Ariadne and Mama went off to plot the wedding some more, Percy broke out the Lafite. The vicar wasn't up to it, but the rest of us settled down for some serious drinking." He glanced sideways at Marian, as if to test the waters. "Lord Ingraham can really pack away wine."

Marian moved closer to the bed. She watched the earl, looking for signs of life. "Is he breathing? Good God, Alistair."

"I hope so," her brother replied. "Whatever will we tell his relatives? The Regent? Good God, Percy?"

"Good God Percy indeed! What, then?" she asked, her voice deadly quiet.

"I was watching Lord Ingraham when I got a great idea, a truly brilliant stroke. I went out to the workshop for that little brown bottle. You know, the one you use to send little wounded animals off to a better world. Oh, Mare, don't look at me like that.''

"Alistair," she shrieked. "You idiot!"

She ran to the bed and jumped on it, grabbing the front of Lord Ingraham's shirt and unbuttoning it.

"I figured it out pound for pound, Mare," said Alistair. "If three drops will cock up a rabbit's toes, I thought that—''

"Oh, hush," she ordered, and laid her ear upon the earl's heart. At least he's still warm, she thought grimly as she closed her eyes and rested her head against his chest.

It seemed an eternity to her, but his heart beat steadily, slowly, as if in the embrace of a deep sleep. Marian sighed, her mind blank with gratitude, enjoying for a moment more that pleasant odor that came from Lord Ingraham's skin. It wasn't the smell of cologne, or cigar smoke, or liquor. It was just he. He was a hairy-chested man, and he was quite comfortable. She rested there a moment, covered with relief, while Alistair hovered nearby.

With a sigh of his own, Lord Ingraham put his arms around her. Marian squeaked in surprise as he rolled over with her in his arms and snuggled his head between her breasts. As she struggled to free herself, he sighed again, ran his hand under her nightgown, and rested it on her thigh.

"Alistair," she hissed, "do something! Alistair?"

She pulled Lord Ingraham's hand off her thigh and he promptly replaced it, wrapping his other arm around her waist. She wormed her way out from under his armpit, looking about desperately for Alistair, who had dropped to the floor in wild laughter.

Shaking with mirth, he got to his knees and stared at his sister. "Mare, you can't imagine how funny you look!"

"Alistair, I'll get you for this, see if I don't," she whispered furiously as she tugged at her nightgown and wrestled with Lord Ingraham's hand.

The earl began to nuzzle her along the line of her jaw with slow, deliberate kisses, murmuring something deep in his throat. She lay still, feeling an urge, totally absurd, to return his kisses and murmur along with him. But his face was scratchy from an overnight beard, and there was Alistair, his eyes alive with humor.

"Alistair," she began, her voice honey-soft, "if you expect me for one moment to extricate you from the ridiculous scrape you are in, you'd better shift Lord Ingraham, and be quick about it. And for heaven's sake, close the door."

The menace in her voice was sufficient to propel him to the door, which he locked. "Look at it this way, Mare," he said as he returned to the bed and sat upon it. "At least we are assured that Lord Ingraham is very much alive." The thought sent Alistair into another spasm of laughter.

"Brother," Marian pleaded. Lord Ingraham abandoned her thigh and began working on the buttons of her nightgown. "Lord Ingraham," she muttered through clenched teeth, "you are amazingly dexterous."

He said something in reply, and she started. He said something else, yawned, and lapsed into sleep again, his fingers still twined in the buttonhole.

Alistair recovered himself and turned Lord Ingraham onto his back again. Marian wiggled out from under him, her face bright red with embarrassment and whisker burn. She yanked her nightgown down and grabbed her brother by his shirt front. "You ought to be locked up. And now, what are we going to do with this poor man?"

Alistair spread out his hands and shrugged. "I thought we could take him in the gig as far as the Picton-Lyme Regis crossing and trundle him onto the next mail coach. You know, put a tag on him reading, 'Bath' . . ." His voice trailed off. "Well, it seemed like such a scathing idea last night." His tone became reminiscent, fond even. "Papa used to say he had his best ideas over a Lafite."

Marian turned away in disgust and plopped herself down at the foot of the bed, careful to stay out of Lord Ingraham's reach. "Gil will be simply furious when he finally regains consciousness."

Alistair sat beside her. "He will be furious no matter where he comes to, Mare. Why not let it be on the mail coach to Bath?"

She regarded her brother in silence and then looked at Lord

Ingraham, who was sound asleep again. She got to her feet and leaned across the bed, touching the scar on his cheek. "We couldn't just put him on the coach. That would be foolish, perhaps dangerous." She opened the jar of salve by the bed and applied a thin layer to his cheek, hardly aware of what she was doing. She rested her fingertips for another moment on his neck below the jawline and satisfied herself that his pulse was regular.

"Alistair, we will have to see that he gets to Bath. We must accompany him."

He stared at her. "Mare, even in my wildest plotting, never did I ever consider such a thing."

"We must," she argued. "Suppose we did put a note on him? Someone could do him harm. Suppose he did not waken in time to get off at Bath? I can't imagine what you were thinking, but now that you have started this deed, we may as well finish it right."

"Mare, do you know, I believe we could escort Lord Ingraham to Bath, take the next coach to Picton, and be back here Christmas Eve."

"We could," she agreed, and sat down slowly. "Alistair, this is all so wrong! Oh, *how* could you do such a thing! Percy will be furious with us, and he should be!"

A variety of emotions crossed Alistair's face. Irritation was succeeded by stubbornness, which gave way to momentary contrition, which was replaced by a look of determination that reminded Marian forcefully of Bertram Wynswich in his wildest moments. She sighed and waited for her brother to speak.

"Caesar and the Rubicon, my dear," he said at last, and looked at her expectantly.

Marian stared at him. "Alistair, you are making less sense than usual!"

Alistair warmed to his subject. "Marian, I do remember something of my Latin. I think even Julius Caesar would see this as a point of no turning back."

Marian uttered a sound of disgust, but Alistair waved her away. "Now listen. I admit I made a shocking mull of this. If we do nothing and remain here, Percy and Lord Ingraham will be furious. If we do something and go to Bath, Percy and Lord Ingraham will still be furious." He looked at her shrewdly. "If we are doomed to censure, the rack, and exile, Mare, why not at least get Lord Ingraham to Bath? It's what you want, isn't it?"

She nodded, in spite of her misgivings. "Oh, Alistair, I just *know* he is breaking his mother's heart!" Marian squared her shoulders. "Papa would call this a 'bold stroke,' would he not?"

Alistair nodded.

"I know it is not right," she said, and touched Lord Ingraham's neck again, feeling for his pulse. "I truly think I want to have done with pranks, Alistair."

"Your New Year's Resolution then, Mare," he said.

"Perhaps . . . just this last time. We may regret this."

"We may."

"But Lord Ingraham might stay away from his mother and sisters for another year."

"He might."

Her fingers still rested lightly on Lord Ingraham's neck. His slow but steady pulse reassured her, where Alistair's words could not. "Then let us get on with it, brother. With what are we to finance this expedition, may I ask?"

He considered her question. "Mare, details don't generally rear their ugly heads when you are deep in Lafite."

Marian sighed in exasperation.

Alistair pursed his lips, and then his eyes lit up. "Mare, I could spout my watch."

It was Marian's turn to stare. Lord Ingraham stirred on the bed, muttering something else, and she ran her hand along his leg to silence him. "What are you talking about?" she whispered.

"You know—spout, pawn, hock," he whispered back. "I can take my watch to Picton and come back with the ready in a flea's leap. Oh, don't stare at me like that. I've spouted this watch at Eton more times than even I remember."

"Alistair, that will never be enough. But do you know, I have that pearl necklace that belonged to Grandmama Wynswich."

"Go fetch it, Mare," Alistair said. "I can be back here in

thirty minutes, if you can get Lord Ingraham ready.''

She looked at the earl doubtfully. ''Alistair, he is so big.''

Her brother was on his feet. ''Just tuck in his shirt and button his pants. I'll help you with his coat and hat, and we can get Daniel from the stable to help us with the gig. Don't just stand there. We've got to act!''

''This is positively my last scheme, brother, I assure you.''

They unlocked the door and tiptoed to Marian's room. She retrieved her pearl necklace from its case. ''Hurry up,'' she whispered. ''We'll be ready when you return.''

With nerveless fingers, Marian pulled on her green dress again. After a moment's thought, she grabbed up two pairs of long woolen stockings and put them both on, then pulled on her boots. She braided her hair quickly and looped the long plaits around her head. Snatching up a bandbox, she threw in a muslin dress, slippers, and nightgown.

She tiptoed back to Lord Ingraham's room. He had not moved. Locking the door behind her and wishing that her heart would not pound so loud, she approached the bed again. His eyes were open a little. Marian stood stock-still, certain that he was watching her.

''Gil?'' she whispered.

He made no response, so she reached out and closed his eyes all the way. To her relief, they stayed shut. Holding her breath, she leaned over him and buttoned his shirt, but not before touching him and noting how soft the hair on his chest was. ''Who would have thought such a thing,'' she said out loud, and then looked around in embarrassment. Ariadne would swoon, she thought as she finished buttoning his shirt.

Looking everywhere but at him, Marian tucked his shirt into his pants and buttoned them, wondering all over again what Alistair had plunged her into. She was at a loss over the earl's neckcloth, and contented herself with draping it around his neck and tying a loose knot. Perhaps Alistair could do some justice to it later. She would wait until her brother returned to attempt the boots.

''Mare? Open up.''

She unlocked the door and pulled Alistair inside. He held out his wallet and showed her the results of his trip to Picton. "It's enough for our travels."

They tugged Lord Ingraham's boots on him as he sang a tuneless little song and muttered under his breath again. "Marian," he said distinctly, and she jumped. He said nothing more, but slumbered on, a slight smile on his face.

Sweating from the exertion of cramming boots onto a dead-weight, Alistair paused and looked down on the Earl of Collin-wood. "This must be what people call the sleep of the just. Look how peaceful he is."

"You're doomed never to know how that feels," Marian said with some feeling. "Brother, Percy will lapse into total uncon-sciousness when he finds out what we have done."

"I left him a note downstairs, propped up on the mantel-piece."

"I'm sure that will greatly relieve his mind," fumed Marian.

Daniel joined them, and he and Alistair dragged Lord Ingraham down the stairs, pausing every few steps. "He's a deadweight, Mare," Alistair panted.

She refused to be moved by pity. "You should have thought of that last night over your Lafite," she snapped.

Marian watched them trundle Lord Ingraham out the front door. She darted back into his room for another look around. His traveling bag lay open on the floor. She whisked the brush and comb off the bureau and added them to the case, strapping it down. She carried it out to the gig and climbed in next to Lord Ingraham, who listed to one side like a ship taking on water. Alistair straightened him up and Marian leaned against him to balance him upright.

The cold air caused his eyelids to flutter. He opened them, looked around him in total incomprehension, and closed them again. His head drooped forward and he began to snore.

"Alistair, how much of that bottle did you slip him?" Marian asked as Alistair chirruped to the horse and they started down the lane to the main road.

"I'm not really sure, Mare," he said, his eyes straight ahead. "I figured it all out so carefully, and then Percy was there waving about a bottle of Lafite, and I just dumped it in his cup."

Marian shuddered. "Brother, our parents should have left you on a hillside to die when you were born. The Greeks did it all the time." Her voice rose to an unpleasant pitch; Lord Ingraham winced and flopped his head against her shoulder.

"No! Did the Greeks do that?" asked Alistair, completely diverted. "How barbaric of them! I would have thought they knew better."

Marian sighed and attempted no more conversation until they reached the crossing. They waited in the gig, Daniel perched in the back holding the luggage, until they heard the horn of the mail coach.

Alistair turned to Marian. "I could probably do this by myself," he offered.

Marian shook her head. "And leave me to face Percy alone? Oh, no! We will pray that by Christmas Eve Percy will be full of Christian charity."

Marian paid the driver, counting out the coins and pocketing the rest, while Daniel and Alistair hauled the inert Lord Ingraham aboard the mail coach.

"I don't know, miss," said the driver doubtfully.

It was an easy matter to allow tears to spring to her eyes. "But, sir, we are returning him to our home in Bath." The tears flowed more freely. "True, he *is* a trifle indisposed right now, but it has been five years—five years!—since our widowed mother has seen him. Oh, sir, it is Christmas!"

By the time she finished her artful declaration, the other coach passengers were peering out the window. One older woman was dabbing at her eyes.

The driver rubbed his chin and then pinched Marian's cheek. She forced herself to twinkle her eyes at him. "For you, miss, I'll do it. But mind you keep an eye on him!"

She curtsied. "Oh, God bless you, sir. Our mother will be endlessly grateful to you."

The coach was full. Lord Ingraham, his eyes half-open, leaned against Alistair, who sat crowded against the window. Marian squeezed in next to Lord Ingraham, who promptly sagged against her, making himself comfortable, his head cradled on her chest.

An older woman sat on the other side of Marian. "Did you say it had been five years?" she asked in an undervoice. She leaned forward for a better look at Lord Ingraham. "Mercy, if he don't look like a pirate."

A parson who was sitting across the way nodded. "This, surely, is a man who has kept low company."

You can't guess how much he would agree with you right now, Marian thought to herself as she touched his hair, admiring the color of it. She looked about her at the other man seated next to the parson. He stared but said nothing. She sniffed. He smelled strongly of fish. He eyed her with considerable expectancy. She leaned the earl toward Alistair and took a deep breath.

"Sirs, you cannot imagine," she said in a conspiratorial whisper to the men opposite them, who leaned forward. "Imagine this: he was traveling to Istanbul and was set upon by Turks."

The woman next to her gasped, and Lord Ingraham stirred uneasily. Alistair opened and closed his mouth several times, while the parson removed his wig, rubbed the top of his bald head, and replaced it. The silent man rummaged in his pocket and popped a herring into his mouth.

Marian took her handkerchief from her pocket and twisted it in her hands. "And there he was, my poor brother, chained to a galley bench and forced to row for the next five years of his life."

The woman burst into tears. The parson clucked his tongue. "I had no idea that the Turkish navy still employed galley slaves."

"Oh, they are not employed, sir," Alistair added. "Gilbert has nothing to show for it."

"I believe the area of the Mediterranean Sea is considerably more backward than England," said Marian hastily. "It was 'Row, row, you blaggards,' every day of his life for five long years." She patted the earl's leg. "And that is why his hair is gone almost gray, and he a young man still."

The woman sobbed louder. "And that terrible scar?"

Marian dabbed at her dry eyes. "He was branded, ma'am,

branded like an animal. That is the Turkish symbol for 'slave.' ''
She sighed and managed a small sob. "And so he will be marked
for the rest of his life."

"It is a melancholy reflection on the state of the world, outside
of England," commented the parson. "I trust he learned his
lesson and will not travel abroad again."

"I am sure he will not," agreed Marian.

"Will not what?" asked Ingraham in a drowsy voice.

Marian jumped. Lord Ingraham's eyes were wide open, the
pupils greatly dilated. He looked about him in complete
amazement. "Where the deuce am I?"

As her heart plummeted toward her toes, Marian grabbed his
hand and covered it with kisses. "And this is the worst part,"
she cried. "He sometimes cannot remember where he is!"

"And that's the truth," said Ingraham. He closed his eyes
again and was soon snoring.

Alistair blinked and retreated like a turtle into the warmth
and security of his overcoat. Marian clung to Lord Ingraham's
hand. "That is the sorrow of it all. Sometimes we even have
to remind him who we are."

"Let this be a lesson to those who go adventuring," ser-
monized the parson as he returned to his bible.

The silent man shook his head and pocketed his herring.

The woman next to Marian dried her tears and picked up her
knitting again. Gradually Lord Ingraham relaxed against
Marian, and soon he was sleeping.

On the other side of Lord Ingraham, Alistair continued his
intense scrutiny of the countryside. Marian made herself as
comfortable as she could and wished that she had found time
for breakfast. She had never cared for herring, but the smell
of it lingered in the coach, and her stomach began to rumble.
The cold was beginning to seep inside the venerable mail coach.
Marian closed her eyes and burrowed in closer to Lord
Ingraham. Before she drifted off to sleep, she roused herself
long enough to notice that the rain pelting down had turned into
snow.

The blast from the coachman's horn woke her. The steady
rhythm of the horses running smoothly in harness was slower

now. They were coming to a village. Marian sat up and glanced quickly at Lord Ingraham.

The earl's eyes were open, his pupils much larger now. Marian bit her lip and watched him as he stared straight ahead, a little frown on his face, as if he were attempting to discover what he was doing on a coach. The last thing he probably remembered was staring into a Yule log and drinking Lafite 'Ol, she thought.

"This is my get-off," said the lady as she stowed her knitting and arranged her cloak about her shoulders again. "And now it's snowing. I hope you'll have a safe enough journey to Bath, my dear."

"Bath?" Lord Ingraham asked. "Good God."

The woman peered at him, and her ready tears began to flow again. "Oh, you poor, poor dear," she crooned, "and you don't even remember where you're going." She reached into her basket and drew out a pair of bright-colored mittens. "Here, take these and wear them in good health. Now that you're back in England, you'll need some warm mittens." She placed them in his lap and patted his knee, all the time looking at Marian. "I'm sure he'll be better, young lady."

Ingraham stared at her, his mouth open, as she nimbly removed herself from the coach, waved good-bye, and disappeared into the swirling snow.

Marian held her breath as the parson took out a stocking change purse and carefully counted out several shillings. He placed the coins on top of the mittens. "I was taking these to Bristol to the Widows and Children's Home for Christmas, but I don't know why you can't have some, young man," he said, and patted the earl's knee, too. "To help you to a fresh start."

Lord Ingraham could only stare, wide-eyed, at the parson. Alistair let out a long, low whistle and slid farther down into his overcoat. Marian's tongue froze to the roof of her mouth.

The parson gathered up his belongings. As he left the coach, he turned suddenly and shook a finger at Lord Ingraham. "Now, remember, laddie, this is the season of forgiveness. I depend upon you as a good Englishman to forgive those Turks."

He was followed from the coach by the silent man who

smelled of fish. As the man passed in front of Lord Ingraham, he dropped a packet of salted herring in the diplomat's lap. "Merry Christmas, laddie," the man said, "and stay out of the Mediterranean."

The coach was empty. Silence filled the air. Marian could feel Gilbert drawing himself up. Before he could speak, the coachman swung down and looked inside. "We'll be stopping for a half-hour. Mind you come inside and warm yourselves."

Numbly, Marian rose and pulled her cloak tighter about her. She didn't dare look at Lord Ingraham as she made to leave the coach, but he grasped the back of her cloak and held her there.

"Not so fast, Marian. You're going to explain to me what's going on."

"Not here," she said, and tugged at her cloak, which the earl showed no desire to turn loose.

The coachman opened the door. "Miss, are ye having trouble with an ugly customer?" He peered closer at Lord Ingraham and then whispered to Marian in a loud voice, "Is this the man I've been hearing so much about?"

She nodded. "We will be quite all right. Oh, sir, could we just sit here a moment? We'll be in directly."

The coachman grunted and tipped his hat to her. "Mind you don't sit out here too long." He pulled his coat tighter about him. "Looks like we brought the bad weather with us."

He left them, and Lord Ingraham twitched on her cloak again. Marian sat down and looked to Alistair for help. Her brother still sat with his neck deep in his overcoat.

Lord Ingraham eyed the brother and sister in turn. He poured the parson's coins into the old lady's mittens and pocketed them. "Well? Who goes first?" he asked, his voice loud enough to make Marian wince. "You can begin by explaining why my eyes feel twelve feet away from my toes and there are occasionally two of you, Marian, if I turn my head too quickly." He rubbed the stubble on his chin. "One of you is enough. Anyone would tell you one is enough."

His eyes held no amusement, and his lips were set along firm, unsmiling lines. "And don't try to tell me I drank too much. I am careful about those things."

Alistair cleared his throat and raised up a little higher from the safety of his overcoat. "Actually, my lord, I drank too much."

"And you feel this way, too? My sympathy." Lord Ingraham took the mittens from his pocket. "Of course, I seem to have the sympathy of everyone on this vile conveyance." He looked about him, turning his head slowly, as if it ached. "And pray tell, what is this humble vehicle?"

"It is a mail coach, my lord," Alistair offered.

"Indeed. And what am I doing on a mail coach?"

Marian opened her mouth to answer, but Lord Ingraham held up his hand. "Wait. Let me guess. Could this be the coach bound for Bath, or would that be too much coincidence?"

Marian nodded, not daring to look at him.

"After I expressly told you on several occasions that I had no desire to go to Bath for Christmas?" he thundered.

She nodded again.

Lord Ingraham shook his finger at her. "And don't go giving me that soft-eyed look of yours! And threaten those tears! And quiver that lip! Oh, Marian, don't do that. Here, take my handkerchief."

She accepted the hastily offered handkerchief and sobbed into it. After a moment in which a series of emotions crossed his own face, Lord Ingraham took her hand and pulled her over to the seat next to him and tucked his arm about her. "I wish you would not do that," he said, and his voice was kinder. "Now blow your nose and tell me what is going on." He tightened his arm about her. "That's my only handkerchief right now, so be economical, my dear."

Alistair cleared his throat again and Lord Ingraham swiveled his body carefully to look at him. "Oh, if my memory serves me, I believe you were about to tell me something about your drinking habits, Alistair."

"I blame this event entirely on Papa's Lafite."

"Don't be so harsh, lad! That was an excellent year," Gilbert said. "I even remember it. Which is more than I can say for last night," he continued dryly.

A thought piqued him and he leaned closer to Marian. "But tell me first . . . I seem to remember this morning. Did I . . ."

He stopped. "Oh, I could never have done anything like that. No. No. It's nothing, Marian."

She moved closer. A chill was coming in under a crack in the door. The earl began to run his hand up and down her arm. She shivered and he looked down at her.

"Did I frighten you a moment ago?" he asked, his voice soft. She nodded.

"Good! Now, Alistair, pray continue."

"I . . . I hatched a scheme, my lord, one that seemed damned near brilliant over wine."

Gil smiled affably. "You're not the first to solve the fate of the nations over a bottle, lad. It's just that most of us have the wit not to follow through. But I ask too much, obviously, considering that streak of insanity in the Wynswich family."

Marian turned her head so the earl would not see her smile.

"But, come, come, lad. Your sister grows colder by the minute, I am none too warm, and I will have an explanation before I leave this mail coach."

"I went to Mare's workshop and . . ." Alistair craned his neck around Ingraham for a look at his sister. "Mare, what is that stuff?"

"Morphine."

"Morphine," Alistair squeaked. "Morphine! Mare, why didn't you tell me ages ago?"

Marian stamped her foot. "Alistair, you nod! I never thought in my wildest imaginings that you would tip that in Gil's brandy."

It was the earl's turn to stare. "Good God, Alistair," he said, "have I offended you in some way? Something I said?"

"No, no! It's just that I thought if you were in a state of euphoria, we—that is, I—could get you onto the mail coach and home to Bath. Mare told me she would be so happy to see you with your own family, and . . . I just took it from there," Alistair concluded miserably.

Ingraham shook his head slowly. "Tell me. When you were a baby, did someone—a nursemaid, perhaps—drop you on your head? On the soft spot?"

Silence ruled the mail coach again. When Alistair could stand no more, he sighed. "But it was Mare's idea that we come along. I was going to put you on the coach with a note pinned to your coat." Alistair groaned and leaned forward, his head between his hands. "I see now that never would have served."

"Thank the Lord for that," Ingraham retorted. "For all you know, I could have been set upon by infidel Turks and forced to row my way across the Mediterranean."

Marian's lips twitched. She tried to smother her laughter, but it was a forlorn hope. She turned her face into the earl's overcoat and abandoned herself to helpless mirth.

Lord Ingraham leaned toward her. "Or kidnapped by gypsies. Or abducted by Mohicans." He started to laugh. "Marian Wynswich, where do you get your crackbrained notions?" He pulled her away and held her at arm's length for a good look. "You're faster on your feet than any a diplomat I have rubbed shoulders with, but thank the Almighty that our country has been spared your services."

He pulled her back to him, held one hand to his head, and laughed until the tears came to his eyes. Marian handed back his handkerchief and he dabbed at his eyes and then made a face.

"Marian, are you totally and completely resolved that I should appear before my dear mother as I am, looking like St. Lawrence the Martyr, roasted to a turn over his grill?"

Her laughter stopped. She touched his face. "Totally and completely resolved, my lord," she said, and took his face in her hands. "Do you think for one silly moment that she will love you less? Honestly, I think men are the vainest creatures."

He kissed her palms. "I bow to your superior knowledge of my sex."

Her face reddened. "Oh, Gil, I know nothing about men." After a moment's sober reflection, she continued. "But if I were your mother, my heart would be breaking about now."

It was Lord Ingraham's turn for a moment's pause. "You are the oddest collection of parts, Marian. You don't flinch at attempting mad schemes that would send most women into spasms, but you have such a sure hand where emotions are . . ." He stopped. "Well, never mind. Here comes the coachman again. And what's this? He looks like the bearer of bad news."

Marian glanced up from a frowning contemplation of the floorboards. The coachman opened the door and the snow blew in. The expression on his face was no warmer.

"I recommend ye find your way to the inn now, lady and gents," he said. "We're snowed in."

9

Marian gasped in dismay. "Oh, never say that," she exclaimed, and looked at Lord Ingraham. "What are we to do?"

"The first thing ye can do is get your bones out of my conveyance," said the coachman impatiently.

"Very well," she grumbled, and drew her cloak about her. The coachman held out his hand for her, but she stopped. "Gil, can you walk?"

He shook his head. "I'm doubtful. Here, Alistair, give me a hand up. Jump down, Marian."

She did as he said, and stood outside in the snow as her brother helped Lord Ingraham to his feet. The diplomat paled noticeably and grasped Marian's shoulder as he descended. She put her arm around his waist, and the coachman did the same on his other side.

"Laddie, you've suffered a lot at the hands o' them heathens," grunted the coachman.

Lord Ingraham managed a smile and a wink over the coachman's head to Marian. "Yes, I was in some danger from the greatest rascals I have ever known."

"Be that as it may, me lad, you're almost home now. And with a brother and sister like these to help you, what more could a man ask?"

Lord Ingraham had the good grace not to look at Marian. "Yes, what, indeed?" he murmured, and then stood still, leaning forward. "Alistair, take Marian's place. My dear, run

139

on ahead. I must pause here now and make a fool of myself.''

She did as he said and hurried toward the inn, flinching at the sound of Lord Ingraham retching in the stableyard. Oh, I could throttle Alistair, she thought. How dare he?

She had reached the door before she turned around and marched back through the snow to the three men, who had not moved from beside the mail coach. Without a word she ripped off a corner of her petticoat. Wetting it in the snow, she wiped off Lord Ingraham's mouth, wet the cloth again, and applied it to the back of his neck.

His eyes were closed, but he opened them long enough to look at her. ''I don't understand why you always know what to do,'' he murmured. His words slurred together.

''Hold that cloth on his neck, Alistair,'' she ordered, ''and keep him moving toward the inn.'' Marian ran ahead, hopeful of a room.

A room was out of the question, a bed laughable, Marian discovered in a brief consultation with the innkeeper. ''We're full, miss, and have been since earlier this afternoon. I can give you a blanket and a pillow and a corner of the taproom.''

She took the blanket and pillow without a murmur and plunged into the taproom, which was full of other travelers, mostly workingclass men and women, bound for home and Christmas on the mail coach. Bags and parcels were perched in every corner. Pipe smoke was as thick as Devon fog, and she heard men hawking and spitting on the floor.

Marian made a rapid about-face and cornered the innkeeper again in the kitchen. ''This will never do,'' she said. ''Have you nothing else?''

''Have you any money?'' he countered as he hacked great slices of meat off a half-done joint.

She touched the coins in her reticule, their coach money back to Picton. ''Yes, I have,'' she declared. ''Please, is there not a room?''

The innkeeper examined the coins she extended to him and shook his head again. ''I can find you a spot under the stair landing, and even that will cost you, miss,'' he said. He put his face close to hers and she drew back from the smell of stale beer on his breath. "Of course, a pretty girl like you should be able to find a bed anywhere."

Marian's fingers itched to slap his red face, but she did no such thing. She handed him a coin, and then another when he still stood there. She parted with another coin. "And please bring some warm milk," she said, waiting for him to move off.

He stood where he was and reached for her waist.

"Touch her and you're a dead man," said Lord Ingraham.

Marian hadn't heard them come in. The earl was still supported by the coachman and her brother, but the look in his eyes was enough to send a little frizzle down her spine.

"I think he means it," Alistair offered, apology in his tone but a look no less venomous on his face.

"I expect he does," added the coachman. "Laddie," he said, addressing Alistair, "I'll be more than happy to take my ease on the stairs here, if you should need an extra arm with a fist on the end of it."

"Thank you," Alistair said. "I'll sing out if I need you."

Marian raised her chin and looked the innkeeper in the eye. "Lead us to that landing, sir, and we'll want the milk directly."

They followed the innkeeper to the stairwell and waited while he shifted a barrel out of the little space. He swiped a dirty rag around and stepped back. "Of course, if I get a better offer for this spot, I'll be moving you."

The coachman rubbed his chin and eyed the innkeeper. " 'Twould be a pity for me to have to blow my yard of tin in someone else's inn yard for the coming year of Our Lord 1815, but I could arrange it."

He stared at the innkeeper, who blanched, looked away, and then disappeared into the kitchen.

The coachman sighed. "Don't just stand there, miss. Help this poor cove."

Impulsively, Marian reached up and kissed the driver on the cheek. Tears sparkled in her eyes. "Oh, thank you," she whispered, and spread out the blanket.

"And I think I can find another blanket in the stable," the coachman went on, his face fiery red. "Nothing fancy, but it'll be warm."

Alistair laughed. "Better back off, man, or Mare will peg you again."

"Lucky devil," croaked Lord Ingraham, and then his head flopped forward.

Alistair and the coachman laid out Lord Ingraham on the blanket. "Brother, pull off his boots and unbutton his pants," Marian directed.

"Marian, my blushes," protested the earl.

"Oh, hush," Marian said gruffly as she untied his neckcloth and placed the pillow under his head. "Drat! This pillow is no better than a block of wood. Alistair, hold up his head for a moment."

Marian scrambled back under the landing and sat down with her back to the wall. "There, now," she said as Alistair lowered Lord Ingraham's head into her lap. She tucked the blanket up higher on his chest. "You will sleep now, and feel much better in the morning."

"And if I do not?" the earl asked, and his eyelids began to droop.

She touched his chest. "You will. I promise." She hesitated. "And forgive us, Gil."

"Done," he said. He grasped her hand as she rested it on his chest, and closed his eyes.

Marian settled herself against the wall and listened carefully to Lord Ingraham's breathing. It was deeper than his shallow breaths in the coach. She moved her hand across his chest to his heart and smiled in satisfaction. Impulsively, she kissed his forehead.

"Do that . . . when I'm awake . . . sometime, Ingraham said, and tightened his grip slightly on her fingers.

She chuckled. "No! Whatever would your lady-love think?" She looked about her. "Besides, I thought you were asleep."

The earl only smiled. "Don't waste them." He slept then.

The wall grew no warmer, but Marian's legs were comfortable from the heat of Lord Ingraham's body. In a moment the coachman returned with two more blankets and Alistair on his heels, followed by a gust of snow.

"Mare, there's a coachman outside who's going to attempt

Lyme Regis. I could stay with Gil and you could be home.''

She shook her head. "I cannot leave him. Go, if you've a mind to."

"Mare, you won't be home for Christmas," he reminded her, "and Ariadne told me you had such plans."

"I suppose I did. Thank you, sir," she said to the coachman, who draped the horse blanket over Lord Ingraham. "But they are of little consequence now."

Alistair shrugged and accepted the other blanket from the coachman, sitting down Indian-fashion.

"If you're needing me, I'll be in the stable with the horses," said their self-appointed guardian.

"Sir, you are so kind," Marian said. "We cannot repay you."

"Tush, it's Christmas, little lady," he said with a smile. "And I did enjoy that look on the innkeeper's mug." He tipped his hat to them and went back outside into the whirling snow.

Alistair wrapped the blanket around himself and hunkered down in the narrow space. Marian thought he slept, but then he spoke out of the depths of his blanket.

"Marian, I'm sorry. I should never have done what I did."

"No, you should not," she agreed in a low voice. The earl stirred and mumbled something and she placed her hand on his neck and pulled him closer.

"It was foolish and ill-advised."

"I'll not argue with that, brother," she said. "And I'll tell you one thing more: you could have done Lord Ingraham serious damage."

Alistair said nothing.

"It is time the tricks ended, brother," Marian said. She reached out with her foot and touched him. "It is time we both grew up."

She knew that sleep would entirely elude her, but she slept anyway, Lord Ingraham clasped protectively in her arms. She woke only because someone was staring at her.

It was Lord Ingraham. "Oh," she exclaimed, looking down into his eyes.

"You can turn me loose now, Marian," he said. "There are no gypsies, Mohicans, or infidel Turks in sight. And I would like to sit up."

She did not let go, but gazed into his eyes. "Your eyes, my lord," she said. "They are much improved."

He grinned. "They were never my best feature, Marian. Usually my classic nose and aristocratic cheekbones are commented upon. So glad my eyes meet with your approval."

"Silly," she declared, and let go of him. "Yesterday the pupils were the merest dots."

The earl grasped the stair tread above his head and pulled himself upright.

Marian watched him closely. "How do you feel?"

"Hungry." He glanced around at her. "But that is your office, is it not, my dear? If I am hungry, you must be on the outer reaches of starvation."

"Well, I am a trifle sharpish," she confessed.

"I know. Your stomach has been rumbling in my ear for the last quarter-hour, at least."

She blushed.

"But what a comfortable lap, dear Marian," he continued smoothly. "I suspect you were not as comfortable, but I thank you."

Alistair peeked around the stairwell, a glass of milk in his hand, which he thrust at Lord Ingraham. "Here, my lord, Marian insists."

He drank it without demur. "What, now?" he asked.

"Now some porridge," Marian said decisively.

"Then you must turn loose your purse strings, sister. The innkeeper looks with no particular favor on us."

She handed over her purse and Alistair departed.

Ingraham moved out from under the stairwell and stood up. Marian watched him closely. "How do you feel?"

"Much, much better. My eyes are only six feet from my toes now," he said. He looked about him. "Where are we?"

Marian got to her feet. Sharp pains dug into her back and she straightened up with difficulty. "A back stairwell. And it took some persuasion to convince the innkeeper that we were good enough for it."

"No room at the inn, eh?" the earl asked, his eyes lively. "Marian, you're hobbling like an old woman. Sit down and turn around."

She did as he said, perching herself on a stairstep while Lord Ingraham rubbed her back. "From the sounds overhead in the taproom, we are still snowed in. Surely these people do not stay here merely because they love the keep. Marian? You're not going to sleep, are you?"

"Gil, you're so good at that."

"A diplomat's art, my dear. I wish I had a crown for every back rub I've given and gotten from traveling about the continent in less-than-commodious carriages. Hold still."

He paused when Alistair returned balancing three bowls of porridge on his arm. Without a word, they fell to breakfast.

Alistair finished first. He looked around him and then wiped his mouth on his sleeve. He tossed Marian's purse in her direction. "Mare, you'd be dumbfounded to know the going rate for porridge when you stay at the only inn in the village during a snowstorm."

Ingraham reached into his pockets. "H'mm. I do believe I donated all my change to the Picton church choir, or I would contribute." He brightened. "Did you happen to bring along my overnight case? I have a wallet in there."

Marian shook her head. "We brought your carpetbag. I remember that your wallet lay on the bureau."

"And why did you not bring it along?" Brother and sister stared at him, their mouths open. The earl shook his head. "Would that you were as scrupulous about harebrained schemes as you are about my wallet." He thought a moment. "Then I suppose you are spending your return mail-coach fare."

"Exactly so," Alistair said.

Lord Ingraham grinned at them wickedly. "Then, when we arrive in Bath, I will direct you to a public house where you can sweep floors, Alistair, and Marian can wash dishes. When you have done sufficient penance, you can earn a ride home to Picton."

Alistair hung his head. "Sir, I do wish to apologize to you for the inconvenience I have put you through."

"Your apology is accepted, Alistair Wynswich," said the earl promptly. "I will exact my revenge soon enough."

Brother and sister looked at each other, and Ingraham laughed. "And I will not offer you any explanation now. Come, let us take a look outdoors and consider our situation."

The snow had ceased falling and the sky was a brilliant blue. Smoke curled from the chimneys of the houses that clustered around the inn, sending neat little plumes into the cold air. The snow shimmered like broad-cast diamonds, scattered at random by a wintry sower.

Marian clapped her hands. "It is beautiful," she said. "Look how the snow clings to the branches."

"Marian, do you wear your boots?" Lord Ingraham asked.

She nodded.

"And did you ever find your other mitten?"

She shook her head.

"Happens I have two, and by Jove, there is money in one." He took the mittens from his overcoat pocket, a puzzled look crossing his face. "I seem to remember widows and orphans in Bristol, or is that part of my morphine euphoria?"

Marian could not look him in the eye. "A parson took pity upon your wretched situation, my lord," she said with a straight face. "That was his contribution to your future."

He shook the coins from the mitten and smiled down at the money in his hand. "It is my immediate future I am concerned with." He stared at the money thoughtfully, as if mulling something around in his mind.

Marian watched him closely, but had the wisdom to remain silent. She crossed her fingers behind her back.

Finally he clapped his hands together, jingling the coins between them. "Well, I suppose all the signs point toward Bath, my dear. Alistair, take this money into our friend the innkeeper and see how much bread and cheese you can purchase with it."

"I shall, my lord," Alistair replied promptly. "And wrap it in brown paper?"

"Oh, decidedly." Lord Ingraham smiled at Marian. "The bread and cheese is for your sister. You and I will chew on the brown paper."

Marian laughed. "Wretch! I am not that hungry."

"Oh, perhaps not, but you are the last person I would wish to have starving with me on a deserted island. But since you have apparently assured the parson that I have abandoned my adventuring, that likelihood will never arise." Marian sniffed and he laughed. "I have something better in mind. We appear to be in Frome."

"Frome?"

"It's a village about ten miles distant from Bath. I would recognize that church steeple anywhere. I, er, climbed it one boring November on a dare. In the buff, I might add."

Marian stared at him, her eyes wide. "You?"

"Shocked, Marian?"

"No, not precisely. I am merely wondering if you caught a dreadful cold."

He shook his head. "It was a mild November, and I have always possessed a robust constitution."

"I don't wonder that your mother was beside herself."

"To this day, my mother does not know of it." He chuckled in remembrance, took her by the shoulders, and looked her square in the face. "And remove that calculating look from your eyes, my dear. This is not information to be squirreled away and used at a later date."

Alistair returned with a cloth bag containing bread and cheese. "Do you propose that we walk, my lord?" he asked.

"I do."

Lord Ingraham placed a hand on Alistair and Marian's shoulders and steered them toward the inn again. "We cannot retrace our journey; the roads are closed to Lyme Regis. We cannot go forward by coach, but I would wager that we can walk the distance." He gave them both a little shake. "When it comes to that, I would wager my money—had I any—on the Wynswiches."

Neither Wynswich had a reply.

"Well? Does this meet with your approval? Or would you prefer to celebrate Christmas at the tender mercies of this particular landlord? Let me refresh your memory: landlords are notoriously ill-equipped on Christmas Eve."

Alistair laughed. "Well said, my lord."

Gilbert bowed in his direction. "I would rather face my relatives—oh, there's a dreadful pun—than spend another night under the stairwell." He bowed to Marian. "Even with such charming company. Shall we go forward, then, comrades?"

Marian nodded. "Only let me fetch my bandbox."

"Excellent. If you would permit me to add a shirt or two to your bandbox? I don't remember what is in my room in Bath." He sighed, and the look in his eyes was faraway. "It has been a long while between visits. Maybe I had forgotten just how long."

They set out for Bath shortly after noon, with the blessing and best wishes of the coachman, who insisted on pressing a coin in the earl's hand. "Laddie, I would only spend it on Blue Ruin, and mayhap you can buy your dear mother a little gift. You've been a long time gone."

"I shall do that, sir, and thank you," said Ingraham.

Marian allowed the coachman to give her a kiss on the cheek. "You're a remarkable lassie," he told her. "If you're ever in need of help, Jeremy Towser's the name, and the other mail-coach drivers know me. The world's wide and deep, and there are rascals afoot in plenty."

"How well I know," murmured Lord Ingraham under his breath.

Marian gave him a speaking look, twinkled her eyes one last time at the coachman, who stood in the snow, hat in hand. He remained there, watching them, until they left the inn behind.

"Perhaps we are rascals," she decided, speaking more to herself than to the man who walked beside her. "But you must own that this Christmas has likely exceeded all your expectations."

She couldn't fathom the look he gave her. Something about his expression both disturbed and moved her at the same time. He was not walking close to her, but that look seemed to slice the distance between them and take her breath away. All the more remarkable to her, he seemed not to be even aware of it.

He stopped walking. "You have it there, Marian," he said quietly, as if he were suddenly out of breath. "I was beginning to wonder if . . ." He paused, and then the look was gone from his face and the familiar good-natured expression restored. "If I would ever have such a good time."

"That was not what you started to say, my lord," Marian said, her own voice as quiet as his had been.

"It will do . . . for now, brat," he teased, and waggled his finger at her. "Pay attention now, or you will land yourself in a ditch. And my loyalty does not extend far enough to follow."

I would wager that it does, she thought as she navigated through the drift toward the center of the snow-packed lane. It was an odd thought, one that she would have quickly dismissed only yesterday. But she had spent the night holding Lord Ingraham in her arms, watching him sleep, worrying about him, listening to his breathing, touching the scar on his face, wishing she could take on some of the pain they had so lately caused him. Something was different; whether it originated from Lord Ingraham or from her, she could not tell.

Lord Ingraham walked on ahead with Alistair. She sighed. What is the matter with me? I wish I were home in Picton. She watched Lord Ingraham, and smiled at his confident stride, even through snow, and noted how nicely his overcoat hung from his broad shoulders. She closed her eyes, committed the image to memory, and then laughed to herself and hurried to catch up with her men.

10

"What, ho? We are beginning to resemble Napoleon's retreat from Moscow."

Marian looked up from the snow-covered tree stump where she had planted herself, and squinted into the white and glaring distance. The walk had seemed like a novel idea only an hour before. The early part of the adventure had taken them down a road sufficiently tamped by local wagons and horses. Then the tracks stopped; soon there was nothing before them but snow-covered road that had drifted until it was difficult to tell where the road edged. It wound on and out of sight through country that she knew she could appreciate in the spring. All was white and still.

Drat these skirts, she thought as she shook the snow from the folds of her woolen dress. It was growing wetter and heavier by the minute. Each floundering footstep in the snow seemed to sink her deeper and deeper.

Lord Ingraham made his way back to her and took her by the hand, to pull her to her feet. "I am sorry I was not paying attention," he apologized. "There's something about being here again. Makes me forget I am not alone."

"Or do you dream you are in Moscow, watching Napoleon struggle through such drifts?" she teased, less out-of-sorts.

"Oh, that was no dream, my dear," he said quickly. Some memory darted across his eyes and he opened his mouth to speak, but reconsidered.

She looked at him and pursed her lips. "Something tells me you did not mean to say that."

He bowed over her hand. "I did not. Please forget I mentioned it."

"I gather from your secrecy there was no official English delegation in Moscow?" she asked, and watched his expression.

There was no change of expression. He had recovered himself completely. "Indeed, there was not." The earl laughed and inclined himself closer to her, as if they shared a secret. "And yet, I appear to have difficulty dissembling in front of you. Move over, brat."

He sat beside her. Marian looked about her. Alistair had gone on ahead, whistling to himself.

"Were you really and truly there?" she whispered.

"I was. Really and truly," he replied, his voice no louder. "This is not a matter generally known outside of the Foreign Office, my dear."

"Then I shall say no more." Marian looked sideways at him. "Only tell me. Were you afraid?"

"Oh, yes. The city was burning around us as our delegation tossed state papers into our own fireplace, flung a firebrand into the offices, and closed the doors behind us."

"And did you watch Moscow burn?"

His hand went involuntarily to his scar. He traced its pattern and then looked beyond the white-covered fields, cordoned by tidy fences. "We fled the city and swam the river. The bridges were crammed with refugees. We watched from the far shore. Ah, God, such a pagan city. Such a beautiful city. I shall never forget the sight."

After another moment's reflection, he slapped his gloves on his knee and put them on again. "But this gets us no closer to Bath. And since you are determined that I should arrive there, let us be off." He held out his hand to her again, but she declined to take it.

"If there was no diplomatic mission, Gil, what were you doing there?"

He made no reply for a moment. "There are events that I

am not at liberty to share with anyone," he said quietly. "Even with you."

She smiled at his words, but they saddened her. She put her hand in his and let him help her to her feet. "Could it be, Gilbert Ingraham, that you are not what you seem?"

Again he was a long time in answering. "It could be " He let go of her hand and shook out her skirt. "No wonder you are such a laggard! I did not consider the difficulty of long skirts through wet snow. This could weigh down much heftier women than you. Do trust me, Marian, above all things, trust me," he said urgently, even as he pointed her toward the roadway again.

She took him by the arm. "Tell me one thing more: did you watch Napoleon leave the city?"

"I cannot tell you anything else."

She shook his arm, agitated in a way that surprised them both. "But you must! You must! In a few months, I will go to live in the vicarage with my sister and mother probably, and I will never, ever, see anyone like you again. I'll never see Moscow," she said passionately. "I'll probably never even get up to London. Our horse you have purchased will see more of the world than I will."

There were tears in her eyes. She stopped and put her hand to her mouth. Alistair, far ahead, was looking back at her. Was I so loud? she asked herself. "Whatever am I saying?" Marian said out loud as she dashed her hand across her eyes. "I am sorry. So sorry."

She tried to brush past him and regain the road again, but he took her by the arm this time. "Marian, you are destined to see much, much more of the world," he said, and smiled at her in a way that she found intensely irritating.

"Oh, don't look at me like that," she protested. "I know I am being out-of-reason foolish."

"You are no such thing," he said. "In fact . . ." He did not complete his thought. "Marian, let me break a trail in front of you. That will help. Stay close, and I will tell you about the retreat from Moscow."

He waved Alistair on ahead, and Marian followed close on

his heels, hopping in his tracks. "I rode with Kutusov and his Cossacks and—"

"How did you ever manage that?" she interrupted breathlessly.

"Hush, brat! They rode like demons. I could scarcely keep up, and I am no poor shakes on horseback. But we followed Napoleon day after freezing day, like fleas on a dog." He looked around him at the white world. "This is nothing to it, nothing to it at all. And then we would wait until nightfall and swoop down to plunder and kill."

Marian shuddered. "Beastly."

"Well, do I go on?" he demanded.

"Perhaps not," Marian said.

He continued in silence, and she longed to know more, but had the good sense not to prod him. She started counting fence posts. After sixteen, she heard him sigh.

"Do you know the saddest thing?"

"I cannot imagine."

"I think it was the priceless furniture and the icons and the jewels those bandits in soldiers' garb abandoned with every step they took. And some of them, some no older than you, just curled up and died beside their loot, their faces frozen to the cold metal. Poor wretches! So much for empire . . ."

She said nothing.

He reached back again and held out his hand, and she took it. "So this is the world you want to see, Marian?"

"Oh, it is," she replied, her voice subdued, but the passion still there like a banked fire.

"Perhaps . . . it can be arranged."

She did not know what he meant. She wanted to ask him, but found herself suddenly shy. She let go of his hand. How strange it is, she thought as she hurried along in Gilbert Ingraham's tracks. Up utnil this two days ago, I thought it was exciting to drive into Lyme Regis and pick out ribbon. How little I know about anything, for all that I have read Papa's library backward and forward.

"Cat got your tongue?"

"Yes, sir," she replied, and said nothing more as they

followed the snowed-in road up a small hill and then looked into the valley far below.

Alistair already stood there, hands on his hips. "Such a view, my lord," he said, and pointed toward several large gray stone buildings that seemed to sprout from the snow and then sprawl before their eyes. "What is it?"

"Ah, how good that you should ask," the earl replied. He pulled Marian up beside him. "Take a good look, Alistair. You are gazing upon your future."

"Eh?"

"I can see that you do not fully appreciate the moment," said Lord Ingraham. He spread out his hand before him in a grand, Napoleonic gesture. "That is St. Stephen the Martyr's."

Alistair looked from the stone conglomeration to Lord Ingraham and back again. "A prison? A workhouse?"

The earl grinned, and Marian noted a malicious glint in his eyes. "Very like, my lad, very like. It is my alma mater, my nourishing mother, my school of schools. And soon, I might add, to become your school, too."

Alistair said nothing for a long moment. He frowned and ran a finger inside his ear. "I don't follow. Perhaps I didn't even hear you right. Weren't you an Eton man?"

"Oh, glory, no," said Lord Ingraham with a look of distaste on his face. "My late father was concerned that his only son and budding prospect for the diplomatic corps should get an actual—let me steady myself—education." He clapped a hand on Alistair's shoulder and drew him close. "How pleased I am to offer this all to you now."

"I still do not follow you," Alistair said, but there was a note of caution in his voice. He tried to edge away, but the earl tightened his grip.

"My dear Alistair, I have arranged with your much-put-upon brother to see that you will be enrolled in St. Stephen's, why, just practically before the cock crows. And you need not thank me. I was pleased beyond words to do it."

Alistair whirled about to stare, goggle-eyed, at Lord Ingraham. "Do you mean, I am to go . . . Oh, surely, not!"

"Yes, Alistair, I mean precisely that. I left no stone unturned."

"But, sir! Surely I cannot be enrolled at this time of the year." Alistair's voice was less a protest than a squeak, the tortured sound of someone with his neck in a vise.

"Alistair, do not fret. You will be relieved to know that I am a trustee of this noble institution. If I were to write the warden and tell him that Attila the Hun was desirous of enrollment, he would have a letter in the box by nightfall, begging Lord and Lady Hun to bring little Attila by the school for a stroll about the grounds. It was no trouble."

The silence hummed. Alistair swallowed a few times and his Adam's apple bobbed up and down. Marian stared at it, fascinated. She held her breath.

"You see, Alistair," said Lord Ingraham in a quiet voice, "I have answered your Christmas wish, have I not?"

"Dash it! No, you have not, my lord," Alistair burst out as he wrenched himself from Lord Ingraham's grasp. "This was the very last thing I asked for!"

Gilbert took him by the shoulders and would not turn him loose. "On the contrary, my lad, it is precisely what you wnat. If—just if—by some stroke of merit or genius, or maybe just damned hard work, you manage to acquit yourself well at St. Stephen's between now and Christmas next, I have it in my power to see you berthed aboard a ship as a midshipman. A dear friend of mine commands a beauty of a ship in the West Indies." When Alistair made no reply, the earl continued. "You'll find no distractions at St. Stephen's beyond oatmeal every morning and cold baths. And when you have proven to my satisfaction that you just might be developing some discipline and are ready for the life you long for, I'll spring you from this pile. But not one moment before."

He released Alistair, who was white about the mouth and darting angry glances at his sister.

"Why are you doing this to me?" he asked when he had some small control over himself.

"I do it for you, and not to you, lad. I do it for your father, Bertram Wynswich, too," he added, and his voice took on a metallic tone. "He was a scamp and everyone loved him—and his horses. But, Alistair, no one took him seriously, and he left your family in tatters. Percy has to work twice as hard to overcome whatever reputation his father left dangling. I'd like to see you become the man Lord Wynswich could have been but never was. I want you to make Percy proud of you."

Without a word of warning, Alistair swung at Lord Ingraham. Marian stifled a scream as the earl stepped aside and grabbed Alistair's arm, pinning it against his back. He pushed him to the ground and let him stay there a moment, his face in the snow. Ingraham knelt down and put his face close to Alistair's.

"You could have killed me with that morphine, Alistair," the earl said so quietly that Marian had to strain forward to hear him. "It was the kind of disjointed, freakish thing that is hardly worthy of you. Percy and I have already agreed upon it: you will dance to my tune for a while."

Lord Ingraham released Alistair and sat back on his heels.

Alistair got up quickly and brushed the snow from his overcoat. He refused to look at Gilbert or Marian. He stalked to the road's edge and stood for a long minute contemplating St. Stephen's, his hands shoved deep in his pockets.

Marian started to speak once, but Lord Ingraham put his finger to his lips and shook his head.

"The West Indies, you say?" Alistair asked finally without turning around.

"Aye, lad, berthed in Kingston. I'll warn you, though, that Captain de Spain is as hard a man as you could hope to meet on a dark night. However that may be, his sailors will follow him anywhere. A better man I do not know, unless it is your own brother."

"Done then, sir, done." Alistair turned around. "I need not scruple to tell you that I am not happy about it."

Without another word, Alistair started down the road at a clipping pace, despite the snow that came up to his knees.

Marian looked at him in dismay. The earl motioned to her and she floundered through the deep snow to his side.

"Marian, we'll let him go on alone for a while. Likely he'll feel like talking later."

Marian nodded. Ingraham started ahead of her again, but she

took him by the arm. "Seriously, why are you doing this for us, sir?" she asked.

He was silent a long moment. "Well, if I have to explain it, then you probably wouldn't understand—not yet, anyway. Let's call it a Christmas gift for hospitality rendered."

"That is a hum," Marian scolded. "You have already said in so many words that Wynswich hospitality is exhausting."

"I have, haven't I?" Ingraham agreed. "Hurry up, brat. You're making me cold just standing here."

Snow was falling again by the time they walked into Brattleford. Nothing moved except the smoke that puffed vigorously from every chimney. There was a tangle of carter's wagons around Brattleford's only inn.

Alistair sat on the whiffletree of one wagon, waiting for them to arrive. "Tired, Mare?" he asked.

She nodded and then quickly amended, "But not too tired to make it to Bath. By the way, sir, how far have we to go?"

"About three miles, as I recall." Ingraham leaned against the wagon. "What's it to be? Do we go inside, throw ourselves on the floor, and plead for sanctuary, or do we plunge ahead?"

"We plunge ahead," Marian said.

"Can you still wiggle your toes, Marian?"

She blushed. "That's not something a gentleman asks a lady."

"Brat!"

"Yes, I can wiggle my toes. Come on, Alistair. Let us show this earl what we can do."

They continued through Brattleford, stopping once to help a carter extricate his wagon and team from the ditch where the horses had wandered. The snowy afternoon was filled with enormous, whirling snowflakes as the sky turned a deep gray and they struck the rough road again.

Marian continued in silence, head bowed against the snow, determined not to complain. Her stomach rumbled, her head ached from the cold, and her beautiful green woolen dress was icy to the waist. If you insist that your Christmas-pudding wish comes true, Marian, she told herself, you had better be prepared for the lumps in it.

Alistair forged ahead. Gilbert joined Marian, slowing his pace until Alistair was out of earshot. "I've been meaning to ask you, my dear." He hesitated, and for a moment the diplomat's polish deserted him. "The other day—good God, was it only yesterday?—I seem to have vague recollections that I was not . . . How do I put this? Behaving in a completely gentlemanlike fashion."

Marian thought back to her struggles yesterday morning in the best guest room and was grateful that the gray and snowy dusk hid her blush. "I can certainly make allowances for your behavior, Gil. You were extremely put upon."

"H'mm. Was that it? I had the distinct impression that you were the one 'extremely put upon,' as you so nicely phrased it."

"It is nothing you need speak of," she added hastily.

"Then I will not, other than to apologize," he stated promptly.

They walked on in uncomfortable silence for the space of several minutes, the only sound the crunch of snow underfoot. "But tell me," he asked finally, "did I enjoy myself?"

Marian only giggled.

Lord Ingraham rolled his eyes. "I thought so. My apologies, Miss Wynswich," he said formally, and then ruined the effect by winking.

It was snowing in greater earnest when they walked into Bath. Night was well along, but the traffic, held up at several points throughout Christmas Eve day, increased the nearer they came to the city. Shoppers hurried on the snow-covered streets, buying last-minute items as shopkeepers stood by the doors, keys in hand. Church bells tolled as the lamplighters strolled down the well-lit thoroughfare, pausing now and then to adjust a lamp where a flame struggled, and then shout holiday greetings to friends passing by. The friendly sounds were muffled by that peculiar stillness that snow brings, wherever it falls.

"What is your direction, sir?" Alistair asked when Ingraham stood still on the sidewalk, as if wondering where to go.

"The Royal Crescent," he replied slowly, the words dragged from his body. Still he did not move. Alistair glanced at Marian and shrugged.

Marian inclined her head toward a shop window that was still brightly lit. Alistair nodded and went to watch the shopkeeper sweeping inside.

Marian moved closer to Ingraham, saying nothing, but looking at him in critical fashion, much as she imagined the passersby doing. She saw a tallish man in a stylish overcoat of definite continental cut, wearing a high-crowned beaver hat. The scar on his face stood out in the lamplight, red and raw, even under his two days' growth of beard. What do they think? she wondered. Do they feel pity? Revulsion?

His hand was thrust deep in his pocket. Marian put her hand in his pocket and grasped his wrist. Startled, he looked down at her, as if unaware that she was even standing beside him.

"I am a great coward, Marian," he said as he stepped out of the lamplight and into the shadows. "Or perhaps it is vanity. I was once accounted a regular handsome man." He fingered the scar. "It is not a face with which to startle one's mother."

"Gil, does she know nothing?"

"She knows that I was burned." He sighed. "I suppose others have told her." His arm went around her shoulder. "It was always easier to find an excuse to stay away from Bath, and truly, I was needed in Ghent at the treaty talks." He looked down at her. "But the talks are over, and you have removed all my other excuses."

"Gil, she will be so relieved to see you," Marian said. "I know . . . I know that I would be."

He clapped her on the shoulder. "I hope you are right. I suppose I must get used to that startled glance that people give me now, that look, right before they recover and then smile and bow and act as if nothing is different."

"You will not know unless you go home, Gil."

He stood still a moment longer and then waited another minute.

"Gil, pretty soon I will not be able to wiggle my toes," Marian warned.

A brief smile flickered across his face. "Well, then, let us go. Come, Alistair. You have made that shopkeeper quite nervous enough. He must think you have designs on his cash box." Ingraham rubbed his hand over the stubble on his chin.

"God knows we look none too respectable, as it is. Thank the Lord, at least I do not still smell of herring."

As they walked, the snow tapered off and stopped. Everywhere the world was white, except for the great wreaths of greenery that adorned the doors of the fine homes, and the candles that winked in windows, little dots of light that transformed the snow into diamonds.

They came to the Royal Crescent, and Marian stood still in delight. "Such homes," she said, her voice soft with wonder.

"Truly, I had forgotten how beautiful it was," the earl said softly. They walked slowly down the middle of the deserted street until Lord Ingraham stopped. He remained there a moment, silent in thought, and then squared his shoulders and started toward one of the elegant row houses.

To Marian's ears, even the door knocker sounded distinguished and restrained, like everything on that magic street. The butler who opened the door was as impeccable as the hall beyond that opened to their view.

The butler looked down at the three of them. "Lady Ingraham is not receiving callers at this hour," he began.

"Washburn," Lord Ingraham murmured, and stepped closer.

The butler peered into the dark night and then his eyes widened. He stepped into the snowy entrance. "Oh, surely it is not—"

"Ah, but it is," the earl contradicted. "Merry Christmas, Washburn."

"Lord Ingraham! We had no idea . . . no idea at all that you were even in England." He practically pulled Gilbert into the front hallway as Marian and Alistair trailed behind. "Allow me, my lord," he said, and held out his hand for Lord Ingraham's overcoat.

The earl unfastened the buttons but did not remove the coat. "My mother?"

"My lord, she has gone to Christmas Eve services."

Ingraham's face fell. "Oh, I had no idea it was that late!"

"It wants but a quarter-hour to eleven, my lord." He peered at Lord Ingraham's face, and Marian felt Ingraham tense beside her. She crossed her fingers. The butler's eyes flickered across

Gilbert's face, but his expression did not change. "Surely my lord has not misplaced his late father's watch?"

Marian felt the earl relax. "Not precisely, Washburn, so you need not scold me. It is ticking in some French tar's pocket, I don't doubt."

"Very good, my lord, if that is your preference," said the butler, betraying his dissatisfaction with a slightly upraised eyebrow.

"So many of my decisions have been made for me of late, Washburn," Lord Ingraham murmured. "That was one of them. And is my mother . . ."

"Yes, my lord, in the same place as always."

"Good." The earl turned to Marian. "My dear, can you still wiggle your toes?"

She nodded. The butler raised his eyebrow a fraction of an inch higher.

Ingraham smiled. "Washburn, these are Marian and Alistair Wynswich, friends of mine from Picton, near Lyme Regis. They will be staying with us a few days."

Washburn bowed. "Very good, my lord."

"Very good, indeed," Lord Ingraham echoed. "Let us be off and do what good Christians do at least twice a year, whether they need it or not."

"Oh, surely we could just wait here," protested Marian. "I know that I look a sight, my lord."

"Yes, you do," he agreed. "Your cheeks are rosy, and even though your eyes look a bit tired, they have a real snap and sparkle to them."

"Oh, do be serious," she murmured.

"I am being serious," he insisted, and then continued in some embarrassment. "If I do not continue on and see this thing through, Marian, I will not have the heart to wait." He looked over her head, his gaze on something far away. "I'd be off to Vienna, or St. Petersburg, or even Washington again, and she would never know I was here. No. We . . . I must see it through. Please come with me."

"I shall," Marian said, with no further argument.

"You, too, Alistair," said the earl. "The Lord must amply

bless rogues and sinners tonight, and we are all that. '

Alistair had the grace to blush. "And more, sir."

Down the stairs they went. Alistair hung back. "My lord, I have not been to church for a long while."

Gilbert gave him a searching look. "You are in desperate need of St. Stephen's, where chapel at six is a preface to oatmeal at seven. Or was it the other way around?"

The bells of Bath were silent as they hurried along. A brisk wind began to blow from the west.

Lord Ingraham sniffed the air. "Alistair, I fancy I can almost smell the sea. It is a good omen."

Alistair only grunted.

"Tell me, lad," the earl asked as they quickened their pace. "These pudding wishes. Is there a time limit? I mean, must they come true by a certain date?"

"Twelfth Night," Alistair declared firmly. "That is the Wynswich rule. Sir, why do you ask?"

Marian giggled. "I think he has made a wish about a lady-love, Alistair. I shall browbeat Reverend Beddoe when we return to Picton, and discern the truth, for I think our vicar knows."

"You'll do no such thing," said Lord Ingraham. "I was merely curious." He tucked his arm through Marian's. "And you are a nosy baggage."

Marian laughed. The sound sparkled in the crisp air.

"You must not encourage her, my lord," Alistair said.

"I wouldn't dream of such a thing." Ingraham tightened his muffler about his throat. "God, it's cold!" He looked at Marian inquiringly and tightened his grip on her arm. " 'Blow, blow, thou winter wind . . .' "

She thought a moment, skipping to keep up with him. " 'Thou art not so unkind as man's ingratitude.' " She laughed. " 'Thy tooth is not so keen, because thou art not seen . . .' "

" 'Although thy breath be rude.' Marian, except for your nosiness, you are excellent in every way."

Alistair grunted again. "I think the two of you have gone quite to pasture yourselves."

The earl nudged Alistair. "Had you an education, lad, you could quote Shakespeare, too."

Alistair opened his mouth to protest, but Ingraham overrode him. "Think how useful such a skill will be when you are trying to keep yourself awake while standing a West Indies watch."

They passed the great cathedral of Bath, which was surrounded by carriages, and grooms walking blanketed horses back and forth. Marian looked at Gilbert, but he did not even slow down.

"Mother never did hold much with fashion," Lord Ingraham explained to her unanswered question. "We go to St. John's."

Christ's Mass was well under way when they quietly climbed the worn steps and entered the little church.

"Alistair, claim us that spot on the last row," the earl whispered.

Alistair moved forward, genuflected swiftly, and slid into the pew. Ingraham did not move. Marian watched his face, reading on it the anxiety that overcame his habitually well-bred expression. She waited a moment and then stood on tiptoe, pulling at his shoulder. He leaned down obligingly.

"Gil, have you a coin left?"

"It belongs to the Widows and Orphans," he whispered back, even as he reached into his pocket and handed it to her.

She took the coin and dropped it in the little collection box beside the row of candles. She found an unlighted one, held it into a flame, and set it carefully in its holder. She could think of no prayer except "Please, Lord," which she whispered to herself.

In a moment she felt the earl's hand on her shoulder. He stood there beside her and then briefly touched her cheek with his. The tears started in her eyes as she followed him to the pew Alistair already occupied.

If there was a sermon, Marian did not hear it. The priest's words were a pleasant blur that reached her across a great distance. She sat nestled close to Lord Ingraham, enjoying his warmth and fighting to keep her eyes open. Alistair had already succumbed to sleep. He was gently snoring on her other side, and the temptation was great to follow his example. It had been an exhausting day, which had followed an even longer night. She thought of her mother, and Percy and Ariadne, and herring and Cossacks and innkeepers, until her mind was a muddle and she wished only for bed.

"Wake up, brat." The earl prodded her to her feet and pulled her after him to the front of the church.

The sharp, choking smell of incense shook the fog from her brain, and she was fully awake again, taking in the greenery that banked the altar and Christmas colors of the altar cloth. Obediently she knelt beside him and waited for Communion.

The priest came quickly down the altar railing, dipping the wafers in the wine, murmuring, and passing on to the next parishioner. He moved swiftly, competently, and then he came to the earl.

"The body of Christ," he whispered, and looked down at Gilbert Ingraham. He paused then, and Marian looked up.

There was no shock in the priest's eyes, but only wonder. Silently Marian blessed him. The priest gave him Communion, but he did not move on. For a moment that seemed to stretch out and fill the whole church, he placed his hand on Lord Ingraham's head. "Welcome home, my lord," he finally murmured.

The earl's cheeks were streaked with tears. Marian longed to tuck her arm through his, but it was her turn for Communion. The priest continued down the row, and those at the altar rose to their feet.

The chapel was a blur. Marian could only follow the earl down the central aisle, her hands clasped together, thumb over thumb. When he turned in, she followed blindly and dropped to her knees, even as he did. She was dimly aware that the woman already seated in the pew next to him went to her knees.

Marian rested her forehead against the cool wood, worn smooth and shiny by centuries of petitions. She added her own wordless plea and sat back on her heels.

Lord Ingraham still knelt beside her, his arms around the woman kneeling beside him in the pew. Where was Alistair? With a start Marian realized that they had not returned to the back row, but knelt in another pew, one much closer to the altar, a pew of privilege. She scarcely breathed as the earl held the woman in a wordless embrace.

Marian could see little of her, except for the salt-and-pepper gray hair that peeked from under a bonnet both sober and expensive. The woman's hands were locked tightly together across his broad back, the knuckles white, as if she did not wish to let him go ever again.

11

A connonading from the guns of Napoleon's Grand Armée would have been insufficient to awake Marian Wynswich Christmas morning. Had the little general rooted his entire artillery directly below the second-story window on the Royal Crescent and ordered his men to fire on Marian Wynswich's window until she crawled to the sill and waved a white flag, it would have been a fruitless effort. As it was, she surrendered to hot buttered toast, placed quietly on the bedside table.

Oh, heavenly smell. Marian sniffed and tried at first to burrow deeper into the feather pillow that smelled so divinely of lavender. But lavender is not toast. She opened her eyes and looked into smiling eyes very like Gilbert Ingraham's.

"Oh," she exclaimed, blinking against the sunlight that streamed through the delicate lace curtains and landed on the bed like a benediction, after the snow of yesterday.

"Merry Christmas, my dear," said the woman, who sat with her hands folded neatly in her lap. "I would have wagered that you would not have wakened for hours yet, but Gilbert told me to save my breath to cool my porridge. He insisted that the application of toast and eggs—and plenty of them—would bring you around." She laughed softly. "It appears that he is right, Marian. May I call you Marian?"

Marian nodded and sat up in bed. "Yes, of course," she said automatically as her eyes went to the well-laden breakfast tray on the table. "And you must be Gil's—Lord Ingraham's mother."

"I claim that rare privilege," she said. "I am Gilbert's much tried and put-upon mother." She placed the breakfast tray across Marian's lap, eyeing the gruel, bacon, eggs, toast, and tea dubiously. "I told him it was too much, considering that in only a few hours we will attempt a family Christmas dinner, but he told me you were equal to it."

"Well, I am," said Marian calmly. "I should be embarrassed, I suppose, but I am hungry."

Lady Ingraham took a cup of tea off the tray and seated herself again. "You do not mind if I keep you company?"

Marian shook her head and took a bite of toast. She rolled her eyes and Lady Ingraham laughed. The older woman sat back in her chair and sipped her tea while Marian made rapid inroads on the meal before her.

By the time she finished the eggs and bacon, Marian had looked up several times at Lady Ingraham, and she liked what she saw; a trim lady with delicate features, enormous blue eyes, and Gil's salt-and-pepper hair. She was older than Marian would have thought, but her back was straight, her head erect.

"You are wondering how Gilbert came to have such an aged mother?" Lady Ingraham asked at last as she set down her cup.

Marian blushed. "I did wonder that," she admitted, and then added hastily, "but surely it is not my business."

The woman shrugged. "Perhaps it is. How are we to know? Let me say that Gilbert is my youngest child by many years. Indeed, his father and I had entered into that time of life when an expected baby causes smirks in men's clubs and lady friends to look askance. I was remarkably *enceinte* at my eldest daughter's come-out in London. Goodness, what a Season."

Marian laughed.

"And so, when most of my childhood friends were contemplating the blessing of occasional, widely spaced visits from grandchildren, I was collecting tadpoles in ponds and pulling Gilbert out of trees." She smiled at the memory. "I would not have traded a moment of it."

She removed the tray from Marian's lap and placed it outside the door. "And now, my dear, I must thank you . . ." Her voice faltered. "Thank you for returning my son to me." She sat down again and took Marian by the hand. "I was so sure I had raised a son of great intelligence. How could he even think for a moment that he would suddenly become repugnant?" She touched her hand to her forehead. "What time we vain creatures waste! My dear, I cannot begin to repay the debt I owe you."

"No payment required," Marian said softly as tears started in her eyes. "It was merely a Christmas wish that came true."

Lady Ingraham dabbed her eyes. "Well, I wondered what Gilbert meant when he alluded to that last night, only he called it a pudding wish. He described how your brother got him drunk and onto that mail coach."

Marian silently blessed Lord Ingraham for fudging that infamous detail. "I was so distressed with Alistair, I assure you, madam, but the opportunity! How could we pass it up?"

"Indeed!" Lady Ingraham laughed and Marian joined in.

There was a quick knock, and the door opened. "Marian, when you laugh like that, I know the pangs of hunger have been assuaged and it is safe to enter. But only with your permission."

Lady Ingraham looked him up and down. "You know you should not! Where are your manners?"

He laughed. "I left them with my luggage in Devon, ma'am, where all good manners go to die! Humor me. It is Christmas."

"So it is," Lady Ingraham agreed in a softer voice. She looked at Marian. "Do we allow him entrance?"

"If he behaves," said Marian.

"Very well, sir. You have heard the terms."

Marian straightened her bedcap and tucked the coverlet around her. "Gilbert, how grand you look. H'mmm, and you smell so divine."

He grinned and came closer, barely brushing her cheek with his. "Do you like it? Mama tells me that a little splash of this on my face will get me whatever I want."

Lord Ingraham did look better than she remembered. His face was shaved, his hair trimmed, his shirtpoints well-starched, his trousers impeccable. He winked at her and tugged on her hair that peeked out from under her bedcap, and Marian's heart flopped.

Ah, God, heartburn. Have I finally eaten too much? she thought.

"What? What? No takers on my comment?" he quizzed.

"No, indeed," Marian replied. "You are much too indulged already. Sir, where is my brother?"

"Alistair is sleeping the sleep of the innocent, something he rarely does, I am convinced," said Lord Ingraham. "And when he awakes, I will present him with a list of required clothing and accoutrements for St. Stephen's, and the direction of my Bath tailor, which should occupy him fully on the morrow. And by the way, my dears," he added. "The road east is at least partially open. I expect Louisa and her brood to pile in here at any moment." He heard a noise in the hall and stuck his head out the door. "And it looks like the maids have come with a tin tub. Marian, I bid you farewell."

"One moment, sir," she said. "Did you carry me up here last night? I really don't remember anything."

"I thought it was a kind gesture when you practically fell out of your chair in Mama's parlor. And, I might add, you behaved in a totally ladylike manner."

Marian blushed.

Lord Ingraham bowed to his mother and edged out the door as the maids entered. He paused on the threshold. "One more thing. I wrote to Percy and your mother this morning, using all my diplomatic arts. I trust we will brush through this. Delivered the letter in person to the Post. The mail coach will be running south by noon, they tell me." He blew Marian an air kiss and left.

Lady Ingraham had watched the exchange between her son and Marian. "I do not know what magic you have been working on my son, but I assure you, it is welcome." She went to the window. "The last time I saw him was at least two years ago, and he was not smiling then. So preoccupied." Lady Ingraham paused a moment, absorbed in her own thoughts. "There are times when I wish he would abandon the diplomatic corps, marry, and set up his nursery at Collinwood. I seem to recall a young woman in London two years back . . ." She traced her finger down the steamy pane of glass. "But these are trying times, are they not, my dear?" She remained at the window in thought for another moment, then blew a kiss to Marian and left the room.

The maids left a can of hot water by the side of the tub, and Marian made it last a long time, pouring a little in, and then a little more, until she had stretched her bath out and her skin was quite wrinkled. She sat in contemplation of her knees until she heard a carriage and horses draw up in front of the house, followed by the sound of knocking. She listened, a smile on her face, as she heard a woman shriek, and then the earl laughing. That is Gil's sister, she thought, and she has just discovered that he is home.

Marian felt a sudden longing to be home herself, back with Lady Wynswich and her crotchets, and Ariadne. She rested her chin on her knees and closed her eyes. There was a wedding to plan. An unexpected twinge of envy gripped her, and she sat up to the fact that the bathwater was getting cold, and she was woolgathering.

While she was drying herself, the maid scratched on the door and tumbled another scuttle of coal on the fire. She was followed by Lady Ingraham's dresser, who placed two dresses on the bed.

Marian sighed with pleasure. The one on top was the kind of dress she only would have dreamed about, simple and butter yellow, with long sleeves and a high neck. A row of the most exquisite lace peeped from wristbands and hem. Marian looked at the dresser, a question in her eyes.

"Lady Ingraham has set aside several dresses for her niece to carry to London for the Season. These two will not be missed." She leaned closer and continued in conspiratorial fashion. "And I do not scruple to add that Lady Elizabeth hasn't the coloring for either dress. She would disappear, totally vanish, in yellow."

"Oh, please thank Lady Ingraham for me," Marian said. She wrapped the towel tighter around her and touched the yellow dress, her eyes wide with delight.

The dresser draped a paisley shawl on the bed. "In case you get cold," she said brusquely. "I don't require two."

"Thank you," Marian said as the dresser nodded and swept from the room.

Thoughtfully, Marian pulled on the undergarments that had been left with the dress. The frock was a trifle long and a shade wide, but by the time she arranged the sash about her middle, pleating here and there, no one but the sharpest-eyed dressmaker would have given it a thought.

The dresser returned later, and arranged Marian's long hair on top of her head. "You are so short, this will give you a little height. Too sad there is not a curl to be seen," the dresser scolded, and then looked in the mirror at her handiwork. "Of course, yours is not a face that needs the distraction of curls to take away from some defect of nature."

It sounded like a compliment, but Marian was not sure. "Miss, tell me," she ventured timidly, "who is below?"

"Lord and Lady Hammerfield and their several children," the dresser replied, "and they are probably romping about the best parlor and upsetting things. Not Lord and Lady Hammerfield, of course."

Marian smiled but said nothing.

"Lady Hammerfield is Lord Ingraham's older sister. She lives to the east of Bath."

"Has he other sisters and brothers?"

"No brothers. He has another sister slightly younger than Lady Hammerfield, who is visiting the Irish estates with her husband and children this season." She fiddled another moment with Marian's hair and leaned closer. "Lady Hammerfield is harmless enough, but do look out for Lord Hammerfield. He has a cutting tongue."

Mystified, Marian looked in the mirror. Her eyes met the dresser's. "I will say all that is proper."

"The less the better around Lord H.," the dresser said. "Well, I expect you will do now. Mind that you drape that shawl about your shoulders." With no more conversation, the dresser left the room.

Marian turned back to the mirror. She felt a slight chill

already. She shrugged it off and touched her hair. It wouldn't have done to have told the dresser that her mother had never yet allowed her to pile her hair on top of her head that way. It made her look much older. Seventeen, at least.

She took a deep breath and left the room, wishing that Alistair was close by to hang on to, wondering how to make her entrance in a roomful of strangers. She nearly turned and fled back upstairs, but Washburn awaited her at the foot of the stairs.

He bowed. "Miss Wynswich, follow me, please," he directed, and left her with no avenue of escape. He ushered her into the parlor, and all eyes turned in her direction. Marian gulped and crossed the threshold, looking about her for support.

Lord Ingraham stood resting his arm against the fireplace mantel, in the company of two other gentlemen. He just stood there, and his gaze made her blush and look away, wondering where his habitual expression of lazy amusement had gone. There was something else in his expression this time, and she did not understand it.

Lady Ingraham came forward, carrying a small girl. "How lovely you look, my dear," she exclaimed as the child nodded solemnly. "That particular shade of yellow quite becomes you. One and all, may I introduce Marian Wynswich? You have already made Alistair's acquaintance. Marian is his older sister, and they have come to spend Christmas with me."

Marian dropped a little curtsy as Lord Ingraham came forward. The amusement was back in his eyes, she noted with some relief.

"My family, Marian. Sister Louisa, brother-in-law David, and nieces Lizzie, Honoria, and Emma. Surtees over there is already educating your brother in the ways of St. Stephen's, I don't doubt."

Alistair glanced up from his conversation across the room long enough to grin at his sister and put both thumbs up. "Mare, no one in Picton would recognize you," he called, and then went back to his discussion.

Marian laughed out loud. "Alistair! How am I ever to even pretend a little dignity with you about?"

To Marian's delight, Lady Hammerfield came forward.

"Brothers have that ability to totally disconnect one, do they not?" She tucked her arm through her brother's and leaned against him for a moment. "And then they are away too long for silly reasons, and we even get to missing them." She looked up at him. "He will tire of us soon enough, particularly when I ask for his London home from which to launch Lizzie this spring."

Gilbert groaned and raised his eyebrows at Marian. "Do you see what you have brought me back to?"

She twinkled her eyes back at him. "And you love it, Lord Ingraham, you know you do."

Washburn announced dinner and they followed him into the dining room. Marian found herself seated between the oldest Hammerfield daughter and Lady Hammerfield. Her mind was blank of conversation, and she was grateful when the daughter leaned toward her. "Actually, I am Elizabeth," she whispered. "Surtees seems to delight in calling me Lizzie, and it has caught on."

Marian smiled. "And I will always be Mare to my brother, even when we are both halt and lame with age. How is it they know what maddens us?"

She felt herself relaxing. The Hammerfields were clambering to hear the earl's story of the sea battle and his French captivity, and she was happy to let the conversation run around her. She watched Lord Ingraham with his family and wondered why she had not really noticed until just this moment how handsome he was.

But it was more than that, she decided after the fish was removed for the venison. Gilbert Ingraham was not the kind of man to leave one in doubt about anything. For all his adventures, he was steady. She thought of her father as she pushed the venison around her plate and listened with half an ear as Lady Hammerfield described Emma's recent bout with chickenpox. Papa could leave me so off balance, she thought. I always know where I stand with Gil.

The thought made her look up from her plate and smile at him. Lord Ingraham, seated at the head of the table, caught her glance. "Marian, we amuse you?" he asked, then all heads turned her way.

"You do," she agreed. "I have always enjoyed amiable people and good food." She continued eating as the others chuckled.

And then Lizzie was speaking to her. "Marian, do you come out this spring? Are you seventeen?"

She shook her head. "Not until March."

"Good God, the infantry," exclaimed Lord Hammerfield in a loud voice, and Marian frowned. She did not understand the remark, any more than she understood why Gilbert Ingraham blushed because of it and then coughed discreetly.

"Perhaps we will see each other in London this Season," Lizzie continued.

Marian shook her head again. "It's not likely. I won't be coming out."

Lizzie stared and then laughed. "How can you bear to waste all those drawing lessons, and singing lessons, and Italian dancing masters, and tutors who insist on speaking only French from nine to three?"

Marian put down her fork and tried to ignore the little hollow spot in her stomach that seemed to be growing. "Oh, I never could draw very well, and my singing is saved for solitary walks. And as for dancing masters, well, I suppose the damp of Devon kept them away."

"But surely you speak French?" Lizzie persisted.

"No, not much, really. Well, not unless you count the little bit that everyone learns who lives on a smugglers' coast." She meant the remark to be lighthearted, and the stares of the Hammerfields baffled her.

Silence grew heavy about the table and suddenly Marian understood. I have no accomplishments these people consider normal, she thought, and I will not have a Season in London. Our home is going to be sold this spring, and I am sitting here in a borrowed dress. She looked at Alistair, and his face was more stern than she had ever seen it before. Alistair understands, too. Her appetite gone, she put her hands in her lap.

"Ah, but Marian can read Greek and Latin better than I can," Lord Ingraham was saying softly. "And I daresay she has read every book in her father's library."

"What is that to anyone?" Lord Hammerfield said suddenly.

"Don't tell me it will become the rage." He brightened. "Tell me, my dear, how you plan to snare a husband."

Something in the tone of his voice raised the fight in her. "It won't be my face or fortune, either, Lord Hammerfield," she said in a clear voice. "But then, it was never my intention to 'trap' a man like a rabbit in a snare. That does neither man nor woman credit, no matter how vaunted the title."

Lady Hammerfield gasped, and Marian instantly regretted her words.

"I have no plans beyond a quick return to Picton, when the roads are clear again," Marian mumbled.

After a tiny pause, Lady Ingraham carried the conversation onto new byways and Marian had only to look interested and remain silent until the endless dinner concluded. She didn't dare look at anyone else, and as the meal dragged on, she fought the ridiculous urge to slap down her napkin and run sobbing from the table. Gil addressed one or two harmless remarks her way, but she could only shake her head and make herself small in her chair.

And then they were through. "I don't know what others' plans are," Lord Hammerfield said as he stood up and stretched, "but I yearn for a spot of quiet in Mama's parlor."

Alistair stood. "And I intend to explore this charming city with my sister." He held out his arm to Marian, and she took it gratefully. "That is our earnest intention, Lord Ingraham," he said as the earl opened his mouth to speak. "We'll just tramp about and admire the place. Shall we, Mare?"

She let him take her from the room. She gave him a look of extreme gratitude and darted upstairs. She had pulled on her old boots, grabbed up her cloak, and ran down the stairs and out the door while the Ingrahams were still in the dining room.

Alistair took her arm again. He was walking fast, but she had no trouble keeping up with him. Marian wanted to wear herself out with walking. She did not trust herself to speak.

They strode the length of Upper Pulteney and onto High. The sweepers had done their work and the sidewalks were clear of snow. The air was cold, but water dripped from every eave, little jewels catching the Christmas Day sun.

Alistair stopped finally on the bridge overlooking a street neither of them could remember, and put his arm about her. "We really don't belong here, do we?" he said, more to himself than to Marian.

She shook her head. "It's one thing to be poor at home, where it's all a joke how Ariadne can stretch a shilling until it shrieks, and I can mend a dress six different ways and escape to Papa's books. Homer doesn't mind if I have holes in my stockings. After all, he was blind."

Her little joke was wasted on Alistair. "Well, we have fulfilled your Christmas wish." He sighed and leaned on the bridge railing. "I am supposed to see Lord Ingraham's tailor tomorrow. Dash it, Marian! What have we got ourselves into?"

They both stared down into the street below and allowed cold reason to wash over them. Marian twined her fingers through Alistair's.

"You will do as you are supposed to at St. Stephen's, and you will get your commission. I will return home and help with Ariadne's wedding, and Mama and I will move into the vicarage. Nothing's changed. Come on, brother, we're getting cold here."

She started to walk, but Alistair held her to the spot. "You're sure nothing's changed?" he asked. "Something's different. Dashed if I know what, but something has changed."

"Nothing has changed," she insisted, wondering why her words carried so little conviction to her mind.

They walked slowly back to the house, losing their way several times and then stopping to ask directions of a lamplighter, who had begun his evening rounds.

The house was quiet when they returned, and Marian sighed in gratitude. "Is no one about, Washburn?" she asked hopefully.

"I rather think not, miss," he said. "Lord Hammerfield is slumbering in the parlor, and the women are looking at pattern books in Lady Ingraham's room."

She couldn't bring herself to go to her room and just sit there. If I have nothing to read, I will brood, she thought, and I don't need that. "Washburn, where is the library?" she asked.

He bowed and gestured with his hand. She followed him, after blowing a kiss to Alistair. I shall find one book and retreat, she thought as she followed the butler. He led her to the back of the house.

She tiptoed past the billiards room when the sound of balls and sticks cracked the stillness. "Surtees, you have gotten much too expert in my absence," she heard Gilbert complain.

The library was blissfully empty. "Thank you, Washburn," Marian whispered. She looked around her. If Papa's library was a sparkling gem, this one was the crown jewels and the Peacock Throne of Persia, all rolled into one. Floor to ceiling was a solid mass of books. She took a deep breath, inhaling the odor of morocco leather until her mouth watered.

Where there were not books, there were portraits, dark oils in handsome gilt frames. She wandered about the room, stopping last to admire the painting over the fireplace. It could only be the Ingrahams of many years ago, with an older man, looking much like Gil, dandling a small boy on his knee. The sisters were grouped about their mother, who bore about her, then as now, an undefinable air of quality.

"Distinguished crew, eh?"

Marian jumped and put her hands behind her back.

Lord Ingraham entered the room and closed the door behind him. He still carried his pool cue. "I didn't mean to startle you."

"I suppose I am a trifle on edge," Marian said. "It is nothing."

He put down the cue and came to her side, looking up at the portrait. "You'll have to forgive my brother-in-law," he said after an awkward silence. "He only sees his children as investments."

A hundred angry words rose to her lips. To her amazement, she calmly sorted through them all and discarded every one. "How sad," was all she said.

"You would not look on your children that way, would you?" he asked after another pause.

Her eyes flew to his face. "Oh, no! A child needn't be accomplished—oh, I detest that word—to be loved. And people are not to be entrapped and snared."

"No, they ought not, my dear," Lord Ingraham agreed. He gestured toward the sofa, and they sat down. "And what would you do, Marian?"

She looked at him, a question in her eyes.

"To get a husband, I mean?" he asked, his own eyes bright with that same expression that had so puzzled her before.

"Oh, now you are bamming me," she said. "Gil, I told you that I did not think marriage would be at all comfortable."

"You are begging the question. That will not do as an answer, Marian."

She regarded him seriously. "If I were to marry—and I say *if*, for you know the idea does not appeal to me—I could only do it for love." She sighed and fingered a strand of hair that had escaped the dresser's pins. "And that much love would probably consume me. I don't do anything by halves. As you may have noticed." She raised her hands palm-up in a gesture of appeal. "But I probably would not mind at all. That is, if I loved enough," she concluded.

The earl chuckled and traced the lines in her palm with his finger. "Well, then, Marian, let me ask you something."

There was a knock at the door.

"Damn," muttered Ingraham. He made no move to rise, but sat with his lips tight together. He let go of Marian's hand.

"Sir? My lord, are you within?" asked Washburn.

Marian looked at Gilbert. "You can't hide, you know," she said. "Servants always know your business."

"If this one knew my business, brat, he would not knock," he said in a testy voice. He sighed. "Yes, Washburn, drat you, I am within. What is it?"

There was a moment of injured silence. And then, "My lord, I have a letter. It is from London."

The earl groaned and opened the door.

"It was locked, my lord," said Washburn, making no effort to hide the wounded tone in his voice.

"So it was, so it was," Ingraham said impatiently. "London, you say?"

"Yes, my lord. The road is entirely open." He held out the letter. "And from the looks of this envelope, it has been to Picton, back to London, and now here. It is from the Foreign Office, so I knew that it must be important."

"Then hand it over."

"And, my lord, the others are assembling in the parlor."

Lord Ingraham pressed his lips tight together again. "We'll be along soon enough." He took the letter and closed the door again, walking to the window and breaking the seal.

Marian looked down at her hands while he read the letter. She started up in amazement as Gilbert uttered a great oath, wadded the letter into a ball, and threw it into the fireplace.

He turned back to the window and stared out at the snow, his hands deep in his pockets. In another moment, he leaned his forehead against the glass and closed his eyes.

Alarmed, Marian leapt up and hurried to his side. She touched him timidly on the back. When he did not respond, she cast aside her better judgment and put her arm around his waist. He said nothing, but he draped his arm over her shoulders and leaned away from the window.

"Bad news?" she ventured at last.

"The worst." He let go of her and then took her by both shoulders, staring into her eyes. "And I have to do it, don't I?"

Mystified, Marian stared back.

"I mean, when your king and country expect it . . ." He touched her under the chin. "I wish . . ."

She managed a crooked smile. "You used up your Christmas wish, Gil," she reminded him.

"So I did." He gathered her close for a second and then released her. "And you must trust me, then, since my wish is gone." He smiled, but his eyes were bleak. "Or at least, not fulfilled yet."

"I really don't understand, Gil," she managed.

"You'll know soon enough," he said grimly, "and you must trust me. Promise?"

"I don't . . . Yes, I promise," she said quietly.

He looked at her another moment, as if memorizing her face, and then offered her his arm. "Come, Marian, we are wanted in the parlor."

12

If I stay far away from Lord Hammerfield, I shall rub through this evening, Marian thought grimly as she entered the parlor and smiled at those assembled. She looked about her. Lord Hammerfield dozed on the sofa, his hands cradling his belly. Alistair and Surtees had resumed their conspiratorial conversation in the corner, and Lizzie Hammerfield was sorting through the music at the pianoforte. All appeared safe enough. Lord Ingraham saw her seated in a chair by the fireplace, and took his leave.

Lord Hammerfield woke at his wife's prodding and looked around in surprise. He stared for a moment at Marian and then chose, to her great relief, to ignore her. Everyone's attention was claimed by Lizzie, who announced a Beethoven sonata and seated herself with some ceremony at the pianoforte.

Marian relaxed. Lizzie performed with a diligence that would have caused the composer no disgust, considering particularly that he was deaf. Lizzie's curls bobbed on the accelerandos, but she kept her tongue between her teeth and both feet on the pedals and came to the end of the music in the measure Beethoven intended.

When his niece graduated to Mozart, Lord Ingraham returned and sat beside his mother. They conversed quietly until Lord Hammerfield harrumphed them into silence. They were all spared an encore by the arrival of the tea tray, with two kinds of Chinese brew nestled among cakes and biscuits and slabs of the same bread that Marian was acquainted with from breakfast. She hesitated between the bread and the little Christmas cakes.

"Take both, by all means," suggested the earl as he handed her a cup of tea. "You must keep up your strength. Don't look at me like that. I have a contest in mind when you have finished."

Marian obliged him, only grateful that Lord Ingraham was not still down in the dumps. He appeared to have made up his mind about something and she was glad to see the hunted look gone from his eyes.

"We will be leaving soon, Mama," Lady Hammerfield said, "although we will allow Surtees to remain with you a few days. He can show Alistair about."

"Very well, daughter," said Lady Ingraham.

The tea tray was removed, and the earl got to his feet. He snapped out his pocket watch, examined it, and then took Marian by the arm and led her to a small table. "Sit."

She sat, her eyes alive with interest and not a little embarrassment at being the center of attention. Lord Ingraham went to a cupboard and returned with a chessboard. As she watched in growing appreciation, he hummed to himself and lined up the players. He picked up a black and white pawn and held them behind his back.

"Choose."

"I'll beat you to flinders."

Lizzie gasped and looked at her mother.

"Would you like to wager that you just said the wrong thing to a belted earl?" Ingraham asked Marian, leaning forward and whispering in her ear.

She nodded, trying not to smile. "But I will beat you."

"You can try, brat. Choose."

She laughed out loud and touched his right sleeve. He produced a white pawn, bowed, and set it before her, turning the board around until white was on her side.

Marian regarded the board seriously, chin in hand, and then looked across the little table to her opponent, staring into his eyes.

"You'll not intimidate me with that ploy," he declared. "In

case you have forgotten, I am a diplomat. I do not reveal my feelings so easily. You can study me for days and you will never know what I am thinking.'' He removed his coat, draping it over the back of his chair. "I can tell this is going to be a long contest. Let us wager on the outcome.''

"Gilbert," protested Lady Ingraham.

"Turning your parlor into a regular gaming hell, eh, madam?'' he said.

Marian giggled. "Don't worry, Lady Ingraham. I can trounce him no matter what the bait.''

"I will wager a copy of Aristole's *Poetics* that you will do no such thing.'' He raised his eyebrows. "Well?''

"In Greek? I have an English copy, the Barnwell translation.''

"Of course.''

She thought a moment more. "I have nothing of value to stake.''

"I contend that you do. Kiss me under the mistletoe over there and procure me another jar of that ointment.''

"Gilbert," Lady Ingraham exclaimed again. "You are absurd!''

"Done, sir,'' Marian agreed. "I was never safer, Lady Ingraham. And you'll have the ointment anyway.''

The game began. It showed no signs of letting up when Lord Hammerfield took his family home, muttering something about chits who play chess.

The earl looked up long enough to flick a careless finger at his brother-in-law and suffer his sister to kiss the top of his head.

Neither gave an inch of ground without careful consideration, a serious eyeing of each other's motives, and deliberation that bordered on the defiant. Lady Ingraham threw up her hands after midnight and took herself off to bed. She was followed shortly after by Surtees. The players barely acknowledged good nights and admonitions. His legs stretched out in front of him, only Alistair remained to witness the battle raging in silence across the chessboard.

The clock struck one. Lord Ingraham untied his elaborate neckcloth and dropped it to the floor. He unbuttoned the top buttons of his shirt.

"It's warm in here," he commented. "Marian, are you too warm?"

"Indeed I am," she said, raising her eyes to his after a minute scrutiny of knight and bishop.

"What a pity! Alistair, be a good fellow and throw another log or two on the fire."

Marian glared at her opponent. "You are unscrupulous, sir."

"I am when it comes to chess." He looked over his shoulder. "Alistair is asleep. Tiresome boy. I shall have to add the logs myself." He made no move to rise. "You see, Marian, I don't care to be beaten at chess, either."

Marian's chin came up. "Go on, say it. You don't like to be beaten by a woman."

"No, that is not it. I merely do not like to be beaten." He reached across the table and touched her cheek. "And there is a world of difference, my dear."

"I could lose, you know. In three moves, at most four, I could give up my bishop and queen so gracefully that you would never suspect."

Lord Ingraham took her by the hand and, before she could pull back, carried it to his lips. "And you could win—in five moves, I think." He released her hand. "If you lose in three moves, Marian Wynswich, I will turn you over my knee and paddle you. So there. Play on, Macduff." He looked at her and laughed softly. " 'And damned be him who first cries hold, enough.' "

"You think you're so smart. The next line is 'Exeunt fighting,' " Marian declared under her breath. "And so I shall. But it is still warm in here."

"Too bad." The earl removed his cuff links and started rolling up his sleeves. He hesitated, and she saw the curious burn pattern on his left arm.

"I am a regular Maori, my dear, tattooed here and there. That's what happens when you chance to lie upon a crisp grate."

In her turn, Marian reached across the table and took him by the arm, turning it this way and that, touching the skin around the scars, frowning at the lack of elasticity.

"They are fainter, of course," he said, his eyes on her face.

"I was wearing a shirt, but no coat. I have similar marks on my hip and thigh. They are fainter still, thanks to my buckskins."

Marian scarcely heard him. She touched the prominent scar on his forearm. "I wish there were some way to remove skin and replace it," she said, "but I suppose such things can never be." She released his arm. "But, sir, do not try to elicit my sympathy by baring your war wounds. I will defeat you anyway."

"I would never be so utterly debased," he replied virtuously.

"Oh, you would! It is your move, my lord."

He raised his eyebrows. " 'My lord,' is it? Dear me!"

The room was silent then, except for Alistair's snores. One move. Two moves. A knight changed hands and Marian moved again.

"Check," she said, barely able to keep the triumph from her voice.

Lord Ingraham considered the move from all angles.

"Checkmate," she said, and leaned back in her chair for the first time all evening. "Make sure it is a good copy, leatherbound, with a signature by the author."

"You scamp," the earl said. "I suppose you will want Aristotle's margin notes, too!"

"If you can get them," she replied calmly, struggling to keep the dimple from her cheek. "And tuck in a letter from Plato and a prescription from Hippocrates, while you are about it."

Ingraham laughed and put the chess pieces and board away. He stretched and stood before the fire, poking at the embers with his shoe. He looked over at her then, and he was not smiling. "If I am to do all that, lady, then I shall insist on a kiss under the mistletoe. There should be some little reward for crossed eyes and an aching back," he complained. "The next time I begin a chess game with you, let it be at noon on a sunny day. Good God, it must be two at least."

Marian rose and pressed her hands to the small of her back. "What a pair of fools we are. Oh, very well . . ." She went to the door and stood under the mistletoe, raising her face for his kiss. She did not know what she expected.

Ingraham took his time getting to the doorway and then he put his hands on her waist. "Such a little waist," he murmured. "How can you eat so much and remain so small? Is there not an animal that eats . . . Ah! It is the shrew!"

She opened her mouth to object and he kissed her. He stepped back a moment, put his hands on her neck, and kissed her again.

On the occasion of her fourteenth birthday, Marian had sneaked out to the garden and kissed the doctor's son. She had received a furtive peck from Alistair's Eton chambermate last spring when he came down for a visit. Both events had been singularized by inexperience and the oddest sort of dissatisfaction. Gil's kiss bore not the faintest resemblance to her previous encounters.

The only way to steady herself was to put her arms around Lord Ingraham, Marian discovered. And his back felt so good that she had to run her hands up and down it once, and then again. For one wild, disordered moment, she thought how scandalized her mother would be, and then she did not give a flea what anyone thought. She thought only of Gil and savored the moment with some enthusiasm.

Just when Marian thought he was coming to a conclusion, he kissed her on the earlobe and then that part of her neck that until this moment had never seemed to serve any useful purpose. And Marian was pleased to learn that it was not at all difficult to stand on tiptoe and kiss him on the ear, too. The notion must have met with his entire approval, because he picked her up so she could reach him easier.

If Alistair had not stirred then and muttered something in his sleep, Marian would have been content to stay in Lord Ingraham's arms until the maids came to clean out the ashes in the grate and open the draperies to meet the morning sun. She gave a little start, and the earl set her on her feet again.

He stepped back and she noticed with some confusion that his eyes were beginning to glaze over in a peculiar manner and his breathing was somewhat ragged. Perhaps the fireplace was starting to smoke a bit. She was having a little difficulty breathing, too.

Lord Ingraham put a hand against the wall to steady himself.

He looked up at the mistletoe in amazement. "Good God, Marian, suppose I had won?" he managed to say.

She could think of nothing clever or witty in reply. She touched his face as she wondered if she could ever get her mouth to form sentences again.

"Good night, Gil," she finally said. "I shall leave Alistair to you."

She hoped he would kiss her again, but he did not. "Alistair will not be nearly as fun," he said.

Marian smiled and said good night again. She tiptoed into the hall, relieved to discover that her knees hadn't turned entirely to India rubber. She looked back at the earl, who still stood under the mistletoe.

He raised his hand to her. "Until later," he said.

Marian climbed the stairs slowly. Halfway up to the first landing, she stopped and looked back, wishing for a moment that he would follow her. And what would you do, then? she asked herself. Don't you even consider it, Marian Wynswich, was her next thought.

She knew she would not sleep the remainder of that night, and she did not, but lay on her back, hands folded across her stomach, staring at the ceiling. She heard Alistair and the earl talking quietly to each other as they came upstairs later, and then their doors closed.

The old house creaked and settled, and she thought she heard the whisper of snow outside. It wasn't until the maid crept into her room the next morning to start a fire in the grate that Marian rolled over and allowed her eyes to close.

When she woke, it was bright midday. Marian sat up in bed and looked about her. Everything was the same, and yet, somehow, it was different. The lace curtains were more beautiful. Even the brass can of hot water on the dressing table had a brighter shine to it. She got out of bed and looked along the Royal Crescent. Snow had fallen, after all, but only enough to dust the street. Servants from each great house were already at work sweeping it away.

Marian watched them for a moment, resting her elbows on the sill, allowing herself to think no great thoughts. Her mind, usually so lively, was a curious blank, almost as if some hand had reached inside her head and scooped it clean, leaving every thought to follow new and original, as if it had never happened to anyone else before.

Her feet grew cold, and as she turned to hop into bed again, she noticed a note was shoved under the door. Marian held her breath and snatched it up from the floor before diving back into bed and ripping open the envelope. She read the missive once and then twice: "Marian. Just trust me. Ingraham."

That was all. She turned it over. Nothing. "How singular," she said out loud. "I shall have to ask him about this."

After another moment of contemplation among the feather pillows, Marian rose and dressed. As she was washing her face, Marian wondered what she would say to Lord Ingraham when she saw him. Thank the Lord it was past the hour for breakfast. The thought of sitting down to bacon and eggs and discussing the weather, or even books, with a man she had kissed in such wild abandon only hours before, brought a rosy glow to her cheeks that no amount of cool water would dash away. Ariadne would never have behaved in such hoydenish fashion, Marian scolded herself, not even with the Reverend Beddoe.

Marian sat down on the bed and then flopped onto her back again. I don't think I was ever so swept away before by winning a chess game. This is odd, indeed. I shall have to ask Lady Ingraham if her parlor fireplace is drawing properly. Something obviously went to my head.

There was a brisk knock at the door. Her heart thrummed a little faster for a second and then resumed its normal gait. Marian sat up and smoothed down her dress. "Come in."

Lady Ingraham entered. "Good morning, my dear. Washburn saved you some breakfast downstairs. Hurry up and eat. I have been commissioned to deliver Alistair to Broad Street to Gilbert's tailor, and while he is suffering at the hands of that exacting man, you and I will walk over a block to Milsom and see what we see."

"Cannot Gil take Alistair to his tailor?" Marian asked.

Lady Ingraham sighed. "My dear son is gone up to London. Just like that. He left directly after breakfast."

Marian stared at Lady Ingraham. "He can't be gone like that!"

"Ah, but he is! He seemed in no very cheerful mood either, and muttered something about business that could not be postponed." She sat down next to Marian. "I don't understand it. He seemed almost bitter, as if he hated what he was doing, and then he smiled at me in the oddest way and said that he would return in a few days with a grand surprise."

The women looked at each other, and Lady Ingraham patted Marian. "I have given up attempting to divine the whys and wherefores of the male sex. Whoever it was that thought women changeable obviously never had any dealings with men."

She hurried out. Marian finished dressing, pulling on the clever little half-boots that Lady Ingraham had declared did not fit her and left in Marian's room the night before. She sat in thought until Lady Ingraham called up the stairs for her to get cracking.

Breakfast was strangely tasteless. Marian eyed the cook's excellent sausage with suspicion, and left it on her plate. The egg went down easily enough, but she barely savored its flavor.

Snow still sparked on the Common, which was the center-piece of the Royal Crescent. Other women were about in their carriages.

"The shops are open, Marian," Lady Ingraham said, "mainly, I think, so we will bestow gifts on the shopkeepers. Once we have relieved ourselves of your brother, we will take a stroll down Milsom Street. I seem to recall a particularly beautiful bolt of deep blue that would look becoming upon your back."

"Lady Ingraham, I cannot expect you to do that for me," Marian protested. "The two dresses you have given me and my own green wool are enough. Besides, Alistair and I will be leaving quite soon."

Lady Ingraham took immediate exception to this. "You cannot. Gilbert made me promise to keep you here until his return. And so I shall."

They abandoned Alistair to the scant mercies of Lord Ingraham's tailor and continued to Milsom Street, where the

stores were crowded with after-Christmas shoppers. The blue
wool was duly admired and purchased and taken directly to Mme
Bresson's dress shop in the next street. Mme Bresson herself
took Marian's measurements, exclaiming over her tiny waist
and trim figure, and promised to have the dress by New Year's
Eve.

"Do you plan a party, Lady Ingraham?" the dressmaker
asked.

"No. Just a quiet evening, I am sure. Isn't that right,
Marian?"

"What? What? I am sorry, but I was not attending," Marian
replied.

Wandering back to Milsom Street, Lady Ingraham led Marian
in and out of shops, trying on hats, considering gloves, and
settling finally on a pair of white silk stockings for Marian and
a bottle of rose water.

Alistair was waiting for them when they returned to the
tailor's. He made a face as he left the shop. "Mare, you should
see the student's robe for St. Stephen's. I shall look like a monk.
Marian, are you paying attention?"

"Oh, I am sorry. Did you say something?" she asked, startled
by his elbow in her ribs. This will never do, Marian told herself. I do not know what is the matter with me.

She spent the evening in front of the window, looking out
at the snow and tracing circles on the frosty pane. Lady
Ingraham was accumulating a list of clothing requests to forward
to her son's Bath tailor.

"I should have this delivered tomorrow," Lady Ingraham
mused as she pored over the list, "for who knows when Gilbert
will be off directly to some new post?" She put down the list.
"In fact, I have decided that must be the big news that took
him to London. I am sure of it. I wonder where in the world
he will go now?"

"Yes, where in the world?" echoed Marian. To her chagrin,
tears came to her eyes and rolled down her cheeks. Thankful
that Lady Ingraham was occupied with the list, Marian remained
at the window until her eyes were dry again. She joined her
hostess finally and took up Lord Ingraham's copy of *The
Odyssey* she had spirited from the library.

It had long been a favorite book, but she found her attention wandering. She sat, book in her lap, staring into the fireplace, which was drawing perfectly tonight. Marian looked once at the doorway, but the maid must have removed the mistletoe.

The morrow brought two letters from Percy, one to Lord Ingraham, which was taken to the bookroom to await the earl's return, and the other addressed to Marian, which ended up on the breakfast table. It was a letter full of admonition and stern counsel. Alistair read through it and then tossed it back to his sister with a shudder.

"One shouldn't be subjected to sermonizing over eggs and toast."

"Perhaps not, Alistair," said Marian slowly as she ran down the closely written lines. "God knows we deserve it, I might add."

Alistair sighed, but said nothing. He finished his coffee in silence, and then took a closer look at his sister. "Mare? Are you quite the thing? You look like your stomach hurts." When she did not answer, he pecked her on the cheek. "I am off with Surtees."

As soon as Marian rose from the breakfast table, the letter still in her hand, Lady Ingraham called for the carriage. "A drive will be just the thing, Marian. Child, are you homesick? You're so quiet!"

They drove to Milsom Street again, where Lady Ingraham picked up a hat she had ordered before Christmas, and then drove out to the parade grounds, which were almost bare of snow. "It is so lovely in the summer to see the young ladies promenading about in their white muslins, eyeing the soldiers in their regimentals." Lady Ingraham touched Marian's hand. "You will return in the summer?"

In the summer I will be ensconced in the vicarage, Marian thought as she gazed out the window. "Of course I shall," she replied. "Only think how diverting that will be."

When they returned to the house, a package was lying on the hall table. Washburn handed it to Marian. The handwriting was the same as the note she had received yesterday. Her heart pounding, she tore off the brown paper and held up a copy of *The Poetics*. A note was stuck in the pages. "The dealer was

completely out of those copies with Aristotle's autograph,'' it
read. ''Trust this will suffice. Yours, Ingraham.''

Lady Ingraham looked over Marian's shoulder at the book.
''I am glad he remembers his obligations. I was beginning to
think he had fled to London because you beat him at chess.''

Marian pleaded a headache that night, so Surtees and Alistair
escorted Lady Ingraham to a recital by an Italian soprano in
the Upper Assembly Rooms.

''After all, Mare, Surtees says I need to acquire a little
polish,'' Alistair said as he squeezed his shoulders into the coat
he had borrowed from his new friend. ''Although why I'll need
polish tacking back and forth among the Caribbean islands, I'm
sure I don't know.''

Marian thanked him for his sacrifice on her behalf and waved
to them from the front door.

It was the truth; her head did ache. Marian dutifully drank
the headache powders that Lady Ingraham's dresser bullied her
into taking, and then climbed in bed. She closed her eyes and
willed herself to sleep, but she could not.

The moon rose and shone in the bedroom window, spreading
across the bed. Marian threw back the covers and went to the
window. Wrapping herself in a shawl, she curled up in the
window seat. Lord Ingraham's book was lying open by her feet.
She picked it up, thumbing through the pages, and suddenly
realized that she was in love with Gilbert Ingraham.

So many idle thoughts had been flitting in and out of her brain
the last two days that she nearly chased that one away, too. But
she could not. It was there to stay. She loved Gilbert Ingraham,
plain and simple.

The knowledge of her feelings, finally admitted, covered
Marian like a blanket warmed by the fireplace. She basked in
the feeling, smiling at the moon and laughing out loud. ''Marian
Wynswich, you are such a fool,'' she chided herself. ''You've
probably been in love with Gil ever since he rescued your kittens
from under Sir William's bed!'' It wasn't until Gilbert Ingraham
had absented himself from her life that she realized half of her
was gone.

Marian cried a little then, sitting in the window seat, and then hopped back in bed, her headache gone. She put her hands behind her head and watched the moonlight cross the bed and creep up the wall. "Hurry back, Gil," she whispered and closed her eyes. "I have something so wonderful to tell you."

Marian felt better in the morning, full of energy again, ready to joust with dragons. Marian, you are the luckiest woman alive, she told herself as she danced about the room and then stopped in front of the mirror. She looked deeper into her eyes. "Maybe I am prettier than I ever thought," she said. She felt beautiful, easily the most enchanting woman who had ever lived.

"Marian! Are you about?"

It was Lady Ingraham, and her voice was tremulous with excitement.

Marian hurried to open the door. "Oh, good morning, Lady Ingraham. Isn't it a beautiful day?"

Lady Ingraham grabbed Marian and kissed her. "Yes! Yes! And see here, my dear, we have a letter from Gilbert. And you can't even guess his news. Oh, I shall ring a peal over his head when he returns. Sly, sly boy!"

She waved a letter about as Marian laughed. "Lady Ingraham, what is the news?"

The woman sat down on Marian's bed and held the letter next to her heart. "He's done it! Oh, and we thought he rushed off to London on business. Marian, you cannot imagine how this pleases me. Gilbert's got himself engaged. He's getting married!"

13

"What?" Marian shrieked. She felt the color draining from her face and turned her head away.

Lady Ingraham was oblivious to Marian's distress. "My dear, how grateful I am you are here. Gilbert has asked me to plan a little New Year's Eve dinner for close friends and a reception to follow. He mentions dancing, if I can produce an orchestra on short notice. There is so much to do. Oh, Marian, say you will help me."

"I will help you," Marian said automatically. Tears began to marshal themselves behind her eyelids, and she felt as though she were suffocating. She wanted to fling open the window and take deep drafts of the cold winter air, but she remained where she was, frozen to the spot.

If Lady Ingraham noted anything unusual, she did not indicate it. She was on her feet again, pacing the length of the room and waving the letter about. "Gilbert says he will be at Collinwood on the thirtieth, where his fiancée, Lady Amanda Calne, will meet him, and they will go over some plans for refurbishing the estate. They will be here on the afternoon of the thirty-first. Sly boy! Have you ever heard of such a man?"

"No, never," said Marian. Tears began to slide down her cheeks, so she bent over to straighten her stockings.

Lady Ingraham finally took notice of her. "Oh, and I have intruded on your morning toilette. When you come downstairs,

I'll be in the bookroom with the cook. Come join us, my dear, and we'll begin planning.''

She hurried out of the room, clicking the door shut as Marian began to sob. Marian was on her feet in a moment, pacing the room, as the tears streamed down her face. As she crossed by the window seat, Marian grabbed up *The Poetics* and pulled back her arm to hurl the book across the room.

She stopped herself in midswing, wiped her eyes on her sleeve, and took a good look at the book. What a foolish thing that would be, she thought even as she sobbed. I would ruin a perfectly good book. Marian set the book down carefully on the dressing table and ran her finger across the binding. Better to keep it as an excellent reminder that men are not to be trusted.

If Gilbert had taken a knife and thrust it up under her rib cage, nothing could have hurt more than the realization that she had been made a fool of. Marian moved about the room. Another turn convinced her that even more painful was the certainty that she still loved him.

Her legs began to shake, so she sat down in the window seat. She drew her knees up close to her face and leaned her forehead against them. And Lady Ingraham says that he will be back here in a few days, and I must help. Oh, God, I cannot. She reached into her pocket for a handkerchief and pulled out the note that Gil had slipped under her door two days ago. '' 'Trust me,' '' she repeated. '' 'Trust me,' '' she said again. Marian crumbled the note into a ball and threw it toward the wastebasket. ''I wouldn't trust you if you were the last man on earth, Gilbert Ingraham.''

Her shock gradually gave way to enormous anger, the intensity of it taking away her breath and leaving her white-faced and silent in the window seat. How could you kiss me like that and then hurry to London and make love to some other woman? she thought. And then you say, ''Trust me.''

She was on her feet again, wild to go home to Picton and sob out her misery in Ariadne's lap. She looked out the window. We could be on a mail coach by nightfall, she thought, and then remembered that they had no money. ''And I have promised

Lady Ingraham that I will remain here," she whispered. "Oh, the devil take Gilbert Ingraham!"

Tense, Marian Wynswich presented herself in the bookroom an hour later, where Lady Ingraham and the chef were scrutinizing a much-rewritten menu. Lady Ingraham looked at her, and the tiny wrinkles between her eyes deepened.

"Marian, you're much too young to lose your bloom." She laughed. "It must be the frantic pace that we set here in Bath. Pull up a chair, my dear, there's work to be done. Thank you, François. Go do your best."

Marian sat down. "I am a trifle indisposed," she said.

"Gilbert would say you were a bit grim about the lips," said Lady Ingraham.

"Indeed he would," Marian replied. "I am sure that what I am feeling will pass away very soon. Now, what can I do for you, Lady Ingraham?"

When they did not show up in the dining room, Washburn brought lunch to them on a tray. Lady Ingraham ate quickly and returned to her lists. Marian shoved the food around until she was tired of looking at it and set the trays outside the door.

By the time the shadows were long across the Royal Crescent, Lady Ingraham had located a string quartet and enough ivy and other winter greenery to shame a forest, and produced a guest list complete with addresses. She examined the guest list one last time and handed it to Marian.

"My dear, my handwriting is so old and shaky that I would be embarrassed to write the invitations. May I leave this to you?"

Marian nodded, her eyes scanning the paper. There were several names on it that Percy had mentioned before in hushed tones, but none was familiar to her.

"The starred ones will be invited first to dinner, and the others to the reception and dance following." Lady Ingraham took another look. "Gilbert specifically requested . . . Oh, there he is. Reginald Calne." She tapped her fingernail on the paper. "I own I do not wish to have his feet under my table, but he is her brother."

Marian looked up, a question in her eyes.

"A regular scoundrel," said Lady Ingraham, "but he lives in Bath, and we must content ourselves. No one has perfect relatives." She smiled at Marian. "Possibly you know what I mean."

Marian managed her first genuine smile of the afternoon. "I do. Mine are singular."

Lady Ingraham tapped her nail on Sir Reginald's name one more time. "Would that he were only singular!" She leaned forward in a conspiratorial fashion. "He games and games, and loses fortunes on the turn of a card, and when we are sure he is in the basket, he comes up with more money. There are some who would like to know whether it 'droppeth from heaven as the gentle rain.' "

Marian nodded, and understood where Gilbert inherited his penchant for sprinkling literature through his speech. "*Merchant of Venice*, madam," she said as Lady Ingraham laughed and touched her cheek.

Gilbert's mother rose to her feet with some stiffness. "And now, my dear, may I leave you to these invitations? Washburn has been going 'ahem and aha' on the other side of that door, and I know he wants me to look over the ballroom." She patted her hair into place. "Other women my age have earned an afternoon's nap. I must still dash around after my son, as I have done for so many years. My hair will be quite gray before he is safely married, I can tell right now."

At least he will not break your heart, Marian thought as the door closed. She picked up the sample invitation and felt her heart turn over and her eyes begin to prickle again.

" 'Lord Gilbert Ingraham, Earl of Collinwood, requests the pleasure of your company at a reception and dance to honor Lady Amanda Calne,' " Marian read out loud. She looked at the mound of cream-colored note cards in front of her on the desk. "It is rather like spinning straw into gold," she said as she sharpened the pen and then dipped it in the inkwell.

Dinner came and went and Marian continued at the desk. The words bothered her at first, but by the time she finished the twentieth invitation, and then the thirtieth one, they had all run together like soup, and it was merely a task that demanded precision and no emotion. Gilbert Ingraham and Amanda Calne were only letters, she told herself, even though that reasoning didn't explain the ache that started in her stomach and spread upward until her head throbbed.

"Mare? I say, Mare, are you still in there?"

She looked up and set down the pen gratefully, curling and uncurling her fingers. "Come in, Alistair," she called, and got to her feet.

Her brother entered the room and flopped in the chair close to the desk. He looked at the uneaten tray of dinner on the table and then up at his sister. "The veal was good, Mare, and you know how you like veal."

She waved her hand over the food and blew on the last invitation she had penned. "It smelled funny," she said.

Alistair looked at her long and hard. "There's nothing wrong with the veal, sister," he said evenly. "Sit down a minute."

She did as he said, and stared back into his eyes.

Alistair crossed his legs and continued his appraisal of her. To her tired mind, for one moment he looked very much like Percy. "Marian, what's the matter?"

She forced a smile. "Nothing, Alistair, nothing. I'm just tired."

"That's a hum, Mare, and you always were a dreadful liar." He got out of the chair and perched himself on the desk to be closer to her. "I don't pretend that I'm anything but a care-for-nobody, but, Mare, I know when something's wrong. Tell me?"

A week ago, Marian Wynswich would have no more confided in Alistair than she would have walked on her hands through Picton. She had learned from sad experience that all her tales of woe were carried throughout the neighborhood and arrived back at her doorstep much enlarged by her brother. But this time, as she looked into his eyes, someone different looked back at her.

"You care, don't you?" she whispered, and reached for his hand.

"I do," he said simply. "You're starting to worry me, and I want to know why." He would not let her hand go, but grasped it tighter, even as he got up from the desk and pulled his chair around until they were sitting quite close together. "It has to do with Lord Ingraham, doesn't it?"

She nodded and then began to sob. Without a word, Alistair picked her up and deposited her in his lap, where he held her close and patted her back, murmuring nothings that made her sob harder at first and then unaccountably feel better. When she sat up and looked about, he pulled a handkerchief from his pocket and handed it to her. She blew her nose vigorously.

"Do you love him, Mare, is that it?" Alistair asked finally.

She nodded. "I know it's foolish. I know I am foolish." She dabbed at her eyes. "I mean, didn't he tell me that there was someone he was trying to work up the nerve to offer for?"

"I remember something like that." Alistair shifted a little and patted his right pocket. "Anytime you say, Mare, we can be off home. The roads are open, and I can spout your pearls again."

She stared at her brother and got up off his lap. "Alistair, I don't understand. You have my pearls back? How is this?"

He grinned. "I've been meaning to tell you. A package came this morning from London with your pearls and a note from Lord Ingraham."

Marian continued to stare. "I really don't understand."

"Well, when we were walking along through the snow on the way to Bath, I might have mentioned the pearls to him." Alistair scratched his head. "I didn't think you'd mind."

Marian brushed aside his explanation. "You know I do not. But doesn't it strike you as strange that Lord Ingraham has such connections as would enable him to recover my pearls so quickly, and get them back here? I mean, he would have to know a lot of people in Picton, and we know that he does not."

Alistair regarded her with a frown on his face. "Funny, I didn't think of that. I was just so glad to see the pearls again. Fancy explaining that to Mama. Or to, good God, Percy."

Marian shoved her hands in her pockets and began to pace the room. She stopped at the window, not looking at her brother. "You say he wrote a note. Did he mention me?"

"He did. I thought it was rather cryptic. Maybe you can make sense of it." Alistair took the note from his pocket and handed it to his sister, who grabbed it up eagerly.

Marian smoothed out the paper. " 'Maybe these will help your sister feel better. Be a good brother right now, please,' " she read slowly. " 'Ingraham.' " She handed the note back to her brother. "Alistair, how odd! He seemed to know I would be feeling bad."

She clapped her hands together in frustration and took another turn about the room. "He knew I would be upset by his engagement, but that did not deter him from affiancing himself to someone. I mean, a gentleman would have waited until we left Bath if he wanted to spare my feelings. I just wish I knew the purpose of all this."

"You're not going to cry again, are you?" Alistair asked anxiously.

"No, silly! I'm too provoked," she retorted, tears the last thing on her mind. "Gilbert Ingraham is either the biggest cad who ever tied a neckcloth, or he's involved in something that we don't understand." She remained in silence for several moments and then sniffed. "That veal does smell better than I thought."

"Ugh, Mare, it's cold."

"Well, I am hungry. If you can't stand it, leave!"

He grinned and went to the door. Marian hurried to his side and gave his arm a squeeze. He looked down at her and his eyes were bright.

"Do stay by me through the next few days, Alistair," she whispered. "I need you."

"I will. That's what brothers are for," he said with a flourish that made her laugh.

She leaned against the door for a moment after he left. "Alistair, there's hope for you," she said to the paneling before she seated herself again, pushed aside the invitations, and pulled the dinner tray closer.

The veal was cold, but far from tasteless. Marian chewed thoughtfully. It very well could be that I am grasping at straws or trying to whistle down the wind, she told herself. Likely Gil has had this bee in his bonnet for many years, and now has become a creature of action.

The more she ate, the greater grew her optimism. If he did not care, he would never have kissed me like that, she considered. Her face colored at the memory. And why would he ask me to trust him?

Marian finished the invitations several hours later, when all the house was still. Tomorrow all the servants would be dispatched to deliver them, and there would be such speculation in Bath. Hopeful mothers of eligible daughters will glower and fret, and young ladies who nourished dreams of their own about the peripatetic Earl of Collinwood will spend time in their rooms and change their New Year's resolutions. She shivered and came away from the window. It may be that I must change mine, she thought.

Marian walked slowly up the stairs and into her room. A welcoming fire glowed in the hearth. Gratefully she put her hands to it and then remembered the earl's note that she had pitched toward the wastebasket that morning. On hands and knees, she rummaged under the dressing table until she found it. She smoothed it out.

"Trust me." The words leapt out at her. "Trust you," she said softly. "I shall, at least until I find out one way or another what this all means."

In the morning, Lady Ingraham uprooted Marian from the breakfast table almost before she had slabbed marmalade on her last bite of toast. "My dear, there is much to be done. I have sent all the servants out to deliver invitations, so you and I will go belowstairs and polish silver." She peered closely at Marian. "I trust you do not mind?"

Marian smiled as she followed her to the door. "It is what I am well-accustomed to at home, Lady Ingraham. Mama always swore that if we could not be beautiful, we could be useful."

"And whoever told you that you were not beautiful?" Lady Ingraham teased in turn.

Marian paused in thought for a moment. "It is something I never gave overmuch consideration." She hesitated for another second and then plunged ahead. "This lady . . ."

"Lady Amanda?"

"Is she beautiful? I mean, do you know her?"

Lady Ingraham handed Marian a polishing rag. "I am acquainted with her. Her parents are Derbyshire folk, and her father is quite active in the Prince Regent's circle of friends. Manda has been out several Seasons.'' Lady Ingraham rubbed at a large silver tea tray, her eyes on the distant wall. ''There was some speculation as to why she had not made an advantageous match before now, but I do not know. Yes, she is beautiful, and accomplished. I suppose you would think that Amanda Calne had been grooming herself for years to become a diplomat's wife.'' She rubbed the tea tray harder, and a tiny frown appeared between her eyes. ''And yet . . .''

Marian remained silent, thinking, Only a week ago I would have pressed and pleaded and jumped about for her to keep talking. I shall be silent and see what I learn.

''And yet,'' Lady Ingraham repeated, ''I cannot quite put my finger on her appeal to Gilbert.'' The tray forgotten, she sat in silence a moment, and then smiled at Marian. ''How I carry on! I am pleased, though. Be sure of that. Gilbert danced to her tune a few years back.''

''And nothing came of it then?'' Marian interjected softly, not wishing to upset Lady Ingraham's flow of thought.

''No,'' Lady Ingraham said decisively. ''He flirted and teased.'' She laughed. ''And did it with a certain dogged determination, as I recall, rather like he was told to . . .'' Her voice trailed off, and the tiny frown reappeared.

Lady Ingraham made no further attempt to explain herself, and Marian stored it up as food for thought, something to chew on later in bed that night when she could not sleep. She rubbed a silver creamer vigorously.

''Are you waiting for a jinni to pop out, Mare, and offer you three wishes?'' Alistair spoke from the doorway. He was draped in the brown garment that was St. Stephen's undergraduate robe. He twirled around to his sister's amusement, crossed himself, and then sank to one knee in front of her.

Marian gave him a push and he toppled over. ''Alistair, the next thing we know you will be in Holy Orders.''

He grimaced and righted himself, sitting in front of her on the floor as Lady Ingraham looked on in appreciation. ''It is a wonder anyone goes to St. Stephen's,'' he said.

''I assure you, Alistair, that parents think it is heaven on earth,'' Lady Ingraham assured him. ''Marian, shall we wager that in twenty years or so, Alistair might look with a kindly eye on morning oatmeal, Greek on hard benches, and bedtime at nine of the clock?'' She laughed as Alistair groaned and flopped on the floor again.

He raised himself up on one elbow. ''Just for that, Marian and Lady Ingraham, you may rub and rub on that creamer, and no jinni will even grudge you one wish.'' He sighed as they laughed, and then he hurriedly left the room when Marian tossed him a polishing towel.

Lady Ingraham retrieved the cloth. ''Gilbert was telling me of your Christmas wishes. Did yours come true, my dear?''

She nodded. ''Oh, indeed! I wished that your son would have the best Christmas ever, and see how it has come true for him.''

''I wonder, has Gilbert's come true?'' his mother asked.

''I do not know,'' Marian said. ''Perhaps he will tell us . . . when he returns.''

There was no word from Lord Ingraham the next day, or the next. Acceptances to the New Year's Eve reception poured in, as well as morning callers who came and sat and drank tea and tried to pry information from Lady Ingraham. Between visitors and tradesmen and quartet rehearsals, Marian made a quick trip to Mme Bresson's for a final fitting on the blue dress that Lady Ingraham had commissioned. It arrived early on the morning of New Year's Eve, wrapped in tissue paper. Marian sighed over it briefly, smelling the new material, touching the beautiful sleeves, and ran it upstairs to her room before hurrying back to the ballroom to hang the ivy.

She was perched atop the ladder under the chandelier, attempting to drape the ivy strands in an artful fashion, when she heard footsteps below. She sat on the ladder, chin in hands. ''Washburn, what do you think?'' she asked, not bothering to look down.

''A little more to the left.''

Lord Ingraham stood below her. How long he had been watching her, Marian had no way of knowing. He reached out his hand to steady the ladder.

''Tell me, Marian, is there not a servant in this house who

will climb this ladder, or do you long for further adventure?''

She looked down then, hoping for a moment that he would have changed somehow, and would not look so good to her. She hoped, that after five days, she would find him not at all to her taste and leave her chuckling over what she could possibly have seen in him.

She was doomed to disappointment. Marian gazed down at Gilbert Ingraham from her perch, marveling that he could have improved so much in such a short time. She said nothing, and began to descend the ladder. The suspicion grew in her that love of Lady Amanda Calne had ripened Gilbert Ingraham. She looked at him out of lowered eyelids, noting with a chill on her heart that he looked so calm and content, much like a cat sleeping in the sun.

''Honestly, brat, I wish you would leave ladders to others,'' he scolded as she reached the bottom rung. ''How would it look if you returned to Picton in three pieces in an egg basket? I fear Percy would not be pleased, and Lord knows, he is long-suffering.''

That was her answer. There was nothing loverlike in his voice or his demeanor. This was not the man who had kissed her with such abandon under the mistletoe. For all she knew, she had dreamed the whole event. A chill spread throughout her body, and she shivered.

''I am quite surefooted,'' Marian said, matching him calm for calm as she prayed he would not keep her long. To her intense irritation, Lord Ingraham continued to regard her, standing too close, saying nothing else.

What are you waiting for? she thought as she took a step back. Are you waiting in anticipation that I will utter some flippant remark, make some outrageous comment? I hope to God I am finally growing up, she thought as she forced a smile to her face and held out her hand.

''I want to wish you happy, Gil,'' she said, her voice softer than she would have liked, but unable to muster any volume.

He took her hand, and his look of calm contentment deepened until she wanted to cry out. ''Thank you, my dear. Coming from you, that means a great deal to me.'' He shook her hand and let it go. "I expect we will be very happy. Only think how much of this I owe to you and Alistair."

"Yes; only think," she echoed, and put her hands behind her back, feeling suddenly very young and very foolish. She wanted to leave the room the quickest way possible, but the door to the ballroom looked miles and miles away.

And then a woman was standing there, a tall woman dressed in a traveling cloak trimmed with white fur. Marian sucked in her breath in spite of herself, and Lord Ingraham looked around. He smiled, took Marian by the hand, and walked quickly toward the woman.

"Manda," he called out, "here is someone I especially wish to make known to you."

Marian found herself face to face with the most beautiful woman she had ever seen. She had all the perfection of a pattern card, with eyes of an impossible shade of blue and ash-blond hair with not a strand out of place. Her lips seemed to curve in a natural smile as she extended both hands.

"Gilbert," she said, and her voice was as soft as dove down. "You did not tell me she was such a pretty little thing. Oh, dear, are you Marian Wynswich?"

Marian could only nod, stunned, as Amanda Calne gathered her close in a gentle embrace and brushed the air by her ear with a kiss.

"My darling Gilbert tells me that I have you to thank for this wonderful turn of events," she said, her voice tinkling bells, little notes that graced the ballroom like summer fireflies. "He told me how you and your delightful brother brought him here and put some heart into him. See the results?"

She extended a hand, shapely and white, and Marian gaped at the diamond on her finger. Marian stared in stupefied silence at the ring as Lady Amanda grasped Lord Ingraham's arm and rested her cheek against him. "The silly boy just insisted! I tried to tell him it was too much, but, Marian, he said nothing was too much for me."

"I am sure he did," Marian managed to say. The room was beginning to dip and whirl as though the evening's entertainment had already begun. She took another step nearer the door, acutely aware of what an elegant couple they made as they stood so close together.

As she edged closer to the door, Lord Ingraham put out his hand to hold her there. "Don't go," he said. "Mama tells me we have you to thank for the invitations and the decorations. She says you even managed the cook this morning when François was all of a twitter because he could find no pheasant."

"Tell us, my dear, tell us," Lady Amanda chimed in. "I love a funny story, don't I, Gilbert?"

He smiled and kissed the end of her nose.

"And you must tell me all about your delightful animals, and how you nurse them to health," Lady Amanda continued, warming to her subject. "Such a clever child you are! Gilbert tells me that you read Greek and Latin."

Suddenly it was too much. A tiny spark somewhere in the back of Marian's brain leapt into a flame. She drew herself up. "Oh, I am remarkably clever, Lady Amanda, but my little stories will simply have to wait." She smiled a brittle smile at Lord Ingraham. "I am certain that Lord Ingraham will not leave you comfortless if I take myself off. He is such a gentleman. There is much to do yet, and you simply must excuse me."

Lady Amanda pouted and sighed. "I own I should feel guilty. It was naughty of us to put you to so much trouble." She looked about her at the decorations. "How clever you are." Lady Amanda detached herself from her fiancé's side and approached Marian. "Perhaps tonight, while I am dressing for dinner, I will let you help me."

"I am all eagerness," replied Marian. "I only hope I am equal to the treat in store for me."

Lady Amanda's eyes widened. "And, my dear, perhaps we will allow you to come to the dinner and the reception."

Lord Ingraham cleared his throat. "I believe we had every intention of that, dearest."

Lady Amanda turned the full force of her smile on her fiancé. "But, my dear, she is not out yet."

He started to say something, but Marian cut him off. "Don't give it another thought, Lady Amanda. I am sometimes allowed out, particularly if I have been very very good." She twinkled her eyes at the earl as she wished him to the devil. "And I have been ever so good. Excuse me, please."

Without another word, Marian turned on her heel and left the ballroom. As she started up the stairs, she heard Lady Ingraham calling to her, but she ignored the woman, went into her room, and locked the door, leaning against it. She was beyond tears, past all emotion except an enormous sadness, greater than any she had ever known before.

That she had been played the fool, she had no doubt. It only remained to get through the evening as she had promised, spout the pearl necklace again, and be on the morning mail coach to Picton before anyone was awake.

Marian stayed where she was until her breathing returned to normal. The lamp on the dressing table had been lit for her. Her gaze rested on the earl's note that she had rescued and so carefully smoothed out. Without a word, she tore it into tiny bits of confetti. Gathering the scraps in her hand, she opened the window and let them go. Her face devoid of all expression, Marian watched the wind snatch them and scatter them up and down the Royal Crescent.

She stood a moment longer at the open window, breathing deep of the bracing air. She closed the window finally, but still stood where she was, looking out. "I would sooner trust Napoleon himself than you, Gilbert Ingraham."

14

Marian remained at the window until the evening sky had turned completely dark and the lamplighters had done their work. Lights gleamed and danced like gems in a necklace, up and down the crescent. How beautiful it all was. She closed her eyes to remember it better, knowing that in the morning she would be away from this place. It only remained to get through this one last night and then hurry home, where she could lick her wounds in peace and quiet, like one of her animal foundlings.

The idea of going down to dinner was repugnant to her. Marian sat down on the bed as shame washed over her. How could I have imagined that Gilbert Ingraham had ever felt the smallest spark of interest in me? she asked herself. Have I that much pride? "If you are so clever, Marian Wynswich," she scolded herself. "why were you so stupid?"

There was no answer. She knew it was time to dress for dinner, but she did not move. I cannot sit at table and watch Amanda Calne and Gilbert Ingraham make love to each other with their eyes. She felt the flush grow on her chest and then rise up to meet her hairline. And what has he told her about me? Have they laughed together about the silly little girl from Devon who fancied herself in love with a peer of the realm? Have I already become a family joke?

Marian sobbed out loud and immediately put her hand to her mouth. Have a little countenance, she told herself. But still she sat where she was. The room grew darker as she drew herself into a ball and lay down. Her eyes closed and she was asleep.

"Marian, I know you're in there. Open up!"

She woke with a start, wondering for a moment where she was.

"Marian!"

It was Lord Ingraham. He was speaking softly, as if he were bending over the keyhole outside her door.

Marian put her hands together under her cheek and listened to him, making not a sound herself, scarcely breathing. She wondered at his audacity, and then wondered why he was whispering so furtively. This was his house, was it not?

Go away, she thought, grateful that she had locked the door, as Lord Ingraham turned the handle quietly.

"Marian, there is no time. I have to speak to you."

Marian said nothing and made no move to open the door.

"Marian! You are endlessly stubborn!"

Oh, I am. It may keep me alive for the next sixty or seventy years without you.

Lord Ingraham's voice became more urgent. "I have to go downstairs and greet my guests. Sir Reginald Calne will be here soon and you must watch him for me."

She couldn't believe her ears. Marian sat up and wiped her eyes.

"If he says anything to Amanda or gives her anything, you must tell me at the earliest opportunity."

Gracious God above, Marian thought scornfully, you are jealous of her brother?

"Do you hear me?"

She nodded.

"Do this little thing for me. I shall explain later."

I doubt that you can.

He was silent another moment, and then he spoke again, this time in his normal voice. "Please, Marian," was all he said, and then he was done, his footsteps receding down the hall.

Marian continued to sit in silence as the guests arrived. She heard them laughing and talking with one another in the entry hall, and every now and then Gilbert Ingraham's voice could be heard above the others, and his laughter.

"I am the biggest fool that ever lived," Marian said, as she began to slowly unbutton her dress. "I might as well be foolish one last time." She would do as he said, she would see the thing through, whatever it was, and then leave. It was a matter of no more than a few hours. She was not such a child that she could not face him with equanimity and do as he asked. He was doing the Wynswich family an immeasurable favor by furthering Alistair's cause, and the least she could do was what he asked.

In a moment the beautiful blue dress was over her head and she was buttoning it up the back. She picked up the pearls from the dressing table and placed the strand about her neck, grateful for one last opportunity to wear them. Her hair was a simple matter. A vigorous brushing and a velvet ribbon at the nape of her neck caught it up simply. She would not disgrace the Wynswiches tonight. Heaven knows they had suffered enough at her father's vagaries. She dabbed on Lady Ingraham's gift of rose water and took one last look in the mirror.

She was pale, so she pinched her cheeks. What she saw in the mirror did not disgust her. The dress was utterly simple and hung in neat lines from high waist to ankle. She draped the dresser's shawl about her shoulders, took a deep breath, and went into the hall, moving quietly to the landing, where she looked over.

Lord Ingraham, resplendent in evening wear, was greeting the last of his dinner guests. Lady Amanda was arranged artfully at his side. The numbness that was becoming so familiar to Marian returned, and she nearly retreated to the safety of her room. She longed for Alistair to hold on to, but he and Surtees had gone to Hammerfield and would not be returning until later this evening. "Drat," she said under her breath. She hesitated only a moment more and then went down the stairs.

Lady Amanda saw her first. "Oh, my dear, how grown-up you look. Such a becoming dress."

"Thank you, Lady Amanda," Marian replied. Her voice sounded far away to her ears, but she noted with satisfaction that it was steady and clear.

Lord Ingraham took her by the hand. He bowed over it as Lady Amanda watched benignly, smiling at the other guests as if this were all her idea. He kissed her hand and then looked into her eyes. "Marian, be watchful," he said softly in classic Greek.

She blinked, but did not hesitate. "I shall be watchful," she replied in the same language, utterly mystified, completely at sea.

Marian went into the parlor, and in a few minutes Gilbert and Amanda followed. Marian knew no one in the room but Lady Ingraham and the elder Hammerfields, so she stood where she was, her eyes on Lord Ingraham as he circulated about the room. Lady Amanda's arm was tucked into the crook of his elbow, kept there firmly by Ingraham's hand over hers.

Marian watched more closely, and her wonder grew. As Lord Ingraham made a stately progress about the room, nodding to friends, stopping to chat, Lady Amanda tried several times to pull away. He merely smiled, and visited, and kept an iron grip on Amanda. As they moved about the room, Lady Amanda's smile became more brittle. There was even a look in her eyes bordering on desperation. Several times she glanced toward a group of men congregated about the fireplace.

Marian looked in that direction and had little trouble in picking out the likeliest candidate for Sir Reginald. He was tall and blond, even as his sister, a striking figure in stark black evening wear. It could be no one else, Marian decided.

As she observed those about her, Marian found herself listening to another clutch of guests close by, who spoke in rapid French, punctuating their animated conversation with softly whispered asides to one another, and occasional laughter. I wonder if they are émigrés, she thought. Gilbert has such interesting friends. She sighed. It was all so romantic. The only Frenchmen who ever visited Picton were smugglers snabbled by the sea watch.

Lord Ingraham, his fiancée firmly in tow, came to stand before her. "Marian, I have asked Sir Reginald Calne to take you down to dinner. Come with us, please, and let me introduce you."

She followed at Lady Amanda's side, noting that the Frenchmen had become quiet, intent on Lord Ingraham. If the earl noticed, he did not show it. He did not loosen his grip on his fiancée as he introduced Marian to Lady Amanda's brother.

"Reginald, may I make you known to Marian Wynswich? I believe you are acquainted with her brother Percy."

Sir Reginald nodded and bowed over Marian's hand. "Charmed," he said.

At that moment, Washburn announced dinner. Sir Reginald tucked her arm in his. "Will you allow me?"

I can say no, she thought suddenly, and take no part in whatever is going forth this evening. I can turn my back on Gilbert Ingraham. The hurt flooded back into her heart; she turned to the earl, opening her mouth to speak.

She could not. There was an expression in his eyes that calmed her, even as she knew now through painful experience that she could be mistaken about that look. If it is my imagination, so be it, she thought. It is my last evening here.

Marian turned back to Sir Reginald, who was eyeing her with a quizzical expression of his own. Marian laughed and touched his sleeve. "I am so naive, sir," she said. "I was about to inquire whether it should be I who has this honor. Yes, Sir Reginald, I will go down to dinner with you."

It was an easy matter to keep conversation flowing at the table with her partner. Sir Reginald knew everyone, pointing out in low tones who presided over which rung of the Prince Regent's circle, who was ambassador to where, who sat on which department in the House of Lords, and who commanded which regiment. Sir Reginald was a garden of information, a flowering of facts. Marian took it all in, noting the glances that passed between the Calnes, even as Sir Reginald rambled on like a river in full spate.

Marian discovered how easy he was to charm, leaning toward him and using her low-cut gown to full advantage. "Tell me, sir," she whispered during one of those moments when their heads were close together. "Those men over there? Are they French?"

"Émigrés," he replied, his eyes on her bosom. He giggled and put his hand over his mouth, leaning closer until their heads touched. "Some say they are spies."

She gave him the full force of her wide eyes, noting as she

did so that Lord Ingraham was looking her way with another of his inscrutable expressions. "Oh, surely not," she whispered back.

Sir Reginald only gave her an arch look and inspected her bosom one more time. During the remove of fish, he managed to place his hand on her knee. Marian turned her little squeak of surprise into a cough, but not before Lord Ingraham looked her way again.

The men remained at table as Lady Ingraham led the female guests back into the parlor. The ladies separated into their own little circles of acquaintance, at leisure momentarily to dissect their neighbors who were not present, and laugh over the dresses of those in other cliques.

Marian sat by the door and wondered if any of them had ever possessed two thoughts to rub together at the same instance.

Lady Amanda strayed to the door several times, and Marian promptly engaged her in conversation. "La, it is hot in here," the beautiful lady proclaimed finally, interrupting Marian in midsentence. "I must go into the hall for a breath of air."

Marian rose. "And I shall accompany you," she said. "It is rather close in here, isn't it? I have long suspected that the fireplace does not draw well."

An expression closely resembling genuine irritation flitted briefly across Lady Amanda's face. "You needn't trouble yourself."

"It is no trouble," Marian declared, and followed her into the hall, which was empty except for Washburn, who bowed and nodded to the ladies and then opened the dining-room doors, almost as if on cue. Marian regarded him thoughtfully.

The men, smelling of cigars and brandy, entered the hall. Lord Ingraham smiled to Marian and blew Lady Amanda a kiss. He came quickly to his fiancée's side and appropriated her again, pulling her with him into the parlor again and then down to the ballroom, where Marian could see other guests assembling.

It was no surprise to the guests when Gilbert led his lady onto the floor for the first dance. No one raised any eyebrows when he kept her on the floor dance after dance, relinquishing her to no one, not even to her brother when Sir Reginald came to claim his sister for a mazurka. Lord Ingraham was constantly at her side, bestowing her with fleeting kisses, smiling deeply into her eyes.

Marian watched his graceful antics with growing appreciation, and the slowly enlarging realization that she was witnessing an adroit, professional performance. She continued to heartily wish Gilbert Ingraham to the devil, but a small light was beginning to burn somewhere back in her brain. What game he was playing, and so coolly too, still eluded her. It was enough to watch and wonder.

And then Sir Reginald claimed her for a country dance, lining up right behind his sister and Lord Ingraham. Twinkling her eyes at her escort, who was much more interested in his sister, Marian danced gracefully through the pattern with him, watchful even as she flirted.

They traded partners and Marian was claimed by Lord Ingraham. "Great double damn," he muttered in her ear as the Calnes danced, close together, down the line.

"Hush," Marian commanded, her eyes firmly fixed to Amanda's face.

Brother and sister came close again and then danced down the line. As Marian watched, she saw what she was looking for. Amanda Calne mouthed the word "library" to her brother.

Marian glanced up at Lord Ingraham. With a wicked twinkle in her eyes, she noted that he was admiring her bosom, too, even as Sir Reginald had done. "And now, my lord, I have a headache and am taking myself off. Good night."

He stared at her. "You cannot! I need you."

They came close together one last time before returning to their own partners. She looked him straight in the eye. "Trust me this time and let her go to the library," she whispered as she danced away at Sir Reginald's side.

Marian had no difficulty in shaking her escort. A few words about the heat, and he was off to the punch table. While his back was turned, she sidled out the door, gathered up her long skirt, and sprinted down the hall to the library, her finger to her lips as she raced past Washburn.

A low fire burned in the library, adding to the pleasant glow from the branches of candles about the room. She took it in at a glance as she ran about the room, blowing out candles, and then opening a window to whisk away the smell of just-extinguished wick. The room was nearly dark as she walked swiftly to a wing chair, pulled it deeper into the shadow, and sat down. She removed her pearls so they would not catch whatever light the fireplace afforded, grateful that her dress was deep blue and her hair black.

She waited.

Time passed slowly. A clock ticked somewhere in the room. Marian's eyes grew heavy, but she forced herself to remain alert. She invented games to keep herself awake. In the middle of one of them, the door opened. Marian leaned farther into the shadows, drawing up her knees. She sniffed and smelled Sir Reginald's cologne. Hiding herself very still, she waited. Let her go now, Gil, she thought, let her go. Trust me.

More time passed. The quartet changed to waltzes. Marian did not know where Sir Reginald had stationed himself in the room. For all she knew, he could have been sitting across from her, staring at her. The thought sent a prickle of fear down her back.

The door opened and Marian heard the rustle of silk.

"Reg."

"Here."

Marian let her breath out slowly and strained forward.

"Chase and Breckinridge, my dear," Lady Amanda said, and laughed deep in her throat. "Tuesday next, above one of the clock."

"You are certain?"

Lady Amanda giggled. "La, Reg, you think you are the only clever one in the family? He tells me whatever I ask. I have only to sit on his lap and tickle his ear. And you told me it would be difficult."

Reginald was silent. Marian heard a small click in the darkness, and Lady Amanda sucked in her breath. "Put that away, you fool."

Marian held her breath. After what seemed like years, she heard the click again and Sir Reginald's voice, silky soft. "Do not enjoy your work too much, m'dear."

"Oh, I do not, Reg. If I had to look at that scarface day after day, I would go distracted." She giggled again. "But, Reg, I do not notice it when it is dark."

Marian clenched her fists. She let out her breath slowly.

"It is dark now, sweetheart," said Sir Reginald, and he kissed his sister.

Marian sank back against her chair as the couple embraced in the flickering light of the fireplace. What monsters are these? she thought. Nausea swept her.

Lady Amanda ended the moment. "Reginald, you grow tiresome," she complained.

He only laughed. Marian's ears caught the smallest crackle of paper. "The next order, dearest," Calne whispered to his sister. "To these specifications. Go to Chartwell this time and ask for Fandamo. Go on, now."

There was a rustle of silk and then the door opened and closed.

Marian waited where she was, barely breathing, as the door opened and closed a second time. She relaxed in her chair, but waited for the quartet to play through one more country dance. She rose to her feet when the music ended, and started for the door.

A hand snaked out and grabbed her wrist. Her hand to her mouth, Marian whirled about and looked full into the smiling face of Sir Reginald Calne.

"I thought I heard a mouse," he said.

There was nothing to do but faint, so Marian wasted no time getting about it, slipping gracefully to the floor as Calne grabbed her about the waist and lifted her up. He deposited her on a sofa and sat down beside her. She waited a decent interval, hoping that she looked as pale as she felt, and then fluttered her eyes open.

The look of supreme skepticism on Sir Reginald's face made her falter. "Have you any idea how you startled me?" she said, and clutched his arm. He made no reply, so she tightened her grip. "I was feeling dizzy from the heat. I thought I would lie down here in the library. I must have fallen asleep."

He still made no reply, and Marian's heart began to sink. Sir Reginald stood up then and stared down at her for such a long moment that she had to fight the urge to leap up like a rabbit and run about the room, seeking a hole to hide in. The tears that sprang to her eyes were genuine.

She held her breath as he reached in his pocket and took out his knife. Watching her expression, Sir Reginald clicked it open and sat beside her again. He placed the blade against her throat as she remained absolutely motionless. He drew it slowly across her neck, rubbing the blade against her skin in a gesture almost caressing. Calne's face looked strangely sensual in the firelight. He might have been preparing to make love. The thought was more sickening than the feel of the knife at her neck.

"I do not believe a word you have said, m'dear," he purred. He kissed her lips and then clicked the knife shut against her flesh. "You are in bad company, and I do not mean only mine." He stood up then. "But you will say nothing or I will ruin your pretty face. I promise you that." He walked leisurely to the door and rested his hand on the knob. "And, my dear, you would be an even bigger fool to trust Lord Ingraham to look out for your interests above his own. He plays a deep game."

Marian closed her eyes. Her hand went to her throat. She lay there in the quiet and listened to the door open and close.

"Oh, you cannot leave," she said, and rushed into the hall. Washburn still stood there, his eyes on the library door. "Tell Lord Ingraham I must speak to him at once in here." She darted back into the library.

The door opened only moments later. "Well, brat?"

Marian sighed with relief and then drew in her breath. "Where is Lady Amanda?" she demanded.

"In close company with my mother and sister. Well?" he asked again, his impatience evident.

It was on the edge of her tongue to tell him what had just happened, but she remembered Calne's parting words and held her peace. " 'Chase and Breckinridge, Tuesday next, above one,' " she said, her voice toneless.

Lord Ingraham clapped his hands together and then grabbed Marian about the waist and whirled her around.

"Set me down," she ordered. "There is more."

He did as she said, suddenly all business. "And?"

"And he gave your lady dear a piece of paper. A small piece, from the sound of it."

"Where did she put it?"

Marian considered. "She was carrying no reticule in the ball-room. I am convinced she put it in the only place a woman would put it." Marian started for the door. "I suggest you check down the front of her dress, Lord Ingraham," she said, amazed at her coolness. "You can do that while she sits on your lap after all the guests have gone. Although in future, you might like to know that she prefers the darkness, or so she said."

"Marian," he murmured.

"And then you take that piece of information to the devil, Lord Ingraham. It is not too much for a spy to do. For that is what you are, is it not?"

"As was my father before me, God rest his soul. It seemed a worthy occupation in England's time of need."

"And you have set a trap for the Calnes, perhaps?"

Ingraham nodded, his eyes on her face. "Does this disgust you?" he asked quietly.

"As a matter of fact, it does."

"Even if I tell you that we now have proof that the Calnes have arranged the sale of cannon to Napoleon on Elba?"

"Even that. I despise double-dealing. I wonder, sir, what kind of a man would bed a woman like Lady Amanda for . . . information." She spit out the word and stalked to the door.

Lord Ingraham bowed his head, but said nothing.

She was in the hall before she remembered. She opened the door again. "There is one thing more, Lord Ingraham," she said formally.

"You have said enough."

"No, I have not," she flared. "I wouldn't dream of depriving you of every particle of information you've obviously worked so hard day and night to get."

"Marian!"

" 'Go to Chartwell this time and ask for Fandamo.' "

Gilbert sprang up from his perch on the arm of the sofa. "Good God! You are sure?" He grabbed Marian by the arm and shook her. "Make no mistake!"

She nodded and jerked her arm from his grasp.

Lord Ingraham beat her to the door, then whirled around, grabbed her by the shoulders, and kissed her soundly on the mouth. He was gone before she had time to take another breath.

She stepped to the open door. After a few hurried words to the butler, Lord Ingraham ran out the front door. Washburn went into the ballroom and returned in a few moments with one of the dark-eyed emigrees. As she watched in amazement, the butler calmly bent the man's arm up behind his back and held him there until two officers came quickly from the ballroom and led him away.

When the men left the house, Washburn clapped his hands together in a triumphant gesture, smoothed his hair, and rocked back and forth on his heels in evident satisfaction. He noticed Marian staring at him from the library door and coughed discreetly.

"Signore Fandamo of the Chartwell Foundry suddenly remembered a prior engagement, Miss Wynswich," he said, not blinking an eye. "I trust the officers will hurry him to his destination."

Marian opened her mouth to speak, and he put a finger to his lips. "Not a word to Lady Ingraham," he asked in kindly tones. "She hasn't a clue."

Marian stood where she was a moment longer and then squared her shoulders and started for the stairs.

Washburn coughed again. "Miss Wynswich, do you not return to the ballroom?"

"No, Washburn. I think I have not the stomach for it, for all that I am such a game goer. Do me a favor, if you will."

He bowed.

"When Alistair arrives with Surtees from Hammerfield, tell my brother that we will leave early in the morning. The roads are clear; there is nothing to keep us here."

He bowed again. "May I speak for myself and the other servants?"

"Please do."

"We will miss you both."

"It's nice to be missed," she replied, and her voice faltered.

Her room had never looked more welcome. With a long, shuddering sigh, Marian locked the door and piled more coals on the fire. As the room grew warmer, she undressed quickly, pulled on her nightgown, and hopped into bed. Her body sank gratefully into the mattress. Marian closed her eyes and waited for sleep to overtake her as she listened to the music downstairs.

It must have been the last dance. Her eyes drowsy, Marian heard the comfortable sounds that departing guests made as they assembled in the hall, talking with one another and waiting for their carriages. Well, Gil, she thought, soon you will have your lady-love all to yourself, and you can abstract her bit of information. I hope you choke on it. She made herself comfortable as the house quieted down.

Lady Ingraham said good night to her son and his fiancée and climbed the stairs. Her footsteps hesitated for a moment outside Marian's door, but she did not knock. I don't know what I will say to her tomorrow, Marian thought, she who has been so kind to me. We will just leave and soon she will forget all about her foolish guests from Devon.

She closed her eyes again and snuggled into the pillow, and then the quarrel began.

The voices were distinct, the words indistinct, but she knew them to be Lord Ingraham and Lady Amanda. Marian plopped her pillow over her head. The voices grew louder, and Marian sat up in bed. She heard the sound of breaking glass, as though someone had thrown a vase. Lord Ingraham spoke, and his words had a certain crispness to them. Lady Amanda screamed, and then the house was silent.

Good God, Marian thought, and crept to the door. She debated whether to go downstairs and then firmly overruled that notion. I will do no such thing, she told herself firmly. This is not, and never was, my business. She touched her neck, running her finger across her throat, imagining that she could follow the track of Sir Reginald's knife. I have probably already said too much.

She went to get back in bed when she heard the sound of a carriage drawing up to the front of the house. Marian hurried to the window and looked down. Two soldiers stood at attention. She watched, openmouthed, as Lady Amanda Calne was escorted to the carriage by Lord Ingraham. The butler dropped her traveling bags about her and stepped back in surprise as Lady Amanda delivered a stinging slap to Lord Ingraham's scarred cheek.

Marian winced and stepped back involuntarily herself, as though she had been struck. "Wretched woman," she said through gritted teeth. "I hope they hang you."

The carriage pulled away. Ingraham stood there, his hand to his face, until the carriage rounded the crescent and disappeared from sight. After another moment, he turned and walked slowly inside.

The fire had died down and Marian shivered. She rubbed her arms and climbed back in bed. "I will go to sleep," she told herself. "I will go to sleep."

It may have been hours, it may have been minutes, but Marian woke to the sound of someone fumbling at her door. Her blood froze to ice and began to flow in chunks through her veins. "Alistair?" she whispered.

"No, brat. Let me in."

"Not if you were the last man alive, Gilbert Ingraham," she said even as she got out of bed and tiptoed to the door.

The door handle turned more violently. "You let me in, Marian Wynswich, or I am going to put a shoulder to this door and rip it out by the frame."

The tone of his voice left her no doubt that he would carry out his threat precisely. Her heart in her throat, Marian turned the key in the lock and stepped back out of his way.

He was still dressed in his evening clothes, but his shirt front was splotched with drying blood. Marian gaped at him.

"It's not mine," he said shortly. "In case you're interested."

She made no comment, but climbed back in her bed, pulling up the covers to her armpits. As she watched, the earl went to the dressing table and picked up the water jug, drinking directly from it. He came over to the bed. "Move your feet," he directed, and sat down, slumping forward with his elbows on his knees. The imprint of Lady Amanda's hand still showed quite clearly on the sensitive skin around his scar. Any words of recrimination she had been saving to fling at him died in her throat.

He finally looked at her. "Happy New Year."

"Oh. Gil!"

Wearily he reached into his vest pocket and pulled out a scrap of paper, flicking it toward her. "It was exactly where you said it was, Marian."

She picked up the paper, which was crossed and recrossed with strange words and numbers. "I do not understand," she said, and handed it back to him.

He pocketed the paper. "It's an exact count of all Allied troops currently stationed in Belgium and France—information bound for Elba. It was Amanda's happy task to see that message through, although how she expected to do that, I haven't a clue." He sighed. "I think Napoleon is planning, and soon, to shake the dust of Elba from his boots." Lord Ingraham ran his hands through his hair and looked down at his own shoes.

"But you have Sir Reginald in custody now, don't you?" she asked. "And that other man? Signore Fandamo?"

He sighed again and lay down at the foot of her bed. "I do—or, I did, except that Bath's jails are full of revelers tonight, and the constabulary thought to economize and put Sir Reginald with Signore Fandamo."

Marian leaned forward and clasped her arms around her knees. "Let me guess. Out of pure meanness, Sir Reginald slipped a little sliver knife with embossed flowers around the unfortunate signore's neck."

Gilbert gave a dry chuckle. "Your aim is off, my dear. He tucked it up tight under Fandamo's rib cage, so he would die slowly." With an oath, Lord Ingraham sat up and grabbed her by the arm. "And how do you know what that knife looks like?"

Marian gently pulled away. "He slid it across my throat in the library this evening."

"God in heaven, Marian, why didn't you say something to me?" he shouted.

She rose to her knees and grasped him by the shoulders, shaking him. "Because it wouldn't have made a penny's worth of difference to you, that's why!" Marian sat back, stunned by the look in his eyes. "And don't tell me that was uncalled-for, Lord Ingraham," she said quietly. "You're as ruthless as they, in your own way, and it's time someone told you."

He regarded her for a long time, and her glance did not waiver. "Check," he said finally, his voice serious.

"And mate," she replied. "Good night, Lord Ingraham."

He did not get up. "I won't deprive you of the rest of the story. Fandamo is dead. He died not twenty minutes ago in my arms, in fact. He worked at the Chartwell Foundry and for Napoleon, too. He told me the names of his associates, and I can now assure Regent and country that there will be no more cannon coming from that place that goes astray. I have already sent word to Chase and Breckinridge Foundry that we will be waiting there Tuesday next. I have shipped Lady Amanda under guard to her father's estate in Derbyshire and—"

"And what makes you think she will remain there?"

"A bit of plain speaking on my part, my dear," he replied. "I told her that unless she wants to spend the rest of her days picking lice out of her hair in Newgate, she would remain there. We don't, as a rule, hang women like that in Britain, although God knows we ought."

Marian said nothing. Gilbert hesitated and then reached for her in the dark. He touched her leg, but she did not pull away. His voice was calmer then, quieter. "Sir Reginald is on the loose now, and I suspect he would like to sever any links between my windpipe and my lights."

"Dear God," Marian breathed.

He patted her leg and rose. "And so you and your brother— who, by the way, has already expressed his regrets at missing this evening's festivities—will be off to Picton in the morning."

"We were leaving then, anyway," she said. "I can either spout my pearls or borrow money from you, Lord Ingraham."

"You needn't do either, Marian. My chaise and four will take you there." He chuckled, but with little evidence of humor in his voice. "Likely it won't be an exciting ride, but I am out of novel ideas to entertain anyone."

He went to the door.

"Tell me one thing more," Marian asked. "Why? Why would Lady Amanda do such a thing?"

He shrugged and leaned against the door. "Boredom, I suppose. Now, Reg was always under the hatches, and I'm sure he enlisted her services because he was desperate for the money." Lord Ingraham looked at her, as if wondering if he should speak. "You may have noticed that Reg commands a certain, ah, hold, over his sister that is a trifle aberrant, shall we say?"

She nodded, grateful the dark hid her blush. "But, tell me, did you plan this whole thing?"

He came back to stand at the foot of the bed. "God, no. I have no life of my own. I had tried earlier to convince Amanda to dance to my tune, but nothing came of it. It was all planned for me in London. Remember that letter I received on Christmas Day?"

"I do."

"They directed me to woo her and bed her and wed her if I had to, in order to dry up this source of ordnance traveling out of England. It only took an amazingly vulgar ring to do all that." He laughed softly. "Would you ever wear a ring like that, Marian?"

"I'd as lief paste a ruby in my navel and move to a harem," she retorted.

"Even if I gave you a ring like that? A real one this time?"

Marian sat back and pulled the covers close around her. "I think not, Gil," she said, choosing her words as carefully as she could. "It would not be a good idea."

He leaned against the bedpost. "I had planned to wrap this up right and tight tonight with the Calnes, explain it all to you in the morning, and propose marriage over breakfast. I have noted that you are particularly receptive over meals." He was silent then, as if expecting a comment from her. When she said nothing, he continued awkwardly. "I realize this is hardly the time and most assuredly not the place, but will you marry me?"

Marian wished she could see him clearly in the darkness, and then was grateful that he was just an outline. Her thoughts tumbled about in her head. Only a day ago, I would have given the earth to hear those words. "I think not," she repeated.

He chose his words just as carefully. "But I think—correct me if I am wrong—I think that you love me as much as I love you. May I ask why not, then?"

"It goes without saying that I am too young," she began. "Imagine what people would think."

"During my drive to London, I had ample time to consider that obstacle, but it did not deter me. So what if people talk? You're worth it."

"It is more than that, my lord," she said, her voice filled with an unexpected dignity that surprised her, even as it gave her the heart to speak. "Oh, Gil! Papa would put it in horse language. He would say, 'Marian, you're just not up to his weight.' And I am not, Gil. The game you play is too deep for me." She felt her eyes filling with tears, and she brushed her hand across them. "I couldn't stand the agony of kissing you good-bye in the morning and then wondering all day if I would ever see you alive again."

"Marian, do you realize what you are saying?"

She held up her hands to ward him off. "I do! We Wynswiches are wild, Gil, but we don't even begin to approach your standards. My answer is no."

He went to the door. "I'll see you off in the morning . . . brat." The word lingered on his tongue like a lover's touch.

"Good-bye, Gil."

15

Packing took only a matter of minutes the next morning. Purposely keeping her brain empty of all thought, Marian tossed her bandbox on the bed, stuffed in her nightgown and slippers, and added the two dresses Lady Ingraham had given her. She paused over the blue gown, fingering the expensive fabric, thinking at first that she would leave it, but reconsidering. Such an action would cause Lady Ingraham undue pain. Marian folded it carefully and placed it on top in the bandbox.

She set the bandbox by the open door and then went to the window for one last look at the Royal Crescent, imagining it in spring, when the leaves were lime green and nursemaids would bundle up their charges and push prams up and down its wide expanse.

"It's a beautiful view, isn't it?"

Marian looked around in surprise. "I didn't hear you," she said to Lord Ingraham, who filled the doorway.

He came to the window and stood close to her, making no move to touch her. "I used to admire the view from here, too. I don't think there is a prettier town prospect in all of England." He handed her a letter. "This came earlier from Picton."

She opened the envelope with a hairpin and read it while the earl continued to gaze out the window, his hands clasped behind his back. He finally glanced in her direction and frowned.

"Not bad news, I hope?"

Marian shook herself out of the gray mood that was settling

229

rapidly. "No, no, I think not," she said, striving to keep her voice light. "See here, Percy announces that he is being posted soon to Vienna for the talks."

"That is a definite step forward," Gilbert said. "Did he say what position?"

"Aide to Lord Trask."

"Excellent fellow!" Gilbert's eyes stayed fixed on her. "But is there more? Marian, what's the matter?"

She roused herself again. "It is nothing, I suppose. I mean, we all knew it would have to happen. But so soon . . ." Marian took a deep breath. "Covenden Hall has been sold. The new owner will take possession in April."

"I am sorry."

"No need to be," she said brightly. "Percy says the new owner paid a wonderful price. It will see us all out of debt, Mama taken care of, and leave enough left over for Ariadne's bridal clothes."

The earl possessed himself of Marian's hands. "And what about Marian Wynswich?"

She shook her head. "If you don't expect much, my lord, then you are seldom disappointed. I will manage."

He squeezed her hands. "Of that, I have no doubt."

Marian gently disengaged herself. "Percy writes that the agent was not at liberty to tell us who the new owner is. Look here," she said, pointing to Percy's neat writing. " 'I expect, and Mama is certain, that he is a mushroom from the City. If only he will maintain this fine old place, I suppose that will make it right.' "

She lapsed into silence and walked thoughtfully to the window again before remembering herself. "Well, my lord, do you come for my bandbox?"

"I do. And Washburn has orchestrated a mighty breakfast for you. He has little faith in posting houses, and every confidence in your appetite."

Marian smiled, because it was expected of her, and started for the door.

Lord Ingraham collected her bandbox and followed. "Wait, Marian."

She stopped, but did not look around.

"About last night . . . Say nothing to my mother. She does not know about my second career."

"Certainly, my lord. Not a word."

Alistair had already tucked himself into breakfast when they reached the breakfast room. "Mare! You look a bit down-pin this morning," he greeted her.

Marian made a face at him and seated herself. "Alistair, you are a scamp."

He put down his knife and fork. "If I am a scamp, you are a decided slow-top! Lord Ingraham tells me that you slept through all the excitement last night, and I missed it."

She smiled. "It appears your Wynswich luck has run out, Alistair."

Washburn poured Marian's tea. She beamed up at him. "Washburn, you are much too polite to say anything about my appetite, aren't you?" Marian teased.

The butler permitted himself the excess of raising one eyebrow. "Miss Wynswich, I would never—"

"Well, then, stand back, sir, for I have a prodigious hunger this morning." She matched deed to word and proceeded to fill her plate while Washburn betrayed not a whisker of emotion and Lord Ingraham looked on in amusement, his arms folded across his chest. Alistair grinned and speared several slices of bacon from Marian's plate as she ate.

Lady Ingraham entered the room then, and Washburn set one baked egg in front of her. Lord Ingraham consulted his pocket watch. "If it should chance to snow again, I recommend that you put up at the St. George in Clareton. Or you may elect to drive straight through to Picton. My coachman will do as you wish."

"Damn!" Alistair threw down his napkin and turned to Marian. "Beg pardon."

"Beg Lady Ingraham's pardon," Marian scolded. "What is the matter?"

"I left my overcoat at Hammerfield, Mare! Surtees had me rigged out last night in his fancy evening clothes and opera cape, and we never thought about it."

"And I missed this display?" Marian asked, rolling her eyes.
"Now, what will you do?"

Lord Ingraham spoke up. "Alistair, you may borrow my
overcoat. It is upstairs. Come, lad."

"Oh, I should not," Alistair said.

"I have another here." He glanced at Marian. "Perhaps I
can come for it in a few days, when business permits."

Marian would not look at him.

Ingraham sighed heavily. "Or perhaps if you just bring it back
here before the term starts at St. Stephen's."

They left the room together, and Lady Ingraham set down
her teacup. She nodded to the butler, and he withdrew. Lady
Ingraham got to her feet quickly and turned the key in the lock.
Marian looked up in surprise, and Lady Ingraham laughed
softly.

"I do not mean to keep you here against your will, child.
I merely do not wish to be disturbed for a few moments." She
sat down next to Marian and took her hand. "I suppose Gilbert
has told you a farradiddle tale that I do not know—or even suspect—what he is involved in."

Marian stared. "He said . . . he said . . ."

"And I suppose he also told you that I had no notion that
his father was involved in spying and that I still remain blissfully
in the dark?"

"I . . . I did wonder how it could be so."

"It was not so," Lady Ingraham burst out, her voice low but
intense. "And I know how he died in Europe." Her grip on
Marian's hand tightened painfully. "I do not wish this for my
son."

Tears sprang into Marian's eyes. "Oh, Lady Ingraham, I do
not wish it either. What am I to do?"

Lady Ingraham released Marian's hand and sat back in her
chair. "My son loves you."

"I will not marry him."

"Good for you, my dear," said Lady Ingraham decisively.
"And do not look so startled! Did you think I locked you in
here to change your mind? I will not do that. Indeed, I do not
think I could, even though Gilbert admitted that his wooing had

gone aground and begged me early this morning to try. But I will not."

Marian put her hands over her eyes until she gained control of herself again.

Lady Ingraham stood behind her chair and kissed the top of her head. "If you thought there was some way to stop him in his dreadful career, I would beg you to try." She made a dismissing motion with her hand. "I do not know how to help him, but perhaps you can."

Marian was silent as Lady Ingraham rested her hands on her shoulders. "No, I'll not encourage any woman to suffer as I did." She patted Marian. "Although when you brought my son to me on Christmas Eve, I did begin to think that one of my fondest dreams would be realized."

"That he would be married?"

"It is more than that. I have always nourished the hope that Gilbert would marry someone smarter than he is. It could only rebound to his benefit." She sighed. "You may be the only woman I have met thus far who would have done. Good-bye, my dear, dear child. And do come see me this summer."

They embraced, and Lady Ingraham unlocked the door, laughing softly to herself. "And Washburn . . . he is the worst of the lot! He was as deep in the game as my husband, and followed him everywhere. I have no secrets in this house." She kissed Marian. "I'm off upstairs. I do so dislike good-byes."

"I, too, my lady," Marian said softly.

Alistair came down the stairs in Lord Ingraham's overcoat. "Look, Mare. He said I should have the beaver hat to match the coat. This is quite a rig-out, my lord."

"Of course! I cut a fine figure in Ghent. I hear the carriage in front. Shall we?"

"By all means," Marian said. Don't touch me, Gil, she thought wildly, or I shall wail and mourn, or throw myself into your arms and not leave this place. And that would be the worst thing of all.

They went to the hallway and the butler opened the door. Marian breathed deeply of the morning air. "What a beautiful day!" she exclaimed, and sniffed the air. "Do you know

Alistair, I believe you can almost smell the sea air from here.''

She started down the steps, but Lord Ingraham grabbed her by the hand and pulled her back into the hallway. "I hate good-byes, too," he declared. "Kiss me, Marian."

Without question she raised her face to his, threw her arms around his neck, and kissed him full on the mouth.

He grabbed her around the waist and held her close, kissing her over and over until she finally put her hands against his chest and pushed. He released her then.

"Mind who you kiss like that, Marian," he said breathlessly. "They could get ideas. *Bon voyage*, brat."

Marian ran down the steps and into the carriage. "Oh, don't just stand there, Alistair," she pleaded as her tears began to fall.

"Catch, Alistair," Lord Ingraham commanded. Marian's pearls flew through the air as Alistair made a one-handed retrieve and swung himself into the carriage. "Your sister can't seem to keep these around her neck, lad. Better not trust her with anything valuable."

Bath flew by in a blur as Marian wept. In disgust, Alistair dug deep into Lord Ingraham's overcoat and pulled out a handkerchief.

She took it, put her face in it, and cried harder; the handkerchief smelled like Gilbert Ingraham.

"Mare, there was a time when you weren't quite so missish," he grumbled before he closed his eyes.

Lord Ingraham's well-sprung coach was certainly an improvement over the mail coach, Marian decided after several miles. She wiped her eyes and tucked the handkerchief, vowing to wash it and keep it. And someday, when I am married with children of my own and they demand a bedtime story, I will tell them about the Christmas when I was sixteen. If they laugh and think that I am bamming them, I will take out the handkerchief with its monogram, and they will not think I have made it up entirely.

They stopped at noon in Glidewell Common, where they were shown every courtesy.

"Mare, we should travel like this all the time," Alistair whispered to her as they prepared to continue their journey. "All it takes is an earl's crest on the door."

The coachman swung himself into the seat again, but they did not move. Alistair finally tapped impatiently and stuck his head out the door. "I say, we could be in Picton by late evening."

The coachman heaved himself out of the box and opened the door. "Begging your pardon, Mr. Wynswich, but I am puzzling about something."

"Eh?"

"It seems to me that we are being followed."

Alistair laughed. "Now, who would ever follow us?" he asked. "You cannot be serious."

The coachman tugged at his cap. "All the same, sir, I think I'll try a back road, and just see if I am right. I know several in the area, and they are only a small distance from the main road. We'll not lose any time."

They started off. Marian wrapped her cloak about her and lay down on the seat. Alistair looked around him with some interest, occasionally glancing back where they had come. After a short while on the back road, he prodded Marian with his boot.

"Awake?"

Marian opened her eyes. "I am now," she said pointedly.

"Mare, I think there may be something to what the coachman said," he stated almost casually. "I see three horsemen through the trees. They don't move any closer to us, but they are following."

She sat up in a hurry and looked where he pointed. "Surely not," she whispered as if the horsemen could hear her. "Why would anyone do that?"

Alistair was silent a long moment. "You know, Marian," he said slowly, "I think it is the crest on the door. Someone knows this is Lord Ingraham's carriage."

Marian shivered as a prickle of fear teased the length of her backbone. "Don't you think we would be better-off on the main road, where there are other travelers?"

"My thought precisely," he said, and opened the coach door, leaning out. "Coachman! Get us back to the main road, and be fast about it!"

"Right, sir. I see a turning place just ahead."

They slowed and stopped. Marian peeked out the window and

saw the horsemen. One, two, three, she counted through the trees. "Oh, I don't like this," she said in a tiny voice.

"No more do I," her brother agreed. "I think that Lord Ingraham has more enemies than even he knows about."

"Oh, God," Marian gasped, "and look at you in his clothes." She stared at her brother, dressed so impeccably in Ingraham's overcoat and hat. She stared out the window again at the riders and then sagged back against the cushions, her eyes wide with terror.

Alistair shook her. "You know who they are?"

She nodded. "Reginald Calne. And he swore only last night to kill Lord Ingraham." She looked down at the floor, unable to bear the horror in Alistair's eyes. "And me, too, if I spoke."

"And here we sit in his carriage." Alistair glanced down at Lord Ingraham's clothes and slowly removed the beaver hat. "I do believe the Wynswich luck has run out, Mare." He started to take off the overcoat and then reconsidered. He stared at his sister for the briefest moment, as if measuring her very spirit and soul. He grabbed her hand. "Marian, sit down on the floor," he said quietly.

It was a voice of authority she had never heard from her little brother before. Without a word, she slid to the floor.

"Lie flat and put your hands over your head, there's a good old thing," he said, and crouched beside her as a pistol ball shattered the window on the side of the coach where he had been sitting only seconds before. The glass rained down on them in a brittle shower. Marian watched as Alistair coolly grabbed a hunk of glass. "Give me that handkerchief."

She handed him Lord Ingraham's handkerchief. He wrapped it about the end of the shard and handed it to her. "Sir Reginald means to part my hair," he whispered grimly as he clung to Marian. "But I'm damned if he'll touch you."

Shouting to his horses, the coachman attempted to turn around in the narrow lane, left muddy by the melting snow. The horses panted and struggled, and the wheels wedged themselves in deeper.

With an oath of his own, the footman leapt from the box to free the wheels. As he struggled around to the back wheel, another shot split the air, and he fell without a sound, facedown in the mud.

"Coachman, get down, and be very fast about it," said a familiar voice through the trees.

Without a word, the coachman swung himself from the box and edged toward the coach door, his hands raised high above his head.

"Coachman, damn you for this," Alistair said in a voice Marian had never heard before. "You're endangering an innocent woman."

Reginald Calne rode onto the lane, a pistol in his hand. He spoke in French to the rider beside him, who dismounted. Another gesture, and the Frenchman pinioned the coachman's arms behind his back. Calne grinned and nodded, as he kissed his hand to the coachman. "Night, night, sleep tight!"

Without a word, and with only a fleeting backward glance at Lord Ingraham's carriage, the coachman was dragged farther into the woods. In another moment, a single shot rang out.

Alistair let out the breath he had been holding. "God, Marian, this man is ruthless."

"I know," she said through dry lips. "Alistair, he will do worse to me."

Alistair squeezed her arm. "Not if I can help it, sister." He stretched out next to Marian and whispered in her ear. "I'm going to open the door and step out."

"No, Alistair," she whispered.

"And when I do, I'll close it behind me," he continued. "Now, hush! As soon as I do that, you open the other door, slide out, and start running. The carriage will be between you and them. Run into that field. There is a fence, and it may be too muddy for them to jump it. You're not far from the main road. Run and wave your arms about. Lord knows I never could catch you when you had a head start."

"Alistair, no," she pleaded.

"Mare, I—"

"Lord Ingraham, do come out," Sir Reginald called. "I have something particular to say to you."

"Very well, Reg," Alistair called in a creditable imitation

of Lord Ingraham's Wiltshire drawl. He rose to his knees and looked down at his sister. "Marian, I never told you this, but I love you. I'm sorry I wasn't a better brother."

Marian grabbed his hand and kissed it, resting her cheek for a moment against his arm. She took off her cloak, grasped the window glass, and edged for the door.

"Oh, do come on, Gilbert," Sir Reginald said. "See, now, I have dismounted. I really do want to look at you eye to eye, anyway."

"Ready?" whispered Alistair.

Marian nodded.

Her brother took a deep breath and opened the door, kicking down the step and standing on it, but not descending. His broad shoulders covered the door window, blocking Sir Reginald's view of the interior.

"You're not—" Calne began.

"No," interrupted Alistair, "but I will do."

Marian opened the door and slid onto the road. She looked at the fence only yards away, deciding whether to go over or under. She started to run, gathering her skirts about her, holding them high above the mud so they would not drag her down. She slid down the little swale at the road's edge and was under the fence before the Frenchman still on horseback shouted and spurred his horse toward the fence.

As she ran, floundering through the mud and into the snow that still deepened the meadow, Marian heard one shot. "Damn you, Reginald Calne," she cried, and glanced over her shoulder. The sight made her redouble her efforts.

The Frenchman had attempted the fence. His horse lay screaming, this side of it, forelegs twisted at an impossible angle. The other Frenchman crawled through the fence, shouting at her. Above it all, she heard Sir Reginald's laughter. It started on a high-pitched note and seemed to rise up a madman's musical scale.

"Marian Wynswich," he called. "Oh, Marian!" He threw himself at the fence and was running toward her across the muddy meadow, skimming low across the ground in his black cloak like a bird of prey.

I will not look back, I will not look back, she told herself
over and over as she ran toward the highway. She expected at
any moment to feel a knife come to rest between her shoulder
blades, but then she knew he would never do that. Sir Reginald
Calne would punish her especially. She closed her eyes for an
instant, wondering if Alistair still suffered.

Her breath came in gasps as she looked toward the road. It
seemed to come up so slowly, as if she ran toward it on
enormous legs, in the middle of a nightmare. As she watched
the road and struggled through the field, she saw a coach.

It was a mail coach, large and lumbering. "Thank you, God,"
she gasped, and started to wave her arm. She ran through a
herd of dairy cows grazing in the muddy winter grass, hoping
that they would slow down Sir Reginald, or at least attract the
attention of the coach driver. She ran on, her lungs burning,
her side shooting out pains.

Another moment, and the fence stretched before her. Without
a second's hesitation, Marian slid underneath it, scrambled to
her feet again, and ran shrieking intot he road. A crofter,
pitchfork in hand, stood before his barn on the distant side of
the road. He seemed frozen there, staring at her. Her heart sank
as she knew she would never reach him before Sir Reginald
was upon her. She cast her whole attention on the mail coach.

"Help me," she screamed as Reginald gained the high road
and grabbed the back of her dress.

Her face streaked with tears, she tugged against him. He
grabbed her leg, digging in with his fingernails, and she
remembered the broken glass in her pocket. She wrenched it
out and dragged it down his arm, even as it cut into her palm.
She raked it over his arm again and again, her breath coming
in animal gasps, until he let go, screaming unspeakable
obscenities at her.

Blood streaming from her hand, Marian leapt to her feet again
and saw the crofter running toward her now, waving his arms.

"No, you don't," Sir Reginald shouted, and lunged for her
again.

Too exhausted to scream, Marian dodged him and imped
down the highway toward the mail coach, which to her eye was

coming faster now, even as the driver whipped the team and shouted to them.

As she staggered along the highway, her bloody hand clasped to her aching side, Sir Reginald made another lunge at her legs and pulled her to her knees. As she struggled under his weight, he grabbed her hair in a painful handful and jerked her neck back. She looked up to see his other hand high above his head, the knife in it open. She closed her eyes.

The mail coach careened by. Marian heard the sound of wheels jamming and the shouts of the passengers inside. She waited for the knife to fall.

And waited.

Marian crouched lower on the highway and watched the coach skid across the highway as the brakes locked. She lay there another moment before she realized that Reginald no longer held her hair. She raised up slowly, cautiously, and looked about her, the glass still clutched in her dripping hand.

Sir Reginald Calne was gone. Marian looked back at the fence. The Frenchman was pinned there by the crofter. She raised herself to her knees, gasped, and fell back again.

Sir Reginald lay under the wheels, his head wrapped about in the coachman's whip. His hand still opened and closed convulsively around his knife. He mouthed something to her and tried to inch himself forward.

Marian stared in horrified fascination, and her fingers went to her mouth.

The coachman jumped down and ran to her. She threw herself into his arms, sobbing and trying to bury her face in his greatcoat. The man put a meaty hand over her head and covered her eyes as Sir Reginald shivered and drifted sideways like a crab and died.

"Little lady, are you all right?"

Startled, Marian opened her eyes. She clutched at the overcoat and stared up into the coachman's face. Her face broke into a smile, even as the tears streamed down her muddy cheeks. "Jeremy Towser?" she asked, her voice doubtful. "Jeremy?"

"The same." He waggled his finger at her even as he held her close. "I told you there were rough numbers in this world, miss.'' He looked down at her. "And why aren't ye in Bath with your mother and long-lost brother? And where is that other one?''

Marian started then, tearing herself from his grasp. "Alistair,'' she screamed, and started running toward the fence again.

Towser grabbed her and held her tight. "Wait a minute, miss! You're in no condition—''

"My brother,'' she gasped, struggling to free herself from the coachman. "Oh, please! He is across the field.'' She looked at Sir Reginald. "And he is a spy. And that man there also. Please, is there a constable nearby?''

"I'll send me second boy on with the coach. We're not far from Clareton.'' Towser called up to two passengers who sat, gaping, on the roof. "Hop down, lads, and help us.''

Marian stood by the side of the road as the men pulled the body of Sir Reginald out from under the coach wheels and laid him by the Frenchman, who was now sitting bound and tied to the fence.

"Send back a constable,'' Towser ordered as he waved on the mail coach and turned to Marian. "These two lads and I will see you across the field. Your brother, you say? The younger one?''

She nodded, suddenly too tired to speak.

Towser took her by the hand, gently working the piece of glass out of her fist. They started back across the field. Halfway across she fainted; Towser picked her up without losing a step and carried her the rest of the way.

Marian was conscious when they came to the fence. "I can't imagine what made me do that,'' she apologized, her face bright red with embarrassment. "You can put me down. I'll not do it again.''

Towser ignored her. He handed her across the fence to one of the men from the mail coach, who set her on her feet, keeping a careful arm about her. She took several deep breaths until her head cleared. There was no movement or sound about the carriage. She started to cry.

"Mare!''

It was not Alistair's voice, and yet, it was. She raised her head from Jeremy Towser's shoulder. "Alistair?" she called, her voice scarcely louder than a whisper. She limped toward the carriage as Towser patted Lord Ingraham's horses into calm.

Alistair lay stretched out on the ground, his head resting in the footman's lap.

Openmouthed, Marian stared from one to the other. She felt herself growing faint again, so she sank to the ground.

Blood dripped down the front of the earl's beautiful overcoat, but Alistair smiled at her. "Mare, close your mouth," he managed to say.

"But . . . but . . ." she stuttered. "And the footman. But you were dead!"

The footman grinned. "Naw, miss. I think I sprained my ankle when I fell, but it'll likely heal."

"But we saw you die."

He grinned wider. "Pardon me, but you saw me dive in the mud. Seemed like a good place to stay until the shooting stopped."

"And he shifted the back wheel just as Reginald fired," said Alistair. "Which is why I have a hole in my shoulder instead of my throat, Mare. Quit staring like that. I could use a hand up."

"Certainly," Marian said faintly, and reached for him.

His eyes fixed on her hand. "Oh, Mare! I didn't mean for that to happen."

She shook her head and looked down at her hand, which was only now beginning to throb. "Never mind. That glass kept me alive long enough for Jeremy to come up."

Marian sat where she was and let Jeremy Towser drape Alistair across her lap. Her arms went around her brother and she placed her good hand tightly over the wound in his shoulder. "Think what a conversation piece you will be at St. Stephen's," she said as she held him close.

Alistair's eyes were closing. "Mare, don't be silly. I think I would like to go home now."

"And so you shall," she said softly, smoothing the hair out of his face and succeeding in smearing more blood around them both. "I can hock my pearls, and maybe we can talk Mr. Towser into a ride on the mail."

The other passenger from the mail coach tramped farther into the woods on the footman's direction, and crouched by Lord Ingraham's coachman. He shook his head and pointed to a spot right between his eyes.

Marian shuddered and hugged Alistair.

Towser helped the footman away from the wheel, and the able-bodied men pushed the carriage out of the mud and onto the road. The coachman climbed into the box and turned the horses about. "Get the footman in, lads," he called down. "And be careful there with that young lad. Lady—Marian, is it?—you can let go. He won't disappear." Towser laughed out loud. "I think he may have nine lives. Maybe you do, too."

"We do," said Alistair. "It's the Wynswich luck. Mr. Towser." He sighed peacefully and then fainted as the men hauled him into the coach.

They left one of the mail-coach passengers by the side of the road to direct the constable to the body of Lord Ingraham's coachman. The Frenchman whose horse had been crammed at the fence had disappeared.

Towser quickly got the feel of the horses and guided the carriage slowly toward Glidewell Common, the town the Wynswiches had passed no more than an hour ago. But it seemed leagues and leagues away to Marian. Alistair drifted in and out of consciousness, but his face was calm.

"I owe you my life, brother," Marian said to him during one of his moments of lucidity. "You were quite ready to die for me."

He only smiled at her. "Oh, Mare, don't be missish. Besides, sister, if it comes down to that, you'd have done the same for me. I know it."

She touched his face. "How is it that you knew what to do?"

"I just guessed. When the riders started following us, I guess I knew then what was going on." He squeezed her hand. "You're not the only smart Wynswich."

"No, I am not," she agreed. "And lately I think I am the most foolish one of all."

Alistair started to speak, and Marian put her fingers over his lips. "Hush, now. We have a mountain of explaining to do when we get to Glidewell."

While the doctor slapped a hasty bandage on her hand and then took charge of Alistair, Marian explained the whole story to the constable, whose skepticism turned to shock and great anger as she told of spies and secrets and Napoleon.

"You need only verify this with Lord Gilbert Ingraham, who resides in Bath," she concluded.

"I know of him, Miss Wynswich," the constable said. "If you'll sign this statement we have taken down, we'll see that you return to Bath with it."

Her chin came up. "I'll sign your statement," she said quietly, "but I am hoping Jeremy Towser will consent to help us toward Picton instead."

The constable rubbed his chin. "I don't know, miss."

Marian began to cry. "I just want to go home." She dabbed at her eyes and then sobbed in good earnest, to the extreme uneasiness of the constable.

Towser came to her rescue. "I think Jeremy Towser can accommodate you, miss, provided Alistair is fit enough." He turned to the constable. "I suggest that you bundle the bodies and the footman into Lord Ingraham's carriage and drive that back to Bath."

The doctor was not difficult to persuade. While the inn-keeper's wife cleaned up Alistair and tucked him in a nightshirt belonging to her husband, Marian changed into another dress from her bandbox. Her hair was a hopeless mess, but she tugged out enough of the snarls, twigs, and bits of rock from the road and braided the rest. She let the doctor swab iodine onto her skinned knees and help her into her boots again, promising that she would have her hand looked at in Picton.

The landlady took the green dress, all bloody and mud-covered, between her forefinger and thumb. "Miss, you'll want me to dispose of this, won't you?"

Marian nodded and pulled on her cloak. "Wait," she said. "I think . . . I think I will put that dress in Lord Ingraham's carriage." She took it back. "Lord Ingraham may find it useful," she said. Lady Ingraham, she thought, perhaps this is how I can help you.

Without further chat, Marian marched down the stair and into the inn yard, where she handed the dress to the footman. "Give this to Lord Ingraham," she directed. "Tell him . . ." She thought a moment and shook her head. "There is no message. Indeed, it needs no message."

The footman took the dress. "I hate to be the one to give him this. He'll be on the road to Picton in jig time."

"Not unless his superiors from the Foreign office tell him so," she commented dryly.

Alistair was ready to travel when she returned to the inn. Jeremy and one of the innkeeper's sons deposited him in the empty mail coach that waited.

Marian propped one of the landlady's pillows behind his head and covered him with a blanket. "Will you be all right?" she asked.

The doctor's sleeping powders were rapidly claiming possession of her brother. Alistair opened his eyes long enough to say, "Home."

"Yes," Marian agreed as she pulled the blanket higher across his bandaged shoulder.

"Home," he said again, struggling against the sleeping powders. "Mare, the pearls are in my coat pocket," he said, his words slurring together. "For Jeremy Towser. Whole mail coach to ourselves. Imagine that." He closed his eyes.

Towser still stood by the coach door. "No need for your pearls," he said gruffly. "The company can manage without them." He shifted his weight and cleared his throat. "But there is one thing I want, miss."

"Anything, Mr. Towser," she said.

"If you think Alistair will sleep through, ride up here beside me and tell me the whole story."

And so it was that Marian Wynswich, bundled in her cloak and wrapped about in Jeremy Towser's muffler, came riding up to the front door of Covenden Hall after midnight in the mail coach. Word had traveled ahead of them, and the hall was blazing with lights. As the coach rolled to a stop, the door was flung open and Percy ran down the steps. He held up his arms for Marian, and she found herself caught in a breathless embrace.

And then Ariadne was there, and Lady Wynswich, and even the Reverend Beddoe, all of them standing close together with their arms around her.

Jeremy Towser watched all this from his perch high above. He sniffed a little, cleared his throat loudly, and looked the other way, muttering something about "the strangest people who live in Devon."

16

Marian had only a fleeting memory of Percy carrying her into the house and upstairs to her room. She remembered a tub of warm water, where her mother and Ariadne washed her, crying over her bruises and cuts, and the smell of shampoo in her hair. She remembered a good fire and a warming pan in the bed, and then friendly darkness. She woke up once with tears on her cheeks, calling for Alistair, but someone—it couldn't have been her mother, but it must have been—sang her back to sleep with a melody she recalled from the nursery. She remembered nothing more.

The sun was low in the sky when Marian opened her eyes and looked about. For the smallest moment, she was back in the bedroom on the Royal Crescent. For another moment, one that made her start up in terror and set her heart pounding, she was running and running. And then she was in her own room again, with its shabby wallpaper, comfortable armchair, and old books piled on the desk. She snuggled herself down deeper into her old mattress and cried out suddenly; every part of her body hurt.

"Marian, where does it hurt?" Percy roused himself from her armchair and pulled himself closer.

She winced and reached for his outstretched hand. "Percy, everything hurts!" The look of dismay on his face required an immediate amendment. "No, no, that is not true. My ears are excellent."

He sighed and poured her a drink of water. She took it from him and he raised her up so she could drink. "That's the girl. Jeremy Towser said Sir Reginald threw you to the ground several times."

"But I didn't feel a thing yesterday—yesterday?—except my hand." More wary this time, Marian pulled her bandaged hand out slowly from under the covers.

"The doctor had to put a couple of stitches in your palm," Percy explained. "Your knees . . . Well, they'll be better soon enough."

Marian turned carefully onto her side and looked at her brother. Why did I never realize before how handsome he is? she thought. And how much he cares for us? Why does it take something like this to make me realize what I have here?

"Percy," she said.

He looked up from his contemplation of her hand. "Yes?"

"Nothing. Just . . . Percy."

He kissed her forehead. "Alistair woke up an hour ago and asked for you. He turned rather belligerent when I would not let him get up and come in here, but he is running a slight fever, and the doctor said on no account was he to exert himself. Ariadne stands guard."

"And Mama? Oh, I do hope she has not been a trial."

Percy added another log to the fireplace and came back to the chair, sitting down heavily. Marian's heart went out to him. He has been watching all night and day, from one room to another. Oh, Percy, God keep you.

"Mama has borne up surprisingly well. Toss a real crisis her way, and she is a brick. The Reverend Beddoe did worry me at first. I thought he would go all to pieces. However, Ariadne is quite expert with the vinaigrette."

Marian laughed, winced, and put her hand to her side.

"The doctor fears you may have broken a rib or two."

She tried to sit up. "I should go see Alistair."

He pushed her back gently. "You'll not go anywhere. He will keep. Are you hungry?"

She shook her head and then gingerly reached back and touched a bump on her crown. "I will never eat again."

Percy grinned and stretched. "You may never eat again, but I will. Go to sleep, Marian."

She closed her eyes obediently.

"One thing more, sister," Percy said. "Gilbert Ingraham waits below."

Marian snapped open her eyes. "He couldn't be here!"

"Then I do not know who is pacing the floor below like a caged lion. And from the looks of him, Lord Ingraham leapt up from the dinner table in Bath, pulled on his boots while he was already in the saddle, and didn't stop until he got here this morning. He wants to see you."

"No."

"Just no? Nothing more?"

"Nothing more," Marian whispered, and turned herself over until she faced the wall.

Dinner was fish broth, which Lady Wynswich fed to her, all the while holding forth about events around Picton in the last few days.

Marian folded her hands over her stomach and listened with equanimity. A week ago, such a conversation would have driven her distracted, but now, she enjoyed listening to her mother.

"There, my dear," Lady Wynswich said finally, and put down the spoon. "Not too much at once, says the doctor. And you know how he scolds if his instructions are not followed."

"Yes, Mama," Marian said meekly.

"Oh, my dear, dear Marian," she exclaimed, kissing her on both cheeks. "There is someone in the parlor who would like very much to come up and sit with you awhile."

"No!"

Lady Wynswich's eyes filled with tears, and she groped in her bosom for a handkerchief. "He is so weary, poor dear. He almost fell asleep over dinner."

"Then he should go to bed."

Lady Wynswich arose with some dignity and took the tray with her.

Marian moved her hand. "Mama, wait. Have you placed him in the best guest room again?"

"Of course. Some of us are not entirely dead to duty around here."

Marian drew her lips together in a tight line. "I merely want to comment that the feathers are coming out of the pillow in that room, and the water pitcher has a crack in it."

"I'll see to it, dear," she said as she backed out the door with the tray. Her eyes had a decided twinkle in them, which her daughter elected to ignore.

Marian did not know how she could sleep that night, after sleeping through the day, but she did, rousing only once to grope about for another blanket. The room had grown colder, and she wondered if more snow were on the way.

Percy got up from the chair and pulled the blanket up around her. He rested his hand against her cheek. Her eyes closed, Marian smiled and kissed the palm of his hand.

"Good night, brat," she thought she heard Percy say, but Percy never would have said that. She was too exhausted to figure it out.

Marian thought to ask Percy in the morning when he came in the room again after breakfast, sat down, and promptly fell asleep, but did not. Is it that I do not wish to know, she asked herself as she cautiously flexed her knees. This subject bears contemplation.

The house was still quiet, resting peacefully in that luminous light that comes with snow. Moving slowly, quietly, so as not to waken Percy, Marian dangled her legs over the edge of the bed. She looked down at her knees, skinned and scraped raw, and raised her nightgown higher. Deep bruises traveled like fingers up her thigh. She shuddered. Those were Sir Reginald's finger marks. Jeremy Towser, you were right: the world is full of rascals.

Even the soles of her feet pained her, but Marian walked quietly to Alistair's room and slipped inside. The Reverend Beddoe watched her, blew her a kiss, and raised his eyebrows in inquiry.

She put a finger to her lips. "I merely wanted to see him for myself," she whispered. She looked down at Alistair as he slept. His forehead was cool, his breathing steady. "I love you,

Alistair," she said, and left the room as quietly as she had come.

The door to the best guest room was open a crack. Marian stood outside it a moment and then peeked in. Clothes were scattered in a trail from the door to the bed, as if Lord Ingraham had not a thought in his head except sleep, and soon.

The fire had gone out. As her eyes accustomed themselves to the gloom, Marian observed that the window by the bed was open slightly and snow covered the floor like powder. He must have opened the window himself, she thought, for the servants would never do it. Such peculiar sleeping habits, Marian thought as she pulled the door to again. A person would have to cuddle quite close to stay warm.

Marian decided that she would eat breakfast that morning, and there was general rejoicing throughout the kitchen. At least, that was the atmosphere according to Ariadne, who brought a weighted-down offering from Cook.

"Marian, Cook seems to think that you cannot sustain life without tea and toast and eggs and a slab of cheese the size of a roof tile," said her sister. "I would never argue with Cook."

They ate breakfast together, Ariadne telling Marian of her bridal plans. "We have decided on April the fourth. The daffodils and jonquils will be in bloom then, and think how lovely! That will be one week before the house must be vacated, so we will have a lovely reception in the front parlor. Mama is making plans to visit our Aunt Taylor in Norfolk then, and I think she means to take you with her."

And I will go gladly, Marian thought. Precious little time alone you and Sam will have if I do not. She sighed and picked the center out of Cook's excellent toast.

Ariadne pulled her knitting from her workbasket, fiddled with it a moment, and then set it down. "Marian! You can't ignore Gilbert Ingraham day after day."

"It has not been day after day," Marian declared. "This is not the Hundred Years' War!"

"Oh, I am sure I do not know what it is," said Ariadne. "He sits so patiently and then paces the floor, and has such a look of agony in his eyes. Marian, I thought you had a woman's heart in your breast somewhere."

Marian ignored her outburst and ate another wedge of cheese. Ariadne threw up her hands in exasperation and left the room. She didn't exactly slam the door, but she came as close to shutting it decisively as Marian had ever heard.

"Everyone in this house has gone mad, in the short space between Advent and New Year's," she said to the wall. She giggled. "It must be the Wynswich secret."

Percy was her next visitor. He came in as she was brushing her hair. "Good to see you feeling more the thing," he commented.

Marian decided that Percy was greatly improved, too, and told him so. He smiled and sat down in her chair with his newspaper. "I did sleep well last night, and in my own bed."

"I thought you were in here."

"No," he said, and did not elaborate. He snapped open his paper and, humming to himself, began to peruse it. "Marian, here is an item of interest. I shall mark it so you can read it at your leisure. It is the terms of the Treaty of Ghent." He lowered the paper long enough to look at her. "Treaties can be such pleasant affairs, sister. Don't you think it a wonderful thing when people can work out their differences?"

"Percy . . . " she began, her voice dangerously low.

"My dear, I know how you like to follow events of national importance," he said, assuming an air of bewildered injury, and then totally ruined the effect with a grin that spread from ear to ear.

"Percy?"

He was silent behind his paper until Marian wanted to throw her hairbrush at him.

"H'mmm? Oh, beg pardon, Marian. Did you want something?"

"I just wondered. Is there other news . . . of national importance?" she asked casually.

He turned several pages and then looked up. "You do mean in the paper, do you not?"

"Of course!"

Unfazed, he flipped back and forth. "Ah. Here is an item you might find interesting. Or you might not. It says here that

Lord Gilbert Ingraham, Earl of Collinwood, has resigned his position with the Diplomatic Corps. Imagine that!''

"What?" Marian gasped.

"That's what it says. It's only a short item, and contains no real information, so I will not bother to read it out loud." He rose. "I am probably tiring you with this silly talk of inconsequentials." He folded the paper, carefully creasing it just so, and tucked it under his arm.

"Percy, you can leave the paper," Marian said. "If you're done with it, that is."

He put the paper on the bedside table. "It is rather thin of news this time of year. I wonder you would want it."

As soon as the door closed, Marian pounced on the paper, spreading it out on the bed and ruffling through the pages until she came to the last item. She read it and sat back in disappointment. It was only a small notice, after all, as if the news had just come and there was no time for more details.

"So you have resigned," she said, and felt a twinge of sadness, even as she congratulated Lord Ingraham silently for his wisdom. "You'll live longer, I suspect."

Lady Wynswich brought in luncheon and didn't even sit down. "There is so much to do, my dear," she explained. "Ariadne and I are driving over to Mrs. Tilby's this afternoon. Mrs. Tilby is making the bridal gown. Perhaps you care to drive with us next week?"

She carried a book in her hand, something Marian had never seen her do before.

Marian pointed to it. "What is that?" she asked.

Her mother stared down in amazement. "I believe it is a book, Marian."

Marian sighed.

"Dear me. I didn't mean to bring this in here. It would only be a waste of your time." She started for the door.

"Mama, you are provoking! Hand it over."

Mama returned to the bedside with supreme reluctance. "It is Richard Longacre's *A Traveler's Guide to North America*. I can't imagine it would be of any interest."

"We do not possess such a book in our library," Marian said, her voice dark with suspicion.

"I'm sure I do not know," Lady Wynswich replied vaguely. "I must have picked it up when I was in the parlor. Let me return it there."

"No," said Marian hastily, and then smiled. "I mean, just leave it here and I will look it over."

An hour later, Marian was deep in the book when the door opened. "Come in," she said absently.

"Mare! I escaped!"

Marian dropped the book and threw back the covers. She hobbled over to her brother, who stood on unsteady legs at the door. "Alistair, Mama will ring such a peal over you," she scolded, and then tucked his arm carefully in hers and led him to her armchair. "But I am glad to see you upright again."

Alistair sank into the chair gratefully. "I am amazed that a little bullet hole can cause such trouble," he said. "And everybody has been fussing and carrying on. Don't you wish they would go back to the way they were?"

Marian sat on her bed. "Oh, Alistair, I think they have already done that. Everyone schemes and meddles and teases. Nothing has changed."

He laughed. "Mare, it's good to see you."

"And you." She picked up the book again. "Alistair, listen to this. It says here that North America has an agreeable climate and all manner of plant and animal life, including birds of rare beauty and—"

"Indians," Alistair interrupted. "And they take scalps."

"Silly!"

"Gilbert told me this morning that . . ." He stopped and shook his head. "No, no, I shan't tell you."

"Tell me what, you provoking beast?" she said, and threw her pillow at him. "Ow! Oh, I know I have a broken rib." She started to cry.

Alistair grasped the pillow with his bare toes, pulled it closer, and reached down carefully to retrieve it. He set it on top of her head and she started to giggle.

"That's better," he said solemnly. He looked toward the door. "I think I hear someone. If Percy finds me out of bed, I will be interred two years at St. Stephen's instead of one. 'Bye, Mare."

She took the pillow off her head and hugged it to her side until the ache lessened. Longacre's book lay just out of reach on the floor. Marian leaned toward it, gritting her teeth.

"Brat, if you break another rib, the doctor will bind you so tight you'll only be able to breathe through your ears." Lord Ingraham came into the room carrying a chess set, which he placed at the foot of her bed. He handed the book to her and took up the set again. "I promised Percy a game in the library, Marian. See you later, my dear."

"Percy is no challenge," she said so softly that she was sure he could not hear her.

"He will do. I fear you would be easy pickings these days, and I never—seldom—prey on the weak."

Marian gritted her teeth. "You are assuredly the most irritating man I ever met."

He bowed and smiled. "And you, my dear, would drive any sane man to suicide inside of fifteen minutes of making your acquaintance."

She sank down among the pillows and picked up the book, staring at it and turning the pages.

Lord Ingraham opened the door. "Marian, it's easier to follow the narrative when you hold a book right side up."

The afternoon wore on. When it was getting dark, Ariadne danced into the room, removing her bonnet, her cheeks red from the cold outside. "Marian, the dress is so beautiful. It is all silk and has the most beautiful lace overskirt. You must come with us next week and see for yourself." Ariadne sat down on the bed. "I thought blue would be a bridesmaid's color, if you think that agreeable."

"I do," said Marian. "Ariadne, is . . . is Gil still below-stairs?"

"No. I saw him walking with Sam. They were quite deep in conversation. When he returns, do you wish me to send him to you?"

It was on the tip of Marian's tongue to say yes, but she could not bring herself to do it. She shook her head. "It is nothing that will not keep."

Lady Wynswich brought her dinner that evening. "We have all decided that it is best that we do not disturb you, my darling.

Alistair is sleeping, and you must be exhausted, too. When the doctor comes tomorrow, perhaps he will let you sit up in your chair for restricted periods of the day.''

''Mama! Do you mean to turn me into an invalid?'' Marian said. ''I would like to go downstairs right now.''

Her mother only stared and put her hand on her daughter's forehead. ''I am certain what you need is rest.''

When she left the room, Marian got up from bed, tugged her armchair to the window, and sat there, looking out across the snowy formal gardens. It is time I gave a thought to what I will do after April. She smiled to herself. If the world were fair, I would go to St. Stephen's and study with Alistair. Or I would follow Percy to Vienna as his secretary.

But the world is not fair, Marian decided, and I am allowed to do none of these things. She continued her contemplation of the gardens, unwilling to surrender to sleep, but forced to concede finally that her mother was right. She was exhausted still. She sat in the chair a few moments longer, wishing that someone would come and jolly her out of the melancholy mood that was descending rapidly.

No one did. Marian Wynswich tucked her long hair carefully into her nightcap, blew out the lamp, and crawled between the covers. She said her prayers in bed because her knees pained her too much to pray beside her bed, as she usually did. Clasping her hands together, Marian considered the usual order of family and friends and king and country, and abandoned them all to someone else's tender mercies. She prayed for herself alone.

The sound of the fire in the hearth woke Marian hours later. It had been dying down when she finally closed her eyes, and here it was, blazing up as if someone had carefully stoked it. How kind, she thought as her eyes closed.

''Marian, don't go back to sleep.''

She opened her eyes again. Gilbert Ingraham stood by the fireplace. As she watched him, he added another log to the hearth and then tugged her armchair close to the bed and sat in it. Marian raised herself up on her elbow. Without a word, he picked up an extra pillow and propped it behind her head. She relaxed again, never taking her eyes from his face.

She didn't say anything when he pulled back the covers from the foot of the bed, raising them to reveal her knees. He smiled at her and touched her cheek, and then opened a jar in his hand. While she watched in silence, Lord Ingraham knelt by the bed and gently dabbed a layer of salve on her knees.

"I didn't know I had a jar made up," she said finally when the silence seemed too intimate.

"You didn't. I followed your chicken scratch recipe and added some touches of my own." He sniffed the ointment. "I couldn't find your lavender water, so I put in a drop of my own cologne." He sat back on his heels. "Well, brat?"

She lay back, grateful down to the soles of her feet as the salve took the throb and ache from her knees. "Oh, Gil," she sighed.

He smiled. "I take that for approval." He touched her knee. "I don't think I can do anything about the scars that you will have, but I seem to remember someone telling me that scars fade." He allowed the ointment to soak in and then covered her legs again.

"Your hand, please."

Without a word, Marian turned it palm-up on the coverlet. With a gentleness that she thought surprising in a man, Lord Ingraham unwound the bandage and looked at her palm. He traced the jagged wound, counting the stitches. In silence, he wrapped her hand again and placed it back under the covers. He sat on the bed and looked down at her.

"Marian, when my footman handed me that dress of yours at the dinner table, you cannot imagine what went through my head."

She reached for his hand, but he was on his feet, unable to meet her eyes. "I thought you were dead. Oh, God! I held up that dress and it was so ripped and bloody." He turned around to look at her, his face ravaged. "It was the worst moment of my life."

He came back to her then, dropped to his knees by the bed, and rested his head on her breast as he sobbed. They were the deep, wrenching tears of a man who never cried, someone trained by masters, she thought, to seldom betray feelings.

Marian rested her hand tentatively on his head, and then put
her arms around him, patting his back, kissing his hair, holding
him close.

"I had to do it, don't you see?" she said finally when he sat
up. "Someone had to pull you up sharp. But, oh, I hope you
burned that dress. What . . . what did you do with it?"

"I hung it in my dressing room." He rested his head against
her again. "My footman said you fought like a tiger."

She looked down at him and touched his hair. "I have no
experience at all with men, Gil, but I harbored no illusions about
what Sir Reginald Calne would have done."

He did not move; she did not press him. He spoke finally,
his voice muffled by her body. "I could go on with it, of course,
but I would never dare live such a dangerous life, not with a
wife and children." He raised himself then and sat on her bed,
his hands on her shoulders.

She wiped his eyes with the sheet. "You could, Gil. But the
price is too high." Marian cupped his face in her hands and
whispered softly. "And don't you think you—and your father
before you—have done more than most men for the good of
your country?"

He kissed her. "But there is always more to do, Marian."

"And someone else can do it."

He sighed, patted her hand, and went to put another log on
the fire. "Do you know, Marian, that article in the *Times* was
a bit hasty. I did not entirely sever my dealings with the
Diplomatic Corps." His tone was apologetic and defiant at the
same time, and she was forcefully reminded of a small boy.
"I'm not sure that I really want to."

"What are you aiming for?" Marian asked when he did not
speak.

"There is a post in Washington, D.C. I have been offered
it and I am considering it seriously. Now, don't look at me like
that, brat. There is no huggle-muggle about this job. It is
merely"—he bowed deeply—"diplomacy. It is using the proper
fork, dancing the latest dance, and trying to help the Americans
overlook that we burned their swampy capital five months ago."

She laughed. "And you want it, do you not, sir?"

"Indeed, I do." He came no closer to her. "I already have a horse. Now I want a wife." He coughed politely. "That, I am told, is all a man needs in America for a fresh start."

Marian was silent.

He watched her. "I'm leaving soon enough, at any rate. I sail from Bristol in two weeks. Do think about it, my dear. Cast aside all the differences we have, all those counts that make this a supremely silly idea, and put your fine mind to it."

"Very well, sir."

"Very well." He snapped open his pocket watch and laughed softly. "Dearest brat, it is two in the morning. And do you know what day this is?"

She shook her head.

"It is January seventh. My pudding wish is up. Good night."

17

Rather than devote her whole heart and mind to the problem at hand, Marian Wynswich was asleep the moment Gilbert Ingraham closed the door. She slept peacefully for the rest of the night, dreaming of nothing more upsetting than salve and treaties.

She woke late in the morning to the sound of snow tickling the windows again. '' 'Ah, lovely Devon, where it snows eight days out of seven,' '' she said, and pulled back the covers.

Her knees looked no better, but the pain was less. Marian smoothed on another layer of Lord Ingraham's salve. I shall name it balm of Gilead, she thought, and laughed out loud. He will appreciate that.

Dressing was an onerous chore. Marian's arms ached, and she knew she missed some of the buttons, but she resolved to wear her hair long down her back and cover the omission.

The house appeared deserted. Marian went slowly down the stairs, remembering that Percy had said something yesterday about Lyme Regis. The door to Alistair's room was closed, and she heard no sounds within, so she did not disturb him. She peeked in the parlor and sighed with disappointment. No Gilbert. The library produced no earl, either. The sole occupant was a maid dusting the books.

"Sukey, have you seen Lord Ingraham this morning?"

"Oh, miss, I do not think he is here. His bag is packed. I

know that, because I heard him ask Sir Percy to see that it was put on the mail coach.''

Marian sank down in her father's wing chair. ''He is gone?'' she asked. ''In this weather?''

''I'm sure I do not know, miss.''

Marian sat very still. She leaned back and closed her eyes. ''Gil, did you take your own advice?'' she said.

''Beg pardon, miss?''

''I'm sorry, Sukey. Nothing.''

Did you put your own fine mind to it last night after you left me? Did you finally think—really think—about the fact that I am poor, not a raving beauty, full of contradictions and whimseys? Did you change your mind? I can scarcely blame you.

She opened her eyes. The snow was letting up. After breakfast she would go out to the workroom and check on Mama Cat and her kittens, and see that Solomon was behaving himself. *I imagine that I can find someone to take the kittens before April. But Solomon? Could there be a place at the vicarage for him? He does such excellent work with mice.*

Marian took a deep breath. And another. And another. She frowned.

''Sukey? What is Cook making?''

''Oh, miss, I do not know. She scattered us out of the kitchen early. I think it is something special. She had such a glint in her eye.''

Marian managed a smile. Trust Cook to concoct something to help take away the hurt. But why would she make that? Marian shook her head and left the library.

The odor was stronger in the hall, and stronger still as she walked to the back of the house and went downstairs to the kitchen. It was a smell of figs and citron, of rum, orange peel, nuts, and candied fruits. It was Christmas pudding.

And there was Lord Ingraham, apron around his middle, cutting up orange peel at the table. She stared at him in amazement, her eyes enormous. He looked up. ''Good morning, brat. Thought you would sleep all day. Cat got your tongue, my heart?''

Without a word, she sat down at the table.

He turned to the great range. "Is this enough?"

Cook inspected the offering and nodded. "Mind you cut the candied cherries smaller, my lord."

"Smaller? Good heavens, are cherries not small enough already?"

Marian smothered a laugh behind her hand.

The earl wiped his hands on his apron. "Well, I ask you, Marian."

"You had better do as Cook says, Lord Ingraham. We never argue with her."

Startled, Marian turned around. "Ariadne?"

Her sister came out of the pantry, followed by the Reverend Beddoe, who carried a bowl of ground suet. Cook inspected the suet and banished the vicar to the pantry again to grind it finer. She shook her knife at him when he appeared disposed to argue.

"Dump it in there, my lord," said Cook when the cherries had been minced to her total satisfaction. "You will be a cook yet." She added Sam's suet when he returned with it, put in another cup of flour, another sprinkle of rum, and then handed the wooden spoon to Lord Ingraham. "Stir, my lord."

He bowed and took the spoon. Marian eyes began to mist over. He looked at her. "Brat, you needn't cry. There are no onions in Christmas pudding."

"I am not crying," she retorted. "There is merely something in my eye."

"Mare, you'r such a silly," Alistair commented from the stairway. He was wrapped in Percy's silk dressing gown, and escorted by his brother, who kept a hand on his arm and helped him to the table. "Where is Mama?"

"Right here, Alistair," Lady Wynswich said, coming from the pantry. "I wanted to grind the nuts just so, and Sam was wondrous slow about the suet. Here you are, Gilbert. Stir a little faster, or it will burn!"

"Yes, my dear," he said, and kissed her on the cheek.

Lady Wynswich blushed.

Marian sat in dignified silence for the space of another minute, looking from face to face, her gaze finally coming to rest on the man at the cooking range. "I suspect a great conspiracy, my lord," she said.

"It is nothing devious or deceptive, Marian," he replied mildly. "I have abandoned deception. You will recall the day?"

"It is January seventh."

"Indeed. My pudding wish was up last night." He stirred the pot. "It only stands to reason, my heart, that if I make another pudding and another wish, I will have until January sixth next year for it to come true."

"That is only reasonable," Percy agreed. The others nodded.

Gilbert turned back to the pot. "And so, my dear, I will have another year to win you over." He looked over his shoulder at her. "By then you will be older—of course, so will I—and wiser."

Percy got to his feet and clapped Lord Ingraham on the back. "Only think of yourself as fine wine, Gilbert, and how well you age."

Gilbert groaned. "Percy, spare my gray hairs! Another word and I will see that you are forced to accompany me to America instead of Vienna." He put his arm around Percy Wynswich and hugged him. "As I think of it, not a bad idea. I fear Europe will be awash very soon in new troubles."

"The idea has merit," Percy agreed. "Let us consider it. Look, Gilbert, I think it is ready. What say you, Cook?"

Cook was dabbing at her eyes with her apron. "Yes, and be quick about it."

"Gather around, Wynswiches one and all," ordered Lord Ingraham. "Who goes first? Sam?"

The vicar took the spoon, closed his eyes, and stirred the pudding, declaring a loud "Amen!" He handed the spoon to his fiancée, who closed her eyes, stirred, and blew a kiss to her sister, who still sat at the table. "Mama?"

Lady Wynswich took the spoon. "I don't know why I should wish Marian so far away," she grumbled, "but if everyone insists . . ."

"We do," they all said.

"Very well, then, I'll do it. Alistair?"

Alistair took the spoon and wished. "I will miss you more than I can say, Marian," he said, his eyes serious. "You're very dear to my heart."

"Alistair . . ." Marian said, and slowly got to her feet.

"Hold off, Marian," declared Percy, taking the spoon from his brother, who seemed to be having trouble with his eyes. "It is my turn first." He gave the spoon several turns around the pot. "You know, of course, that our is the most wonderful family that ever lived in Devon," he said. "Even if we are not together in our home for any more such Christmases, the memory of this one will keep us close together. I wish for you, Marian, as we all have done. And on our behalf, I thank you for the years and years of Christmas wishes you have lavished upon all of us."

"Percy, I . . ." Marian began, and took the spoon.

"Oh, no! I insist it is my turn," declared Lord Ingraham, taking the spoon from her hand. He put his arm around Marian's waist and held her close. "It's the same wish I made two weeks ago. Is that permissible, Alistair?"

"Oh, yes, as long as you still mean it."

"Oh, I do. Even more." He closed his eyes and stirred. He let go of Marian and looked into her eyes. "And now, my dear, it is your turn."

She took the spoon, but did not stir. "Gil, are you sure? Have you really thought about this?"

He went to the table, where he had left his coat, and came back with her copy of *The Poetics*. "Did you not miss this? I found it in your room in Bath after you left. See here, where I have underlined?"

He held the book up for her and she read the Greek lines, gasped, and laughed. She tried to stir the pudding. "Gil, my hand is too sore. You will have to help."

He placed his hand carefully around hers and they stirred the pot together as everyone gathered closer.

"Done, Cook," Marian declared, and threw her arms around Gilbert Ingraham. "I love you, Gil," she said, and kissed him.

Lady Wynswich and Ariadne started to cry and the reverend had to sit down at the table.

Percy took the book out of Lord Ingraham's hand, read the underlined passage, and chuckled. Alistair looked next, only to shake his head. He looked at the earl and sighed, "I know, I know. The value of an education! But, sir—or do I say, brother?—explain for those less gifted in the Attic languages."

"It merely says that one should always prefer the probable impossible to the improbably possible. As there is no one more impossible than Marian Wynswich, I knew that Aristotle would win out. Marian, will you marry me and follow me to the ends of the earth, forsaking all libraries?"

"Yes."

Gilbert picked her up, whirled her around, kissed her soundly, and sat her on his lap. "Will you marry me next week? We sail in two weeks."

"Of course. But I have no dress."

Lady Wynswich blew her nose and wiped her eyes. "Of course you do! You don't really think Mrs. Tilby was making that dress for Ariadne, do you? She isn't to be married until April, after all."

"Mama," was all Marian could manage, but it said everything.

The silence threatened to bring a flood of tears, so Gilbert put Marian off his lap and reached for his coat again. "Lady Wynswich, you have reminded me. I have something here for Percy, but I suppose it is for everyone. Percy?"

He handed an envelope to Percy, who opened it and then stared at Lord Ingraham. "You?"

"I cannot deceive you." The earl winked at Marian. "Indeed, I have promised not to practice any further deception. I was the purchaser of this fine old home. And I return the deed to you as my wedding gift."

Alistair whistled. "I do not know that Mare is worth all that, my lord."

"That and more, you scamp," Ingraham declared, and set his beloved back on his lap.

Marian put her arms around him and rested her head against his chest. "How odd this is," she murmured. "Just a moment ago, I said I loved you and I thought I could never love you more than I did right then. And now I love you more."

He gathered her close. "It could become a habit. You may even love me more after next week's wedding, or even after our dreary ocean voyage, possibly even after our children are born, and after we have traveled here and there, and had an occasional heartache. It's a theory, anyway, and I am resolved to test it."

The other Wynswiches found pressing activities to occupy themselves for the next few moments while Lord Ingraham and his dear brat theorized.

"And I shall apply immediately for a special license," he said when he caught his breath again. "The Archbishop of Canterbury is a friend of mine."

Alistair groaned. "Oh, do not mention our name. He has two grandsons—"

"And they are perfect idiots," declared Lord Ingraham. "I mean to recommend St. Stephen's to the archbishop when I write to him."

Alistair groaned again, dragged himself to his feet, and stirred the Christmas pudding vigorously. "For me, this time, Mare."

Gilbert kissed Marian and cast a musing eye on the pot. "I would like to eventually trounce you soundly at chess "

"You and who else, my lord?" Marian asked.

He smiled down at her. "No one else, brat. My wish stands."

SIGNET REGENCY ROMANCE
COMING IN JANUARY 1990

———————— • ————————

Dorothy Mack
The Reluctant Heart

Elizabeth Hewitt
A Private Understanding

Irene Saunders
The Doctor's Lady

———————— • ————————

27 million Americans can't read a bedtime story to a child.

It's because 27 million adults in this country simply can't read.

Functional illiteracy has reached one out of five Americans. It robs them of even the simplest of human pleasures, like reading a fairy tale to a child.

You can change all this by joining the fight against illiteracy.

Call the Coalition for Literacy at toll-free **1-800-228-8813** and volunteer.

Volunteer Against Illiteracy. The only degree you need is a degree of caring.